SILVER HUNTER

SILVER BROTHERS SECURITIES

LACEY SILKS

MYLIT
PUBLISHING

"Security is mostly a superstition. Life is either a daring adventure or nothing." ~ Helen Keller

"I'm gonna kiss you, Hunter."
I leaned in and took his hesitant lips. His moustache tickled and
carried the forest's scent.
He pulled away. "Grace—"
"You don't want me. Oh, God, this is so embarrassing. Here I
am throwing myself at you and thinking we could—"
"Grace, stop. I just need you to look up for a second."
"What?"
"Look up."
I followed his finger to the night sky and the bazillion of stars
forming streams of light. A shower of commas splashed across
the sky.
~ Silver Hunter ~

They call me a cougar, but he calls me his Queen.

On his eighteenth birthday, Hunter came over to fix my motorcycle. He didn't leave till morning.

Three years later, he's still working as my pool boy—and so much more. But I'm not ready to introduce him to my friends. He isn't ready to make a commitment. And neither of us is ready for a life together.

One thing I *am* ready for? To have his baby. All I need to do is convince him…

Silver Hunter is the seventh novel in the *Silver Brothers Securities Family Saga*. This book can be read as a standalone novel. Intended for mature audiences.

Life was good; and tonight, my hard work building a beauty empire would be rewarded and all of my dreams would come true. Well, almost all of them, because babies didn't arrive like the award I would receive this evening, and my clock was ticking.

I pinned the last bobby pin into my hair and lowered my arms. Curled strands glittered in gold, forming a flowing fire. The hair creation matched the sparkling dress hugging my body. My mother had called in a favor to a designer from Paris, and a month later, the custom-made gold-chained gown fit me like a glove.

A loud splash drew my attention to the outside. I paced to the balcony where the setting sun bathed the backyard in orange. Below, Hunter was walking up the pool steps, carrying what looked like another toad in his hands. He crossed the lawn to the lily pond and crouched. A giant toad hopped off his hand and into the water. That made the third toad he'd saved this week.

He rinsed his hands in the pond water, shook them off, and stood, pulling his fingers through his hair. The column of his back muscles twisted. He turned around. The permanent tan from the time he'd spent landscaping the backyard glowed in the evening light. His beautiful chest, dusted with hair, was young and firm, with room to grow.

I watched him cross the lawn back to the house. He stopped and looked up to the balcony where I stood. His piercing blue eyes were drowning with sadness. His head fell forward, and my heart sank.

I'd known Hunter Silver since his diaper days. He was my uncle's nephew on my mother's side, and our families spent every holiday, birthday, and celebration together. And boy, had he grown up fast. For his eighteenth birthday, I bought Hunter a bike and asked for a few lessons on my broken Harley, which he was eager to fix that evening. Let's just say, he fixed more than my bike. He'd begun as my boy toy, and three years later, he was saving frogs from my pool.

As soon as he stepped inside, I hitched my dress to my thighs and hurried to meet him downstairs. Hunter wouldn't reject a quickie before I left, and I was ovulating.

"Hey, baby. Another toad in my pool?"

His beautiful blue eyes met mine. Jesus, he would make a gorgeous baby. He stood, dripping wet, his gaze unapologetically slithering down my body. I swallowed with an audible click, drawing my tongue over my dry lips. His shorts clung to his muscled thighs and his healthy dick, lifting my arousal and setting my blood on fire.

"Holy fuck, Grace. You look stunning. Like a queen. My Queen."

I twirled in the spot, and his gloom vanished. The half-smile and two dimples were a good start.

"You like it?" I asked, wiggling my ass.

"What are you supposed to be? An Oscar on fire?"

He stepped closer, his eyes swimming with lust, and a little bit of disappointment.

"Exactly." I cleared my throat.

"But you're not getting an Oscar."

"This award is the highest honor I'll ever get, so it's like an Oscar to me."

"You look beautiful. The dress is the perfect choice. Wish I could be there to see you accept the award." He kissed the tip of my nose.

The punch in my gut briefly knocked me off task. I stepped closer and dragged my manicured nails down his drying chest. "What can I do to make you feel better?"

"I'll ruin your makeup if I have my way with you"

The rumble from his chest vibrated along my skin. I pushed my thigh through the slit in my dress and lifted the other side, exposing my panties. I was willing to beg him to ruin me, but if I did, he would, and I'd be late. But there were other ways.

"If you stay below the belt, you won't ruin my hair or makeup."

His mouth twisted into a sly grin, and my heart kicked up a beat. He leaned into my ear and dragged his lips over the cartilage, whispering, "What if I want to ruin you, Grace?"

Yes.

His fingers skimmed up my arm, and his needy breath drew shivers down my spine.

"Touch me. There." My lips trembled over his.

He slid his hand through the slit in my dress and up my thigh. I gripped the dinette table as he dipped his palm down the front of my panties. My eyes rolled back in my head and my legs instinctively opened. His long, skilled fingers dragged through my wet flesh, and stopped.

"Aren't you ovulating, Grace?" he asked, withdrawing his hand.

Shit.

"I'm thirty-two, Hunter. It's the perfect time to have a baby."

"I'm not ready for offspring."

"But my business is booming, and we're happy and together—"

"If we're happy, my love, why aren't I escorting you tonight?"

"Hunter, we've already talked about this."

His shoulders dropped, and he strode to the kitchen where he poured himself a vodka on ice. He lifted the glass and pointed my way. "No, Gracie. *You* talked about it, and because your reputation is more important than me, you chose not to take me." He took a sip. "What are you afraid of?"

I was worried about Hunter. Last Christmas, he took a tumble down the stairs at the salon and pissed himself when he reached the bottom. Alcohol and Hunter didn't mix well.

"I never thought you'd be one to care what people think about you because you have it all. But you hide me like a dog in a shed. Is it really me you want tonight, Grace, or my sperm?"

I swung my hand, aiming for a slap, but he gripped my wrist before my palm connected with his cheek.

"Fuck you, Hunter. This is exactly why I can't take you to serious events." I yanked my wrist free.

"The least you can do is be honest. Why won't you take me? What am I to you? I fix your car and your bike. I bring groceries and cook. I take you out on dates like all boyfriends do, while most of my friends stay out and party from Monday to Sunday. I go to school, I work, and I'm in what I hope is a committed relationship. Yet you're embarrassed by me."

He took another swig.

"Hunter, you're wonderful—"

"But?"

"But you go to school, and you're twenty-one."

"Yet I'm old enough to make a baby. What's going to happen after you're pregnant, Grace? If you can't introduce me to your friends as your boyfriend, how would you introduce me as the father of your child? Would you even want me in your life?"

My child. I sighed internally.

"They would talk about you, wouldn't they? Fucking Cougar Court." He motioned south to the front of my house. My neighborhood girlfriends, all single businesswomen over thirty, liked to talk.

"We should change your address to Gossip Court."

My neighbors hadn't welcomed Hunter with open arms, but let's be honest. I did live on Cougar Court, and we all lived up to the street's name. When Hunter first moved in, Lexie came out for a jog around the court every time Hunter washed my car in the middle of a heat wave. Carly loved Hunter's help with the lawn mowing, and he'd drained Susanne's pool for the third year in a row after the company botched up the liner. But after he helped them, he was mine and all mine. Day and night, he fucked me like an animal, and I screamed past the open windows. But as amazing as he was, taking Hunter to a party would be like adding fuel to a fire, and when flames flared, so did Hunter. The bounty hunter-in-training at Silver Securities lived up to his adventurous name.

"Hunter—"

"Grace, all I'm saying is that I'd love to be seen as more. I'm not one of your aunt's manservants."

I brushed my hand over his cheek and curled his dark hair around my finger. This evening wasn't starting out the way I'd imagined, but I'd be damned if it didn't end with him between my thighs and deep in my vagina.

"Please don't insult me, Hunter. You know how I feel about you and how much I want you."

"Do I? Your friends don't know I exist, and your neighbors think I'm your boy toy."

I drew back my hand, and his curl sprang off my finger. "My family knows about you, and that should be enough."

"Yet it isn't enough to earn a permanent spot in your life."

The grandfather clock struck six times, and I let go of my

dress. If he wasn't hard in thirty seconds, we'd run out of time. I curved my hand over his dick, but he stepped aside.

"Fine. You wanna be this way, then be this way. I gotta go, but I'll see you later tonight."

I lifted to my toes in front of him and planted a long kiss on his plump lips. When I returned, I'd straddle him if I had to, and I wouldn't let him go until he came hard. His tongue sneaked between my lips, igniting my need, but he pulled away too quickly, bracing his forehead against mine. "Have a great time, Grace."

His soft voice fed my guilt.

"I won't be late—I promise."

"It's your night. Take your time. Just don't let some phantom man steal you away."

"Phantom?"

"The party's Halloween-themed." He kissed me again and whispered against my lips. "Remember, you're the queen of this party. Better get going if you want to make it."

His words buzzed against my mouth, as shame burned a trail through my heart. But I'd come back in a few hours, and everything would be normal. The hallway camera showed a limo pulling up to the front gate.

"A queen is never late." I kissed him back.

By the time Hunter had laced the gold high heels around my calf, the limousine was parked at the front and the clock was striking the half-hour mark. He helped me inside the limo and waved as I drove away.

A pang of regret sank my heart into my chest. Hunter was the kindest and smartest boyfriend; but most of my friends were pregnant or on their way to being pregnant, while Hunter made bets about how far he could ejaculate. It was far. I'd seen it. Except the sperm didn't go where it was supposed to go: inside my drying womb.

Twenty minutes later, my limo parked at the curb in front

of the venue gardens. White and gold fabric was draped over the erected Greek columns at the front, and floodlights illuminated the entrance overgrown with vines. A valet opened the back door. Camera lights flashed, and security closed ranks. I stepped out onto the rolled red carpet, and someone bumped me in the shoulder. A security guard squeezed between us, guiding me to the door. Thank God Hunter had hired his company's private team.

I stepped past the gates, and the crowd's noise settled into a hum. The sound of falling water trickled from a central fountain, and I let go of the tension in my shoulders. A warm breeze blew by, swaying the fairy lights on the trees. Beyond, a tent with tables and a stage had been erected on the main lawn, which was decorated with flowers and vines and looked like a fairytale garden.

I walked up to a tall gentleman smiling my way. He was dark and handsome, in his late thirties, and fit the description I'd given to Aunt Mary right down to the neatly trimmed growth on his face.

"Grace Wagner. You look beautiful."

"Xavier Morrison?"

He smiled and extended his hand. I hooked my arm into his.

"You're early," I said.

"I didn't want to keep you waiting. It's a pleasure to meet you. I took the liberty of getting your favorite drink; non-alcoholic, as per your preference sheet."

He motioned to the wait staff, who immediately brought an aloe-coconut water.

"Thank you. That's sweet. Have you read everything on that preference sheet?"

"My apologies. I wasn't supposed to mention the pref— Never mind. I promise not to slip up again."

My brows furrowed, and I looked at him from the side. He

was more handsome than the profile photo I'd received from Aunt Mary. His firm jaw, dreamy eyes, and confidence were toxic. One day, Hunter would mature, and I could take him to events, but now… For now, I had to make this work.

"No worries," I said. "What about your costume?" He was wearing a tuxedo with a long black cape. "Let me guess. Magician?"

"No." he reached into his jacket pocket and removed a black mask. He looped the elastic around his head and adjusted the front. "Tonight, I'm Zorro."

Cute.

We headed to the front table, where Xavier pulled back my chair. I took my seat beside my other date and my best friend, Emma Silver. Hunter's younger cousin was wearing a feathered mini skirt and a matching top embroidered with gems. The modern cowgirl outfit on her body made her look like a Victoria's Secret angel. My parents occupied the seats across from me, along with my Aunt Mary.

Emma glanced over at my date and leaned into my ear. "Where's Hunter?"

"Home."

"Why?"

"Because he's too young to be my boyfriend today, Ems."

Emma may have been even younger than Hunter, but she had the maturity of ten Hunters and knew how to behave at award nights.

"Eleven years is nothing. You two are meant to be."

"It's a lot at his age. He's not ready for things. He's not ready for a family."

My mother shushed us from across the table, and I shimmied my ass to the chair's edge. The lights dimmed and voices hushed, as everyone focused on the stage.

"I'm not ready for kids either. I've babysat enough of my

nieces and nephews for three lifetimes. Besides, I have school, and Eric is my brother's best friend, so it's not like that's going to happen."

"Enjoy life before settling. Have fun while you can."

Emma rolled her eyes. "Says the woman with an escort as a date because her boyfriend's too immature."

"He has a good heart but makes bad choices."

"He chose you."

Touché.

"If I wanted a lecture, Ems, I'd sit beside my mother. I grew up with four brothers, my twin included. Trust me, you don't need your brother's permission to date. Just have fun, test out the goods, and see what he's like."

"He's a cowboy, rides horses, and reins in cattle. What else is there to know?" Emma reserved the dreamy look on her face for Eric Waters, a well-established cowboy. And since Emma Silver always got what she wanted, it was only a matter of time before she got Eric.

Someone kicked me underneath the table, and I jumped, catching my mother's deadly stare. "You'll miss it," she hissed.

The MC walked out to the front of the stage and tapped the mike. The room's focus shifted my way as soon as he introduced me as tonight's guest of honor.

I walked up to the stage, my knees wobbling and heart pounding. Bright lights heated my face, condensing my sweat into drops. My speech flew out of my head as soon as I took the mike. I barely remembered the words as I accepted the Contessa award. I thanked my team and my parents, my aunt, and the rest of my family for their support and influence. My salon's popularity couldn't have grown without them. I gripped the golden award, lifting the trophy toward my family's table, when my gaze caught a figure in the back corner by the bar. He was dressed in a black suit with a matching cape, and was leaning against a maple tree. A white mask covered half his face. The wind blew, branches swayed, and he disappeared into the tree's shade. The applause settled, and the MC walked me down the stairs and back to my table, where Xavier pulled back my chair.

"Congratulations, darling."

I set the award on the table, took a deep breath, and hugged my parents and my aunt. This was the night I'd waited so long for, yet it didn't feel complete. Celebrating without Hunter wasn't the same.

"Are you all right?" Xavier asked.

"Yes, thank you."

The commotion settled as servers brought out the first course. Soft dinner music played overhead but did nothing to settle my nerves. I scanned the room until I felt someone's stare on my back. I glanced over my shoulder, but no one was there. My heart hammered in my chest, and my hands shook.

"Can I get you anything to drink, Grace?" Xavier asked.

"A glass of rosé would be nice, thank you."

Xavier snapped his fingers, and a moment later, a chilled glass stood in front of me. I gulped half down before my bladder reminded me it had filled twenty minutes ago.

"Excuse me. I need to use the washroom." I pushed my chair back, and Xavier stood as well.

"Do you want me to come with you?" Emma asked.

"No, it's all right. Your food will get cold."

I turned on my heel, crossed the dining area, used the washroom, and broke away from the party and into the gardens. Moonlight illuminated a path with clumps of white carpet roses, and the smell of lavender filled the air. A warm evening breeze blew through my golden hair. I stood by the back fountain, watching the water splash, and then turned at the sound of approaching footsteps. A man in a cape similar to Xavier's walked toward me, except his mask was a Phantom's. I squinted. The corner of his mouth lifted, and a dimple sank into his cheek.

"Hunter? Is that you?"

"Hello, Gracie."

Oh, no.

His deep voice chilled me to the bones. Hunter only called me *Gracie* when he was drunk. He walked forward, somewhat confident on his feet, yet swaying. I looked around the empty gardens. If someone saw him like this with me, I'd be ruined.

He removed the Phantom mask from his face and pulled his fingers through his hair. On a sober night, the move was sexy. Tonight, not so much. The vodka stench finally reached me, and I recoiled.

"What are you doing here? You were supposed to stay home."

"I'm here to replace your date."

Fuck.

He stepped closer, rocking back and forth, and I stepped back.

"You're drunk. You need to go home."

"Come on, Gracie. The night is still young." He moved forward and took me by the arm, but I pulled away.

His brows drew together. "You'd rather sit beside an escort?"

"Xavier's a friend."

He burst out in laughter. Part of me hoped someone would hear him and escort him out. He stumbled forward but regained his balance as I took him by his arm. God, how he stank!

"I don't like it when you're like this."

"I'm like this when you treat me like I'm nothing."

I let go of his arm and poked my finger into his chest. "Don't you fucking blame your drinking on me." The force in my whisper surprised me.

"I drink because you're ashamed of me. Say it isn't so, Gracie."

"It isn't so. I won't be the scapegoat for your problem. We had a deal. You promised—"

"You made a promise as well, Gracie. Remember when I had my tongue in your pussy?"

He stepped closer. Suddenly, that same vodka breath I despised warmed the side of my neck, and I quivered.

"Or all the times I fucked you in your beautiful gardens, similar to these? Was that not a promise to cherish you? Did I suck you wrong?"

He didn't. The lump in my throat tightened into an unbearable knot. In bed, Hunter Silver outdid every man I'd ever been with. I'd taught him well, but he'd needed little teaching and enjoyed listening to my instruction. Then he fucking outperformed in every way.

"Do I not deserve a spot at your table, Gracie?"

I sucked in a sharp breath.

"Or did Xavier fuck you much better?"

I yanked myself away and swung my hand to slap him, but he caught my wrist in mid-air. I focused on his tight grip and my shaking hand before my gaze drifted slowly to his, and my mouth opened in shock.

He let go and stepped backward, toward the dining area, looking at me like I'd made the biggest mistake of my life. I breathed through my nose, desperate to salvage the situation and get him out of here.

"Hunter? Whatever you're thinking of doing, don't. Please."

"Are you embarrassed to introduce your boyfriend to your guests, Gracie?"

I quickened my pace, but I was already too late. He turned on his heel and headed straight for the stage, where he tapped on the microphone. The echo brought everyone's attention center-stage. The lighting technician flashed a beam Hunter's way.

"Oh, no." I covered my mouth with my hand, afraid to walk back to my table. Instead, I stood near the stage stairs, staring at the man I loved like he was my worst enemy.

"Don't do it, Hunter. Don't ruin this," I whispered, breathing to the beat of my heart and still afraid I'd run out of air as soon as he sucked it out of the room.

"Good evening, everyone."

The two hundred people fell quiet.

Here it comes.

Hunter's mother frowned from the table occupied by his parents. Jacob and Teresa Silver had brought big business to my empire. How could I not have invited them? But now that I saw my Hunter there, slurring his words, I regretted my decision to leave him at home.

"My name is Hunter Silver, and I'd like to 'gratulate my Gracie on her beautiful Oscar. She deserves it. She deserves it all, but she's been hiding me from you all. Not my dick. She doesn't hide from my motor."

"Oh, no." My whisper fogged in the cool air.

The more his speech slurred, the quicker my heart raced in my chest. He tilted his hips forward and wiggled them like he had a trunk for a penis.

"I may be younger, Xavier"—Hunter pointed into the crowd —"but with youth comes stamina, and my Gracie likes stamina."

His hand flew to the left, directing the crowd's attention to where I stood. I covered my face with my hands, hoping the ground would open underneath me, but a beam of light shone my way. I slid my fingers open enough to see Hunter turn my way. Someone from the dining area was making his way to the stage as Hunter stated, "I'm good enough to fuck for sperm, but not good enough to have dinner with. Come on, you guys, help me give her a hand. Gracie! Gracie!"

He clapped, enticing the crowd, but the room stayed silent. Humiliation burned through my body and rage coursed through my veins. Someone dragged Hunter off the stage. I was pretty sure I peed myself that night.

And I threw Hunter out on his ass before he sobered.

Chapter 1

Hunter
one year later

I dug my elbows into the ground and clicked the night vision switch on my headgear.

"Three out front and one in the back," I said to my partner.

"One more inside with the girls." Rachel was from the Costa Rican independent division of hunters. Like me, she searched for scum to execute. We'd clicked the moment she greeted me at the airport. Rachel had dual citizenship and worked for both the Costa Rican and the US agency to bring down human trafficking. Her team had hired me privately.

I focused on the group of bound girls huddled in the corner of the house. My jaw clenched until my molars ached.

"There weren't supposed to be girls here," Rachel puffed through her nose.

I found a golf-ball sized rock and gripped it in my fist. "There are now. The mission's changed."

The house was set in the middle of the jungle, and backup was at least an hour away. Our bounty, Mr. Pierce, worth a twenty million dead and thirty alive, was supposed to be hiding here. I'd been counting on cashing in the thirty, but he was nowhere to be found.

Rachel shimmied closer and tugged at my vest. "You mean, the mission's aborted."

"I'm not leaving those girls," I loud-whispered.

"The mission was to get Mr. Pierce. That's all."

"He's obviously not here, and we both know that's not his name."

"Whatever. Mission aborted."

If I continued, the consequences wouldn't be light. We had a deal. No spooking Pierce; and the moment I went after the girls, he'd get the word, vanish, and we wouldn't get paid.

Fuck money.

I crawled behind a tree closer to the house. Rachel swore in my earpiece. A moment later, she was on the ground next to me.

"You don't have to come," I said.

"I'm not letting your ass die on my watch, you stupid fool. There are five of them."

"That's two and a half each."

"And how do you propose we split the last one?"

"We won't have to worry about him if he's down. Eleven o'clock. Get ready for a distraction."

I focused my lens on the guard as he went on his rounds and checked the clearing's perimeter, swatting mosquitos. We stayed low until he passed.

"Hunter, what did you do?" Rachel elbowed my ribcage.

"Nothing yet."

I gripped the rock in my fist, rose to my knees, and launched it into the forest. The wind blew, the trees swayed, and we couldn't hear the rock hitting the ground. My fucking bad timing always got the best of me. I found another rock and threw it closer to the path, where it rolled down a slope and drew the guard's attention.

"Who's there?" He shone his flashlight over the path.

"Go check it out." The other guard waved him away.

"There. That should help." I moved Rachel aside and took my position, removing the dart gun from the holster at my thigh. I took the blind shot before she stopped me, and the dart hit the guard's back. He jerked, turned around, and dropped to the ground.

"Carlos?" his friend called out, and rushed his way.

"That was a risky move," Rachel said.

"Leaves two out here for you and two inside for me. Stay low, and see you soon."

I hunched down behind the shrubs, but the commotion alerted the guy at the rear door. I pressed the trigger and darted him before he turned the corner. Rachel shot one of hers down by the trees. I knew this would be easy. The brawny guard remained inside with a group of bound girls. There were nine of them. The smell of gasoline hit me as I crossed the threshold. I stepped around the trash scattered on the floor and pressed my back against the wall before rounding the corner. I removed a lens and checked the reflection from the main room.

A muscled gorilla stood in front of the bound girls with a handgun. His face was smeared in mud, and his body cast a demonic shadow in front of the candles on the table.

Rachel should have darted the last guard by now, and she'd take the front entrance to cover me. I moved forward and accidentally kicked a bottle. The guard lifted his gun, and I took my shot into his arm. He swatted the dart off his shoulder, stumbled, and I shot another dart into his thigh. The man was a beast; I should have used my gun. He fired two rounds. The first bullet hit my thigh, missing an artery, and the second one got in between the gear, right into my pelvis.

Fuck!

A scream tore from my lungs as I stumbled and fell to my knees in a room full of confused girls. On his way down, the guard tumbled into the table, knocking over the candles, and flames caught a corner mattress.

Rachel. Where's Rachel?

My vision blurred. I removed my headgear and pressed my hand over the wound. Blood gushed from between my fingers. I could taste it in my mouth. And just like that, the sound of the cracking fire and crying girls disappeared.

I tried to call out for Rachel, but only one name left my lips: "Grace."

Four years later

"Come on, Hunter. I don't want to be late!"

Rachel's scream echoed from the ground. The beauty of an eco-lodge without easy access was the solace from the crazy world below. Living in a jungle hadn't been on my radar when I moved to Costa Rica. The day after Grace's award night, I'd flown down and never looked back. Well, that's a lie. Of course, I looked back every fucking day and night; but Grace had been right to kick me out. I'd humiliated my queen on one of the most important nights of her life. I didn't deserve her.

I combed through the nest of facial hair and tied my dreads up in a bun.

"Hunter, the clock is ticking," Rachel called out.

Her words struck deep in my chest. Grace used to say the same thing every month she ovulated. Four years ago, when Pierce didn't show and we should have aborted a mission, a bullet had cut through my insides. Rachel had saved my life; but the injury had caused irreversible damage. I no longer had a ticking clock.

"Coming."

I kicked the looped rope into the hole in the floor, gripped the line, and lowered myself to the ground.

"You didn't have to get me."

"I was afraid if I didn't, you wouldn't show up."

Today we were celebrating. After five long years of hunting, we'd finally dismantled Pierce's sex-trafficking ring.

"Why wouldn't I show up?"

"There are at least a dozen women down in the village ready to propose, *cariño*."

"Can I tell them I don't swing that way?"

"Sorry, buddy, but that's my line."

"I can't believe you're leaving," I said.

I was ready for a vacation, and Rachel was moving on to another project.

"And I can't believe you're staying."

"Unlike you, I have nothing to return to." I hopped on my motorbike and turned on the ignition.

"You won't know unless you try."

"I tried for years and failed."

"So what? You're gonna stay here for the rest of your life cooped up in your tree house—"

"Eco-house."

"Whatever. You're cooped up in your *tree house* like a castaway while a gorgeous and talented woman is waiting for you back home."

"She's not waiting for me. She hates me. Trust me, I know."

I took the lead through the overgrown path to where she had parked her scooter beside mine. I had reached out to Grace several times, but she never returned my calls. She'd made it clear she wanted nothing to do with me, and I had to accept it. Besides, I could never give Grace what she wanted the most; not anymore. She was better without me.

Rachel gripped my arm and turned me to face her. Her throat lurched with a hard swallow.

"I'll miss you, Hunter. You're an excellent partner, and work won't be the same without you."

I took her into my arms. "I know I haven't said it, but thank you for saving my life."

"That was a good call, four years ago, Hunter. If it weren't for you, those girls would have never seen their families again."

"Yeah, it was." The choice might have cost me a future with Grace, but it had been the right one. "I'll miss you, but no goodbyes yet. Like you said, today we're celebrating."

She wiped off the tears I pretended not to see flowing down her cheeks. We rode for fifteen minutes down the mountain into the village on the jungle's edge. Flowers littered the road to the communal building, and cheer and singing filled the soul. Kids waved from the roadside. An elderly woman sat in a chair by the bakery, clapping.

Officially, this was the fourth village we'd liberated from human trafficking. Women now slept safely at night, without fear they'd be stolen from their beds. After we rescued the first group of girls, Pierce's kidnapping efforts doubled, and our efforts to nail him quadrupled. But with the villagers' help, we'd finally lured the bastard into a trap he couldn't escape.

"Hunter, this is beautiful. Look at what they've done. And it's all for you."

Lanterns lit the building's perimeter. A crowd gathered near the entrance, waving us in.

"It's not just for me—because I didn't save these girls alone. If it weren't for you, we all would have burned in that building. Now, let's go inside and party."

I joined Rachel for the first round of drinks but stuck to water with a lime wedge for the rest of the evening, ensuring my friend, who was getting married in three weeks, was safe. We danced and laughed, played games with the locals, and I was pretty sure I received three proposals.

"*Cariño*," the women called after me. "*Cásate conmigo.*"

"*Lo siento, hermosa*. I'm spoken for," I lied through my teeth, and Rachel laughed every time, playing the role of my girlfriend.

"*Beso, beso, beso*," the girls cheered, and Rachel lay a fat guaro-tasting kiss on my lips. My blood flow turned south.

Fucking Rachel.

Like Grace, she was older, gorgeous, and definitely not into me. Unlike Grace, she respected me.

Whatever.

Keeping the truth hidden about her fiancé was easier for Rachel, and having a sane and trustworthy partner was easier for me, so I went along with the light-hearted con. I spun my partner on the floor and caught her before she tumbled.

"Are you ready to take a break?" I asked her.

"What? Me? Break? No. It's fiesta time." She spun once more and reached for a shot of guaro. I swept the drink off the table before her.

"You've had enough, babe. It's time for a break." I lifted her powerful body and threw her over my shoulder. All the weight she carried as muscle nearly tipped me over as she playfully slapped at my ass. "You're not being fair. You're stronger. Put me down, Hunter."

"Not gonna happen."

I walked through the snickering crowd, winking like I was taking Rachel for a fast one, and made my way outside into the hot night air. I gently set her on the ground and held her steady.

"Are you all right, Rach?"

"Yeah, I'm fine. Just had a little too much guaro." She braced her hands on her knees, resting. I helped her to the bakery bench, where she sat down.

"Take it easy for the rest of the night. Hangovers in this heat are brutal."

A woman walked outside the community hall to the shade underneath a tree and lit a cigarette.

"Is that why you don't drink?"

I passed Rachel a bottle of water I'd swiped from the table before leaving.

"I drink," I said. "Just not in the amounts I used to, and not when I'm upset. Drink your water."

She tilted the bottle and took a few gulps, then pulled her hand across the mouth, sweeping the stray drops.

"Are you upset today?" she asked.

I shrugged a shoulder and puffed out. "What can I say? My partner is leaving."

She pouted. Truth was, there was nowhere else I was needed.

"You know, if I weren't into Katrina, I would be into you."

"Sorry I don't have a vagina."

"I'm just saying, Hunter. It's time you found someone. Actually, it's time you called Grace."

"Drink more. This water isn't clearing your head fast enough. I'm taking you home."

We walked down the overgrown path to where Rachel lived, near the village kitchen. She helped with the daily community meals and had bonded with the local girls, keeping them safe. The five hundred yards to her home weren't far, but Rachel chose a circuitous path, swerving from one side of the road to another, tripling our distance.

As the noises from the party lowered behind us, the sound of chirping crickets lifted in the night. A scuffling of rocks sounded from behind us, and we stopped, but I didn't see anyone on the graveled street. Rachel gripped my beard and tugged it her way, dragging my gaze away from the street.

"What will you tell the locals about your fiancée leaving? You should come with me. Better yet, go see Grace."

"That ship has sailed. Be quiet for a sec."

I eased her hold, and she removed her hand from my beard, suddenly sober. She looked down the street to where I was focusing.

"What is it?"

I shook my head. "I thought I heard something. Let's keep going."

I walked Rachel to her apartment, tucked her in, and locked the door behind her. She never locked it, but I had a feeling I wasn't alone tonight. The village was safe because of our security measures, but no security was unbreakable.

A gust of wind blew by. I took the back staircase and tiptoed by the wall. I turned the corner and caught the woman who had followed us in a chokehold.

"Who the fuck are you, and why are you following me?"

She coughed out, and I eased the grip around her neck, allowing her to lower the scarf off her head. Underneath was a beautiful burgundy and purple balayage. I only knew that from the years I'd spent at Grace's salon.

"I was afraid my hair would draw the wrong attention." The woman's face came into view.

"Beth?"

"What the hell happened to you?" She pulled on my beard.

People had to stop doing that.

"I barely recognize you." She slid her hand over my arm. "And what the hell happened to your body?"

"I've been undercover. The more girls I keep from crossing the borders, the less Silver Securities has to worry about back home."

"This is where you live? With another woman?"

"No, this is not where I live. Beth, what the hell are you doing in Costa Rica?"

She removed the flowing scarf from around her neck and fanned her face. Her chest rose in search of air. "Do you know how hard it is to reach you?"

I did. I'd gone off the grid for a reason. Actually, for more than one reason.

"What's going on, Beth?"

She let out a shaky breath. "The DA has launched an investigation surrounding the Hartley case. There's some confusion about Hartley's estate and last will. It will be disputed in court."

"Chad's the only son left. How can there be any disputes? I guess there's his sister Simone, but she renounced her family, and Tristan has her at a good facility."

"That's the thing, Hunter. Jeff Hartley had illegitimate children, and Chad is after every single one of them. One was murdered last week. You need to come home. Grace is in trouble."

She pulled open a garage side door near the kitchen and gestured me inside to the scooters.

"I see you're prepared. What does Grace have to do with the Hartleys?"

"Grace is on their hit list. I'll tell you everything on the way back. My plane's ready and waiting. Help me with these."

I helped her get the scooters outside and followed her down the gravel to the dusty road.

"I have to shower and change."

She stopped, turned around, and poked her finger into my chest.

"What you have to do is put on your charm and protect my daughter."

Chapter 2

grace

Hair dryers buzzed, scissors clipped, and the smell of dye and coconut shampoo filled the air. Lush hanging plants hung over the marble walls. The renovated space and the new name represented everything I'd dreamed of in an outstanding salon. An independent woman. Appointments booked months in advance, and five long years after my reputation was tarnished, Gracie's Salon was thriving. After I dumped Hunter's sorry ass, I squeezed all the lemons in my life into lemonade. It turned out, there was nothing better for business than gossip and bad publicity. At least, I liked to spin it that way. And technically, I didn't dump Hunter, because I knew he'd come back. Except he didn't. He left, thinking a phone call would fix things. His family had told me he was working somewhere in South America on an operation. And so I moved forward, not back.

I pulled my pants and underwear down over the right side of my buttock and pushed in the needle.

Breathe.

The IVF injections unnerved me ever time I poked myself, but this was the last one in the cycle. After my egg retrieval this Friday, the wait would be over. Nearly. My pre-babies would be frozen until I found the right donor, efficiently selected from a list of reputable candidates.

I removed the needle from my skin, disposed of the syringe, and pulled up my pants. Someone knocked on my door.

"Come in."

Frankie popped his head inside my office, his purple tips shimmering in the light. "Hey, Emma's here with a weird appointment. I think you should check it out."

"Define weird."

"It looks like it needs the works. Definitely not a celebrity. More primitive. There's something raw about this caveman."

Emma's unannounced visit to the salon with a homeless-looking person wasn't her first one. She dragged in these off-the-street cases, all costs covered by her family's company, and, well, she was my best friend, so I couldn't say no. Besides, I trusted her, so I found no reason to reject the work.

"Why can't you take the appointment?"

"She requested you do the job specifically."

"A caveman, you say?" I raised an eyebrow.

Frankie's forehead creased. "I called dibs, but Emma wants you."

"You should've said I'm in a meeting. Thanks, Frankie. I'll take it."

But only because it was Emma's request.

I closed my office door, crossed the spa and the salon, and took the glass staircase to the waiting area. A nauseous stench caught my attention before I reached the front where Emma was standing with what, in fact, did look like a caveman.

What the hell is that?

I should've left the job to Frankie. If that thing showed itself amongst my clients, I'd lose my business. I ran down-stairs to the front before they could come upstairs. I approached with caution, but Emma had already set her warrior puppy eyes wide, reminding me I was going into a battle we both knew I would lose. Emma always won. Always.

"What is that?" I pointed to the Neanderthal. He towered over us both, like an animal. The growth on his face hid most of the skin. Thick dreads fell down onto his forehead. I had no idea how he could see anything. He was wearing a dirty coat and giant army boots, both well worn and out of date.

I shuddered and lifted my gaze back to the tumbleweed of a beard.

Is that a feather in there?

The smell of alcohol drifted over on his breath.

Oh, the stench!

I backed away.

"It's fucking Pepé Le Pew."

Except Pepé Le Pew looked presentable. This caveman looked like a gorilla; no offense to gorillas.

"He's drunk. He was celebrating a recent assignment and got carried away, but he's safe. I promise." Emma nudged him forward and the full weight of his body fell into mine, knocking me off balance. I straightened and shuffled around him towards Emma.

"Ems, you should have known better. This thing is… I don't know what it is. Is it human?"

He twitched.

"Stop calling him *it*. He's from Allie's branch and works undercover. He's family, and he needs a cut."

He needed more than a cut. The man needed a miracle only I could perform.

"This assignment is from the Silvers? " I poked a finger into his bulky arm. It bounced off his coat and the steely body underneath. Dirt crumbled to the floor.

I looked back up. "Is he dangerous?"

"Very dangerous." Emma replied.

"You just said he was safe," I said through gritted teeth.

He twitched again, and I jumped.

"Okay, he's not dangerous." She backed to the door. Like I said, Emma always won.

"He can't stay here, Ems. This is a prestigious salon, and I can't afford another scandal."

Truth was, I could afford it, because all publicity was publicity. But I would not allow a man with a bird's nest on his face to pass to the second floor.

"He also needs a shave." She made her puppy face again. She was lucky she was cute, and I loved her like the sister I had never had. My younger brother Cash often took private jobs for Silver Securities, but I had no clue what the hell he did. My twin brother Nick and the two older brothers, Axel and Ace, owned a criminal law firm and a chain of strip clubs. Thank goodness I'd inherited my Aunt Mary's creative side and opened a beauty salon: away from chaos, criminals, and assholes my brothers put behind bars.

"You know, if it were me, I'd just shave him everywhere, if you know what I mean."

I knew what she meant.

"Maybe wax him where necessary." She circled her hand around his groin. "That ought to bring him back, don't you think?" She winked.

The caveman shifted away, and I rolled my eyes, dejected. "I won't hurt you."

"So that's a yes? Great!" Emma squealed.

I took a whiff. "When was the last time he washed? A century ago?"

"I'm not sure if I can give a time frame."

"Ems, I don't have scissors with blades sharp enough to conquer the forest on his face." I pulled her outside the front door. The caveman stayed in his spot. "And I'd have to order at least a gallon of wax. Besides, this is not a charity salon. And even if it were, I couldn't just let *it* parade among all my clients."

"I already told you: Silver Securities is paying for it all. Mr. Silver said whatever the charge, bill him."

"Your uncle?"

"My cousin."

"Which one?"

"Doesn't matter." She waved her hand. "I gotta go. I owe you big time, but I have this thing with this guy."

"Oh, no! You're not leaving me alone with *him,* are you?"

She backed away.

"Grace, I'll do anything. I promise."

"Emma…" I warned.

"Love you so much, Gracie. You're the best friend every girl should have." Emma hurried to her illegally parked convertible Mercedes and hopped into the driver's seat.

Shit! I glanced at the salon's front window. The caveman peeked our way from behind a flowering eucalyptus. When I turned back to Emma, she pulled away and merged into traffic.

"For fuck's sake, Emma. I'll get you back. I promise," I called after her. Tires screeched as she took the corner, and my arms dropped to the sides.

"You didn't even tell me his name," I whined to myself, and stomped back to the front entrance.

I grabbed the caveman by his arm. "Come."

His crisp jacket crumpled in my hand. The thick layers of dirt on the outside had me worried about what I'd find underneath.

"Fucking Emma." I pulled him by the sleeve to the alley where Gus dropped off our products. I entered the code at the panel and opened the side delivery door.

"Follow me and stay close." I pulled on that dusty jacket again. "Actually, hold on. You're gonna make a mess. Take this off."

I went inside, grabbed a fresh robe from the storage room, and passed it to the caveman. He didn't move.

I growled. "Fine. I'll get you out of this inside. Don't make a sound." I wiggled my finger in front of his face. The corner of his mustache moved a fraction.

The spa covered two floors: showers, steam-rooms, saunas and mudrooms were downstairs, massages and personal care upstairs. We crossed the mud-room, where an appointment with a cucumber masque was marinating in the tub. I guided the caveman across the room and into the private shower area. A smell of mold and mildew, moss, and raw earth wafted around him. I grabbed the lavender air freshener and pressed the nozzle, spraying the surrounding air.

His nostrils fluttered, taking in the scent. I lowered the canister and set my hands on my hips. "Please, tell me you've showered before."

A muscle twitched in his jaw, and I wished I could see his eyes. I adjusted my glasses and watched as he tugged at his oversized coat. A row of buttons popped with the pull. He slipped off the coat and tossed it aside. My head flew with the throw, then back to the muscled man standing in front of me. He looked more like a bear than a gorilla. A thick, burly bear with the strength of ten men. Brawn and mystery oozed from the man, stirring a primal urge in my belly.

"Take off your pants." My voice quivered.

The corner of his mustache curved, or so I thought. I ignored the higher shift of his forehead and followed his over-worked hands to his hips. He gripped the joggers and bent in half, stepping out of the pant legs. The path up his hairy calves, knees, and lean thighs three times the size of mine led to a surprise. Mr. Caveman went commando. His healthy cock hung low and to the side, holding my stare longer than appropriate. Then again, there was nothing appropriate about the moment. I bit my lip. I hadn't seen a thing that large since…

Well… It had been a while. My nipples ached at the sweet memory of Hunter's lips around them. As much as I hated what he'd done, I missed him.

I slowly looked up, afraid the caveman would catch me ogling his obvious pride, but he just stood there, frozen. Dreads covered his face and eyes. He definitely needed a cut, and possibly a psychiatrist.

It's just a job.

I squeezed in between him and the wall, reaching inside the shower. The knob slipped in my grip and I stumbled into the caveman, then quickly pulled back. The man's brute strength held me up as I peeled away from his body. Was he also a brute in bed?

What the hell, Grace? I shook off the stupid thought, but it was already too late for the rush of arousal in my veins.

I cleared my throat. "Now that we know each other, you should tell me your name." I tapped at his elbow, guiding him further inside the shower, but he didn't move. "Come on. Give me a break. You have to shower and wash before we attempt to get that gorilla costume off you."

Water dripped down his arm where the shower reached him from the side. Layers of dirt trickled down his skin and onto the tiles, revealing a bronzed complexion, taut skin, and a gallery of muscles.

"Here." I shoved him underneath the stream and closer to the shampoo dispenser, pumping a dab on my hand.

He didn't move. Except now the shower had soaked his naked glory. My right side was wet, and if my client finished her mud bath before the caveman showered, I would die of embarrassment. We had to cross the mudroom to the private waxing area.

I reached for his hand and slid the shampoo off my palm and into his. He stood like a statue, and my hope trickled down the drain.

"I'm going to kill Emma," I said to nobody, removed my shoes, and stepped inside. The overhead rain shower drenched my shirt and pants. I removed my glasses and set them blindly on a holding shelf.

"Get down." I pushed on his wide shoulders, and he dropped to his knees. I dabbed more shampoo on my palm and spread the goo into the scalp between his dreads.

A primal moan rumbled through the falling water and made my limbs go limp. I stopped.

What was I doing? I was standing in a shower with a naked Neanderthal, washing him because Emma had told me to.

He swept the dreads off his face while I wiped the water off my eyes, half blind.

"You make a habit of washing cavemen, Grace?" I hadn't heard the familiar voice in five long years. It aroused anger and pure lust all at once.

It couldn't be, could it?

I gulped through the thickness in my throat and connected my gaze with Hunter's piercing blue eyes. His hooded stare, broken with strands of dreads, nearly stopped my heart.

"It's…it's you."

"Were you expecting a real caveman, Grace?" He stood up in what felt like slow motion, his full naked bear's body so close to my drenched skin that my thoughts vanished. My heart had lost its rhythm about a dozen times by then, and I could barely breathe.

"Wh…what are you doing here?" My lip quivered.

A ricochet of flying bullets blasted from somewhere inside the salon, and I jumped into his arms.

"Looks like I'm just in time."

Chapter 3

Hunter

"What's going on?" Grace fumbled to get her glasses off the shower shelf, nearly dropped them, and set them on her nose. She hadn't worn glasses before. Another gunshot went off and I whipped my head toward the second floor..

"Get your phone." I grabbed her by her wrist and dragged her out of the shower. While I appreciated Grace's steamy reception, her life was in trouble. Beth had told me that we had a few days before the Hartleys made Grace a target.

"The phone's upstairs, and I'm soaked."

I noticed. Her white shirt clung to her skin, outlining her lacey bra and pebbled nipples, messing with my concentration. I grabbed my joggers off the floor and slipped them on.

"What the hell happened to you, Hunter?"

"Not the right time, Grace."

I took her hand and led her through the mudroom, where a fear-stricken client was clinging to the corner of the bath. A scream tore from the second floor, and she shuddered. I lowered to her ear. "You're going to be all right. Stay quiet and don't move. We're gonna get help, but if anyone asks, you didn't see us."

She nodded eagerly. I grabbed a few cucumber slices off a tray and stuffed them in my mouth, pulling Grace along to the delivery door in the back.

"The door leads to the alley, and the alley leads to the front."

"Grace, you need to trust me."

She tugged on my hand, squeezing. "I can't leave my employees."

"Don't worry, they won't kill anyone because they're looking for you, and once they realize you're not there, they'll leave."

"Who's they?"

"Chad Hartley's goons. We need to get to the rooftop."

"Why me?" She was shaking and looking around like she'd never been in her salon.

"Not the right time, Grace."

"You're going in your joggers? What about shoes and shirt?" She was in shock.

"Better in my joggers than with a bullet in my chest. And I can run just as fine without shoes. Now, come on."

I opened the back door, and we hurried to the metal staircase. The building was attached to a row of other buildings. We crossed the hot rooftop and scaled down the staircase at the side to where my brother had parked my car.

"You don't have your clothes, but you have your Bugatti?"

"James dropped it off."

I pressed my thumb to the door and opened the passenger side. Grace hopped into her seat, and I went around to the driver's side.

The sound of sirens echoed from nearby.

"I told you the police would get here quick. Hold on."

I pressed the gas pedal and merged with traffic. A fleet of cop cars raced on the other side of the street. At the third light, I took a left and pulled into the underground parking.

"We're staying at a hotel three blocks from the salon?"

"Yes, it's my hotel room."

"It's only three blocks away from the salon."

"That's correct."

"Three blocks."

"I promise, you'll be safe."

She shook her head, and I glanced at her from the side as I slid into my parking spot. "What can I help you understand, Grace?"

"How do you come to the salon, looking like you do, and not call or text or…anything?" she stuttered.

"From what I remember, you liked what you saw."

"Hunter, can you be serious?"

"Doesn't change the facts."

She puffed out a frustrated breath.

I clicked her seatbelt free and took her hand into mine. She was trembling. "I came to your salon straight from the airport. My brother James left the car for me, and I'm hoping he didn't forget about the clothes in my room. Come on, let's get changed before you catch pneumonia."

I got out of the car, walked around, opened her door, and took her hand. She shook in the elevator, so I wrapped my arms around her and held her all the way to the suite. I stepped in front of the door panel to scan my retina.

The lock clicked open, and I pushed the door, letting her through. She stepped inside and wrapped her arms around herself again.

"You're safe here, Grace." I walked past her. "And we both need a proper shower."

She turned and walked in front of me, blocking my way. "I'm not showering with you."

I swept the dreads off my eyes. "You were willing to at the salon."

"That's when I thought you were—"

"A caveman?" I lifted a brow. "You prefer cavemen, Grace?"

She jerked back, and her brows drew together. "Not a caveman—a bear. I thought you looked like a bear with all that hair over you." Her cheeks flushed bright red. "They didn't have razors where you've been? Or showers?"

"No razors. I fell off my scooter on the way to the airport with your mother."

"My mother?" She set her hands on her hips and began pacing across the room, shivering. "How did my mother end up wherever you were?"

"You'd have to ask her that, but she's the one who came to Costa Rica to get me."

"Let me guess. You had no cellphone."

"I lived off the grid."

"She had to get you again *why?*"

"How about we shower first, Grace?" I motioned to the washroom. "I really don't want you catching pneu—"

"Pneumonia. I know." She threw her hands up in the air, and I pointed to the washroom once again. She rolled her eyes. "I'm still not showering with you."

I followed her into the oversized washroom with a double shower. A two-sided fireplace glowed between the glass walls.

"Is this a presidential suite?" she asked.

"No. This suite belongs to the Silvers. Family use only. Pick your shower."

"I don't remember you talking in short sentences." She snorted. "Turn around. I have to undress."

I shook my head, but I obliged. She had nothing I hadn't seen before, but it was definitely a long time since I'd seen it, so turning around was the better option. I heard her shuffle with her clothes and then twist the faucet.

"Okay, I'm inside."

Her white bra and panties hung over the shower door. She stood on the other side, underneath the rainwater, the curves of her silhouette outlined behind a flickering partition. I stepped inside the other shower and twisted the knob. My pulse raced, blood rushed south, and I submerged myself beneath the stream. The cold water did little to cool the heat rushing through my veins and my throbbing dick. What the fuck was happening to me? I was over this. I was over her.

"I like the new line of lingerie you're wearing," I said.

"How did you know?"

"It looked nice underneath your white shirt." A picture of her nipples poking through the soaked fabric flashed in my mind. "Everything looked nice."

She didn't reply, and I imagined the shade of her skin flushing pink. I braced my arm against the wall and felt my grip on my hard cock. The urge to find a release grew as I pumped. I stepped back and bumped into the glass wall.

"Are you all right?" Grace asked, and I let go of my dick.

"Yeah, just slipped."

I soaped up the sponge and washed myself from the head down. It had been years since I'd taken a long shower, but nothing could replace washing underneath a waterfall. Grace finished well before me. The heat of her stare as she passed by the shower burned into my back. Or maybe it was my imagination? I gripped my cock once she left and tried to whack one out again, but it didn't work. It wasn't the same without her.

Fuck me.

My body ached, and my mind spun from the constant attack of the past in my head.

This is a job. She is a job. That's all.

I got out of the shower and wrapped a towel around my body. Grace was sitting on the corner of the bed in a pair of fluffy slippers and a robe. She was looking out the window at the setting sun. The orange glow cast a warm shade over her neck and chest. Her legs hung off the bed, swinging lightly. The robe shifted to the side and slipped off her thigh. She looked so fucking beautiful.

I cleared my throat, and she looked up, quickly covering her leg.

"I found some clothes." She pointed to the closet.

"Your mother said she'd leave some for you."

She swept her hands down her legs and hopped off the bed. I felt the corner of my mouth lift.

"I wanted to dry off before I got dressed."

"No problem." I paced to the closet and picked up a fresh pair of joggers. I dropped the towel to the floor, slipped on the pants, and returned to the bedroom.

"How long are we staying here? Together?" she asked.

"Is my company after five years not welcome for longer than two hours?"

"That's not what I'm saying, Hunter." Her voice vibrated with nerves. "But I have employees to check on, and my business. And I'm sure the police will want to speak with me."

I picked up my phone and scrolled through my family's group chat. "I can assure you everything is taken care of, but if you insist on an honest answer, you won't return to Gracie's for a while. That's not up for negotiation."

"We're negotiating?"

"Gracie's? You named your salon after the one name you hated me calling you?"

Her face reddened. "You called me Gracie when you were drunk, and don't change the subject."

"That still makes little sense, Grace."

"Argh." She let out a frustrated breath.

"What is it?"

"Nothing." She threw her hands up in the air. "It's just weird looking at you like this."

"I thought you were into cavemen?"

"Bears. I said bears, and not that I was into them, but that… Now, where are my glasses?" It was cute how her voice trembled. She stomped across the room, found her glasses on the table, and set them on her nose. Her freckles popped and her eyes widened. The glasses suited her, and again, I didn't recall all these cuteness factors from when we were together. It messed with my head, but awakened the need to protect her and make her happy.

I strode her way and guided her to the bed. She sat down, and I poured her a glass of spring water.

"Thank you," she whispered, sipping.

"Food should be here soon."

"I'm not sure I can eat."

"Hydrate, at least. Seriously, why 'Gracie'?"

She set her glass aside. "It was a statement of independence. After you left, I wanted to pave my own path, and 'Gracie' reminded me how the man I loved put me down. I stood back up after you left, and I do so every morning."

Her use of the past tense for me—*loved*—stung deep in my heart. I grabbed an elastic band from the side drawer and pulled my dreads into a bun. Her lips parted as she watched me, and the jugular at her neck pulsed strongly.

"I'm sorry for the pain I caused you. I know it's too late, but I'm truly sorry."

She patted the bed beside her, and I sat down.

"So, tell me about this attack. Why are the Hartleys after me?"

Someone knocked on the door. "Room service."

I grinned. "I'll tell you everything I can, but first, we eat. I'm starving."

"Hunter—"

"I came to save you straight from the airport—you know, like a knight in shining armor—and this body needs to be fed. I haven't had a bite since the flight."

I opened the door for the private suite butler, and he rolled in a cart full of every item I'd dreamed of in Costa Rica: pizza, burgers, hot dogs, and fries. Plus a few leafy salads and vegetarian options for Grace. The butler set the food on the table and left. I locked the door.

"Make yourself comfortable."

"Who's going to eat all this?"

"We are."

"I'm not hungry."

I pulled back her chair, and she took her seat.

"Not even for coffee ice cream?" I asked.

She eyed the table and smiled when she spotted the tub of her favorite. I passed her a spoon.

"So, we're leaving this hotel room when?"

"Not today."

"Tomorrow?"

"What's the rush, Grace? Is it the beard or the hair?"

She lifted her gaze and snaked it over my face, shoulder, and chest. A sparkle lit up her eyes, betraying her control. I'd recognize that wanton look from miles away. Her chest rose and fell with heavy breaths, eyes searching for an answer. The jugular on her neck pulsed while my blood rush to my dick, and the first doubt I'd keep my hands to myself crept in.

She pulled the spoonful of ice cream between her lips, and I nearly lost it. She set it back in the tub and sighed. "I have an appointment this Friday for egg retrieval. I took my last IVF shot before you came to the salon."

I cracked my head to the side, and a pinch of regret flew down my spine. "Retrieve them next month."

"I would rather not go through another cycle."

"You're still young, Grace."

"Thirty-seven is not young to have kids. My uterus is shriveling, and my eggs are scarce."

"Why not do it the old-fashioned way?"

"I'd rather pick a candidate based on a profile sheet. Sperm donors don't lie."

"Sociopathic ones do."

"They filter the sperm bank at Cryogenics."

"Filter?"

"Screen. Young, healthy, and good-looking donors with Master's degrees."

I snickered.

"What's so funny?"

"Documents can be altered. Trust me."

"Are you offering, Hunter? Because last time I checked, you didn't want any offspring."

"Sorry, Grace, but I don't have a Master's degree. Also, I never said I didn't want offspring. I said I wasn't ready for one."

"Argh." The chair she pushed back squeaked over the hardwood floor. "I can't stand this. I'll be perfectly safe with my brothers. I can stay with Scar."

Her twin was working on her case and wanted Grace out of the loop. I stood up, pushed away from the table, and grabbed her by the wrist as she headed for the door.

"What the fuck, Grace? How about 'Hunter, thank you for saving my life'? And you're not going anywhere."

She tried to wiggle out, but I bear-hugged her before she could. I tightened my arms around her, the thin robe she wore separating me and her fucking poking nipples.

"That's right, because it's always about you," she spat back.

That was fucking wrong, and she knew it. Our life had always been about her and her high-class socialite friends and all the babies she wanted—but not with me. She never considered I wasn't ready for kids. And now that same future I once saw with her was impossible.

"Let me go."

I allowed her to slip out of my hold, aware that I was still blocking the exit. She puffed out a frustrated breath, plopped on the bed, and flicked on the television.

"I should check the news since I'm your prisoner."

"I prefer 'guest.'"

The first news channel blasted about the attack at Gracie's.

"Wait, Grace." I gripped her hand.

"Fine. Then tell me why you're holding me here, and why the Hartleys are after me."

I sat down on the bed beside her and turned down the television's volume.

"There was a mistake in the will," I lied. I'd promised to let Beth to tell Grace the truth on her own, and I didn't break promises. Not anymore.

"Chad Hartley thinks you're part of their estate settlement."

"Why would they think that?"

"Because there was a mistake in Jeff Hartley's will. Your mother's working on it."

"My mother?"

"It's a sensitive matter, and she didn't want to involve anyone else."

"But she involved you."

"I guess she knows what's best for her daughter."

She allowed a little smile, but just then a headline flashed across the screen's bottom, drawing her attention.

ANOTHER MURDER LINKED TO THE HARTLEYS AT CENTRAL PARK

I watched as she focused in on the details. She clasped her hands over her legs and looked back at me with fear-stricken eyes. "Was that bullet meant for me?"

I didn't reply.

Chapter 4

grace

Hunter shut the drapes, checked the door locks, and left to his room.

"Pffff." I puffed out a breath of relief.

When I went to work this morning, I never imagined I'd end up in Hunter's hotel room. I never imagined him back home again. I'd dreamt about it, but my dreams and reality rarely aligned.

I tossed and turned well past midnight, but sleeping was out of the question.

Hunter.

Hunter Silver.

Air whistled out of my lungs.

He'd morphed from a fit young man to a man. A bear. A deliciously warm bear who wrapped me into his body like I belonged there. His heat consumed me when he held me. I turned onto my right side while twisting the sheets. A sliver of moonlight peeked in between the curtains.

The flick of his night lamp drew my attention to the frosted glass door leading to his room. The shadow of his body crossed to the second washroom. I stayed still, secretly hoping he'd come in to check on me, but he didn't. The faucet's running water triggered another hot flash, reminding me of his shower, where he'd stood underneath the stream, his arm braced against the wall, rinsing his head.

I'd slept with Hunter many times. We'd made love, fucked, orgasmed, and conquered positions I'd never dreamed of. He'd never faltered, and the sex was great, but the new statue of muscles and strength underneath the shower stirred a fresh desire in my belly. I imagined the brute force of his body pressing me into the mattress, my skin yielding to his. I could orgasm just by looking at him.

Hunter finished in the washroom, turned off the faucet, and returned to his bed. I waited until the light went out and shifted in bed, switching sides.

And then he shed the towel at the threshold of his walk-in closet, like he couldn't move further in for privacy. His shoulders stretched wider than I remembered, and stacks of perfectly aligned muscles sculpted his body all the way down to his ankles and feet. Midway, his tight, hairy ass flexed with every move. He bent over with his taut behind on full display, pulled on the joggers, and turned around.

My mouth dropped open when he approached me. Hanging loose, long, and to the side, the bulge underneath his pants shifted with each step. Higher, where the band hung around his hips, a V-cut dipped into the muscles and his hair-sprinkled abs.

He had little hair over his abs, but I'd seen everything below. His back and ass needed as much care as his groin.

Ahh, that fucking groin and everything it promised.

Feeling warmth swoosh through my veins, I shifted to my back and removed the covers.

Air.

Except it smelled like him and tasted like him. A better him. A stronger him. A man I hated and yearned for. A man who could have given me a baby the easy way, but who hadn't wanted kids. Maybe it was for the better. That sexy beard would scare a kid. My palm twitched at the thought of tugging on his growth and raking my fingers through his facial hair. The dreads didn't suit him and I missed his curls, but those piercing eyes underneath, the only ones able to sink deep into my soul, held my body captive the same they had years ago, when…

… when he was drinking and humiliated me.

I yawned.

But the years we'd shared were never lost. Camping trips, hunting yet never killing an animal, and yachting. Adventure ran through his blood, but what I needed was stability. And alcohol was an enemy we'd both fought since the beginning. He was my soulmate—until he became the man I despised. The man I loved to despise who called me 'Gracie.'

"Grace, Grace. Wake up."

Hunter's gentle voice and warm touch on my thigh forced my eyes open. The room blurred around me, and my body stilled as warmth spread upward from his palm. He reached to the side table.

"Here are your glasses."

His hand returned to my thigh, and I fumbled with the glasses.

I lifted my head and looked down to where his palm was resting on my leg. "What are you doing?"

He took his hand off my thigh. "You were thrashing in your bed. I was holding you down."

"I… I'm fine now," I lied, and dragged myself to sit against the headboard and away from him, suddenly aware that my choice of outfit for the night showed everything I wanted to hide, including my engorged breasts and protruding nipples. My eggs would be so ready for retrieval this Friday.

"Yeah, you look great."

As if on cue, my ovaries pulsed. I shook off the heat, and I finally noticed the mop on his head.

"Hunter, what the hell did you do?"

"I tried to give myself a cut so I wouldn't look like a caveman."

Caveman wasn't a bad thing.

"And you opted for scarecrow?"

"I'm hoping you can fix it, but I don't have the tools."

"I do. At the salon. Oh, my God. My salon." I shot out of bed, half-ignoring his enormous bear's body.

"Relax, Grace. Everything is fine."

I whipped around to face him. He stretched out on the bed in a pair of boxers. Fucking concentrating around him would be impossible.

"How can you say everything will be fine? I nearly got killed last night. They attacked my employees... I don't even know how they're doing."

"Everyone's fine."

I linked my arms over my chest. "How do you know?"

"I checked in with Frankie."

"What about the salon?"

"It's a crime scene. The police are collecting evidence." He placed his hands on my shoulders, gently pressing the pads of his fingers into my skin. "There's no need to worry, Grace. I'm taking care of everything."

I stepped back. His hands fell off my shoulders, but their heat remained.

"I have an appointment at the clinic this Friday."

"I remember."

"So, you're letting me go soon? Today?"

"We're moving back to your house as soon as it's ready. Gabe is installing a new security system as we speak. We're making sure the house is bug-free and safe, so you're free to move around your property as you wish."

"No 'but'?" I shook my head. "Wait—did you say 'we'?"

"I'm not leaving your side, Grace, until Chad is behind bars. Or dead."

"Dead? Who would kill him?"

"You're not the only one who's a target. The illegitimate siblings are coming after one another. Jeff Hartley was a gem, wasn't he? The Hartley genes hold firm when it comes to money and fortune."

"That murder on television last night—"

"Is the second related murder. There's one more person on the list—and you."

"Fuck." I hadn't realized I'd said it out loud. "How long do you think it will take?"

"You're tired of me already?" Somewhere underneath the hair growth, I knew a dimple had sunk into his cheek.

"I'm a fan of taking my time, Grace."

My body heated.

"But I'll try to make this quick and painless."

I didn't want it quick and painless. I wanted it long and slow until my veins burned and my ovaries blossomed.

He bent down to my ear. "Your safety requires full cooperation."

"Define 'cooperation.'" My throat screamed for water.

His lips hovered a whisper away, and his fresh minty breath curled around my face. "You do as I tell you."

I swallowed to clear the knot in my throat and opened my mouth as his command surged through my body, pulsing through my heart and veins. My body shuddered and the faint squish in my panties forced my knees together. I turned away from him and faced the walk-in closet.

"I have to change."

I stepped inside, locked the door behind me, and leaning against the back.

What the hell was happening to me? I drowned my lungs

with air, filling them with the smell of Hunter and his wooden-musk. His new rugged scent stirred long forgotten urges and needs. The constant warmth heated my blood and turned my body into an inferno. I pulled myself away from the door and rummaged through the rack of clothes, settling on a pair of breathable sweats and a tank top. The air was thick with my sweat and his smell. My hormones bounced through my body. The injections were getting to me, but by Friday, it would all be worth it.

I braced my hands on my knees.

"Control yourself, Grace. And breathe."

I lifted and looked at the door like I could see Hunter standing on the other side with that mop of his head. It didn't match his bear body. I gathered myself, compelling control back to my limbs, cracked my neck to the side, and opened the door.

Hunter was standing by the window with a cup of coffee in his hand. A pair of joggers hugged his hips, and all my control eroded. My gaze held steady on the slant of his dick. I shut my eyes.

Distraction. I need a distraction.

I squared my shoulders and looked him firmly in the eyes, reaching out. "I need my phone."

"How about a coffee first?" He pointed to the side table with the steaming mug. A hazelnut aroma reached me, and my mouth watered.

"Thank you. I still need my phone.

"For what? "

"To call a friend."

"Again—for what?"

"You know, you were never this controlling before you left."

"You were never on a hit list before I left. And I'm not controlling, Grace. I'm cautious. I have a job to do."

"So I'm a job now?"

"Drink your coffee. You'll feel better." He transferred the cup to my hands. The flicker of anger in my chest faded with the touch of his fingers on mine. I sipped on my coffee while he strolled to his room and returned with his phone. All sexy and beary. Was that even a word?

"Who do you need to call?"

"Frankie. I need a favor. I can't let you go out into the public like this. I need an update on the salon, and he can bring a good pair of scissors and razors."

His mustache lifted. "I was hoping you'd help me with the hair."

"It would be embarrassing to walk around like that. All hairy and primitive." I waved my hand around, catching the delicious path down his abs.

He passed me the phone, and I dialed Frankie's number and gave him the hotel's address. We ate the breakfast waiting by the window in the dining area, and an hour later, a knock sounded at the door.

I pulled away from the table, and Hunter flew in front of me.

"Wait. Stay there."

"It's Frankie."

"Not until I verify." He turned to the door. "What's the code word I gave you?"

"Caveman," Frankie replied, and Hunter released the lock and opened the door.

"Whoa there. I wasn't expecting a bear."

I smiled, rolling my lips inward.

Frankie slipped through the two-foot space between Hunter and the wall, looking him over. He nearly tripped running toward me.

"Hi! It's so good to see you." He dropped the bags of supplies to the floor and charged my way with open arms. "Hey, sweetie. I've been worried sick about you, but this man called yesterday and today and said he's keeping you safe, and the police confirmed your safety, but I couldn't believe it and wanted to see it on my own."

"Frankie. Calm down. I'm okay. How are you doing? How is everybody?"

He took a deep breath and began again. "They trashed the salon. I don't know how much the renovations will cost, but I gather it will be a pretty penny. A gold one... No... Maybe diamond. Everyone's okay, but they've been worried, and Casey sprained her arm when she slipped on the floor. Martina broke three nails, and Sofia burned herself when she hid in the steam-room. Other than that, everyone's okay."

"Breathe, Frankie. Breathe." I took his hands in mine and practiced the same labor technique I'd watched online. It was the only one I knew, but it worked.

Frankie calmed and brushed his fingers through my waves. "Jesus, honey. Let's see what we can do about that hair."

"You're here for him, not me." I turned him around to face Hunter.

"Frankie, meet Hunter. Hunter, Frankie."

"The caveman? Yum. I see why you need my help."

"Your help?" Hunter asked. "I thought Grace was doing me."

"Honey, I can do you better than your girlfriend."

"I'm not his girlfriend." I grabbed the bags of supplies off the floor and carried them to the washroom. "And Frankie specializes in trimming men, so unless you want me to touch your dick, he's doing the job."

"My dick? Why does he need to touch my dick?" Hunter leaned against the doorframe with one arm. His biceps stretched and muscles bunched. Jesus, he looked delicious in that bear suit, but a trim would make him irresistible.

Fucking hormones.

I physically shuddered, shaking off the lust. Thank God, Frankie was here. "Are you ready?" My voice quivered.

"Fine. But he's staying away from my dick." He pointed to Frankie. "And you're going to fill me in on everything you saw at Gracie's."

The sound of my name, the way he used to say it, didn't evoke the rush of dread I expected.

Frankie walked past us into the bathroom, picked up the bags of supplies I'd set on the floor, turned on his heel and carried them across my room. "I need a better space." We followed him to Hunter's bedroom, where he cleared a table, moved it to the bedside, and set up the equipment. He found a pair of scissors and clipped them between his fingers. "Let's get trimming. This will take a while."

He pulled Hunter into the bedroom and pushed me out the door.

"Wait," I said. "Leave the beard. Clean it up, but leave it."

Hunter's mustache twitched with what I assumed was a smile. I enjoyed reading the subtle movements underneath his facial hair, like they were secretive, and for me.

I was patient and paced the room for the first hour, then the second. Halfway through the third, I knocked on the bedroom door. "How much longer?"

"Longer," Frankie called out.

I cracked my fingers and massaged the stress out of my shoulders five times before the bedroom door opened, and Frankie sneaked through the crevice, past me.

"He's all yours. He wants to come out, but you need to finish the job down under. He won't let me move the goods, and from what I can see underneath the towel, the goods need a trim."

"Okay, okay. Thank you so much." I hugged him tight. "We'll stay in touch."

"Definitely. I can't believe this is the man you've complained about over the years."

"What do you mean?"

"He's a protector and a provider. The things he did in Costa Rica—"

"He told you about Costa Rica?"

"I'll tell you this much: I'd let any man who called me his queen butter me up like a pancake for breakfast, so take a hint, Grace."

My heart thumped harder, but the inviting image of a mature Hunter that Frankie painted was difficult to frame. I folded my arms across my chest.

"I didn't complain. I vented."

"Sure. Good luck with the caveman."

The bear, I corrected in my mind.

"Lock the door behind him," Hunter called out.

Frankie hugged me once more and left. I double-checked the locks, straightened my spine, and returned to the living room. I pushed the bedroom door wide open and stilled. Hunter lay naked on the bed, with a towel over his head and another one tenting over his hips.

"I can feel you staring." His voice rumbled through the air.

"I want to see your hair."

"After you're done. I'm afraid if I look at you... Well, it's just better with my eyes covered."

I cleared my throat. "All right. Don't move."

As I approached the bed, he turned into the same statue I'd met at the salon and didn't budge. I grabbed the trimmers and removed the towel from his hips. His cock lay long and thick, curving up to the V near the hip bone. I touched near his navel, and his dick flexed.

"Please, make it quick."

Yet I just wanted to take my sweet time.

"Okay, time for the *big* reveal." Her voice pitched.

I smirked underneath the towel. Sixty long minutes had passed before I moved a muscle. Well, all except one muscle. I'd experienced torture before, but nothing close to the torment Grace's fingers evoked when she moved my cock to one side, then the other. And she repeated the motion a few times, eyeing the area, until I stood tall and proud, giving her access to my fucking pubes. She raked her fingers through the hair growth around my dick, and I was gone. That had been fifty-nine and a half minutes ago, and I was still hard. And my balls ached.

"Come on, Hunter. Take the towel off your face. I want to see your cut."

And I wanted to see her. I wanted to see when she finally recognized the man who'd left her. But through those agonizing fifty-nine and a half fucking minutes, as she breathed hot and heavy over my balls, trimming them, I wanted her to forget that same man. I willed my dick to lower, but Grace's touch won.

Distant nerves rolled down my spine before I tugged at the towel's corner. Grace was standing near the bed. Her gaze slithered over my body as mine did over hers. She was wearing a tank top, with her bra sticking out above the neckline, and skin-tight shorts. Or maybe underwear? I scanned back up to her engorged breasts, full lips, and wide eyes, which painted a picture of a wanton woman. And those fucking glasses were like a fantasy. My dick filled with more blood.

"Hunter." She covered her mouth with her hand. "You... You look good."

She stepped closer, her breasts and protruding nipples in line with my eyes, and she touched my beard. An itch crawled its way up my cheek, and I wished she'd tug it.

"Frankie did well with the trim."

"Let me see." I sat up and slipped off the bed, past Grace to the full-length mirror on the wall. The clown cut was gone and... Fuck, I'd aged. I hadn't seen this face in five years and barely recognized the jawline. I pulled my fingers through the shorter cut and stepped away from the mirror. The side view of a damaged body, overworked but manicured, was reflected back. It had been a while since I'd seen that man. Actually, I wasn't sure whether I'd ever seen him before.

"You look good."

"You said that already." My biceps flexed, and my dick hardened into a rod. *Fuck, I looked good.*

"I mean, real good."

Her tongue clicked, catching my attention, and I laughed. "Thanks."

Her cheeks flushed bright pink. "I'm sorry. It's just that a lot has happened in the past twenty-four hours. The attack and the spa and the attack and...and you're back."

She stared at me like a lost deer in the woods, her long lashes fluttering for answers. Where was the confidant woman I remembered?

I faced the mirror. "Frankie's not the only one who trims well. I look larger. You trimmed me the way you like me."

Her head flew up. "What?"

"The manscape." I turned back to face her and pointed to my crotch, instantly feeling her eyes on my hard dick. "It's the same way you used to trim me."

She folded her arms underneath her breasts. "That's because it's hygienic. You said you wanted a cleanup."

"*I* said nothing. That was Emma."

"So you heard me, after all."

"Of course, I heard you. I enlisted Emma's help to get to your salon so I wouldn't scare you."

"Fucking Emma." Her lips pursed, and she pointed to my dick. "Put on a pair of pants before that thing shrivels up."

"That thing?"

"Your dick," she mouthed, like her lips were begging to taste me. But any shriveling while around Grace was impossible, so she had nothing to worry about. My balls, on the other hand, were fucking ready to explode. I had tossed and turned at night, catching a few silent minutes during the times Grace actually slept. Twenty-four hours ago, I was in a different world, and now I'd returned to invade hers.

I walked to the closet, turned around to face her, and pulled on the joggers, adjusting the tilt of the tenting fabric. She watched me dress with her mouth wide open, then let out a frustrated breath. I could so easily get rid of that frustration.

"You vented to Frankie about me," I said.

"You eavesdropped?"

"Frankie left the bedroom door ajar." I walked up to her and touched her shoulder.

She flinched.

"I'm sorry to have hurt you, Grace. I truly mean that. I'll make sure you're back on your feet as soon as possible. I promise."

"Thank you."

"And I'm very proud of your achievements and how you've... How you didn't let me get you down."

Her shoulders jerked with a careless shrug. "All for nothing. Look at me now. No baby, no family, a demolished salon, and a target of the Hartleys."

"And none of it is your fault."

Her brows narrowed, like she was thinking through a dilemma. What was there to think about? She was the victim.

"I know that."

I rubbed my hand up and down her arm. "We'll fix everything, one step at a time. I'll arrange a visit with your mother."

A knock echoed from the door, and I jumped to the closet where I'd stashed my gun. Grace grabbed my arm.

"Relax, Hunter. I ordered lunch. Burgers, pizza, and fries included."

I grabbed her by the shoulders and switched my position with hers, forcing her inside the closet. "Stay here."

She squeezed past me, and I maneuvered her into a corner, pinning her against the wall with my full body. She gasped, and her brown eyes filled with questions. Her heart thumped underneath her skin, and her curves and longing breaths tempted me to take this in a completely different direction. Instead, I pointed my finger in her face like I was scolding a child. "I said, stay here."

She swatted my hand away. "I'm not a dog."

I pressed more weight into her. "You will listen to me and you will never, and I mean ever, open the door for anyone. Do you understand me, Grace?"

Her pursed lips tightened into a thin line. "It's your butler, and he's verified. There should be no reason—"

"This is not up for negotiation. I will handcuff you if I have to," I warned.

She sucked in a sharp breath. "Says the half-naked man with

a constant hard-on. Go ahead, open the door and greet your butler with that thing."

"Stop referring to my dick as 'that thing.'" My nostrils flared and my eyes must have darkened because Grace's skin peppered with goosebumps, and I instantly regretted losing my temper. I pulled away at the flash of disappointment in her eyes.

She swept her hand up and down her throat like she couldn't talk. I looked at the camera on the side panel. It was him. I opened the door, and our butler rolled in the cart full of food. He took one look at me and didn't look up again. He set the food on the table, left, and I locked up. Grace joined me in the main room.

"Caveman," she grunted, a sly smile tugging at the corner of her mouth.

I lifted a brow. "Not a bear anymore?"

"You're trimmed and shaved. Everywhere." She tilted her head, elongating her neck.

"I still have a beard." I tugged at the landscape over my face.

"Who said I liked beards?" A shrug rolled over her shoulder, and I smiled.

She said so, before Frankie left.

My stomach rumbled audibly, and she snickered, pointing to the plates filled with food. "You better eat, bear. I wouldn't want you to eat me instead."

She caught onto her words a second too late, and I couldn't help myself. "You're very mistaken, Grace. I promise you, all the hours of licking coconut shells and sucking on pulpy fruit in Costa Rica didn't go to waste."

Her lips parted, and time stood still. Had it truly been five fucking years? Because it didn't feel like it. It felt like no time at all had passed between us. Except she looked better. She had ripened like a fine queen and aged better than wine, balancing our age gap with pride. I had been too hard on her, and she'd had every right to put me in line when I was drinking.

"Would you like some wine?" I lifted the bottle of her favorite. My hard-on prevented me from sitting comfortably beside Grace.

"No, thank you. I'm getting my eggs retrieved on Friday."

That ought to do it.

From the new intel I'd read through last night, the clinic was Hartley's target, and I wouldn't allow Grace to set a foot near the place. I poured her a glass of sparkling water and one for myself.

"I appreciate your apology. Earlier, you know. But I also have to thank you."

She bit into her veggie burger.

"Thank me?"

"If it weren't for you, I'm not sure my salon would have grown to the level that it has. I found a purpose after you left. I concentrated on the clients and the business until the long hours paid off."

I thought she was plenty successful when we were together. Despite the giant trust fund she had inherited from her grand-parents years ago, Grace wanted to work. She'd used part of the money to start up her business and made herself a millionaire.

I cleared my throat. "So, I was a nuisance."

"That's not what I said. You were…young."

"I'm twenty-six, Grace. I'm not sure that's old. Some would say I'm in my prime."

She bit her lip and checked me out. "Fine, you were younger, and…different. You seem different now."

Her voice caught in her throat, and the blushing shade returned to her cheeks and arms. I sipped on my water to clear my mouth. She finally looked up and met my gaze. "I owe you an apology as well, Hunter. I shouldn't have excluded you from that night because of public perception. Fuck the public."

Well, that was new. I dared to smile and finished my fries. "So, I'm forgiven?"

"For that night? Yes, you are."

And for everything else?

"When are we leaving this hotel room?" She set down her fork and pulled away from the table.

"Tonight."

A chill breeze swept through the room, and I put on my shirt.

"Perfect. I can't wait to get home."

I couldn't wait either, and realized what I'd missed the most in Costa Rica: her company.

"I have an appointment at the IVF clinic."

"Grace, I'm sorry, but you'll remain under my supervision and on your property at all times."

"What?" She stomped toward me, her hands set firm on her hips.

"The case with the Hartleys is pending."

"And how long will that take? Because unless you say less than forty-eight hours, I don't want to hear it. I'm going to that clinic."

"Is a baby with a stranger more important than you? Because you know, if they kill you, the entire pregnancy plan will be ruined."

"You want to know who really ruined me, dear Hunter?"

There it was. I knew she was holding something back. She might have forgiven me for that night, but not for everything else I'd taken from her.

"Don't go there, Grace."

"You stole everything I wanted, and now you want to take it away again. You...you...you ruined everything. If we'd had a baby, we could have formed a family. I will not let you turn my dreams into nightmares."

"Fuck, Grace. Calm down."

I guessed she hadn't forgiven me for everything. This woman titillated my every nerve and tested my patience with her dreams. I got it; she wanted a baby. But sometimes we didn't get the things we truly desired.

I went to the bar, poured myself a glass of guaro, took a long sip, and returned to her room. Grace turned around from the window, and her arms dropped to the sides. A gray shade instantly replaced the pink tone of her skin. Her lips turned white, and her body trembled.

"Grace?"

"You're drinking."

I looked at the glass in my hand and back to her. "It's just one drink."

"You used to say the same thing." Her voice cracked, more with fear than disappointment.

I set down the drink and paced her way.

"No." She pushed her arm out front.

I ignored the request, took her arms, wrapped them around myself, and closed my frame around her shaking body. I tightened my hold around her, smoothing back her flowing hair and kissing her temple.

"You don't need to worry about the drinking, Grace. I'm not the same man."

"That's an alcoholic's excuse."

"I'm not an alcoholic, Grace. I was young and stupid. I had no clue how to deal with life and stress, and Costa Rica was the best thing that could have happened to me. I don't know how to show you, but I will never hurt you that way again, my Queen. I promise."

Her trembles settled, and she looked up, showing a crinkle of a smile. I swept a tear off her cheek with my thumb.

"And you can deal with all the stress now? Because as you can see, I attract stress like honey attracts bears."

I allowed a crooked smile. "I wouldn't be here with you if I had no self-control."

She inhaled a settling breath and remained in my arms. It felt so good to hold her again, but I couldn't take the road that would ruin her dreams. I couldn't hurt her any further.

"Grace?" I pulled away. "I promise you won't see me with a drink again."

She swept her hand over her eyes, blinking her wet lashes.

"All right. So what's the plan now?"

"We go home."

Chapter 6

grace

The smell of coconut and cold water filled my house. A hint of disinfectant hung in the air. Hunter had driven us home and immediately run upstairs to shower. He used to live here, unofficially. The day after his eighteenth birthday, he came over to change the oil in my car. Two days later, he cleaned up the pool and fixed the cracked window in the pool house. He playfully sprayed me with a garden hose that afternoon, got all muddy, and washed himself in the same shower where he was now in upstairs. That first time, I didn't know he'd step out naked. I didn't know I'd want to see him that way again. The second time, he went skinny-dipping in my pool at night and didn't know I watched him through the window, touching myself. When he surprised me half-naked in the gardens the third time, I couldn't let him go. It all seemed like yesterday.

I put on the kettle and searched the downstairs for my laptop. Silver Securities had installed surveillance cameras inside the house and through the exterior gardens. The team updated all locks and entry codes, lit up the driveway, and changed the front gate to reinforced steel. I rummaged through my home office, checking the bookcase and all cabinets, but came up empty. My phone remained at the salon, but the laptop had to be in the house. I wanted to update my cycle tracking and get in touch with Emma, asap.

I couldn't find it downstairs and went to the master bedroom. Hunter had left the washroom door half-open. The sound of the running shower stirred butterflies in my stomach. It had been a while since I'd had butterflies anywhere. Five years of worry and regret had not passed quickly enough. My days filled with his absence and nights with dreams I'd once had and lost. And now that he was here, all different and *beary*, completely in control, I couldn't shed the flicker of hope. His bright eyes pierced through me, igniting sweet memories. I couldn't stop looking at the changed man.

Bear.

A bear with two stacked columns of abs that narrowed into a v-cut near the hips. Melon-sized biceps ripened around his arms, and when he turned around, chiseled carvings ran down his backside. Bullet scars marked his abdomen, rising questions I was afraid to ask. But he was beautiful to me and would remain beautiful no matter how many scars he had. The silver streak of hair, shared by all the Silver brothers, curled through the darker locks. I looked nothing like my brothers.

The shower turned off, and I lost my train of thought. I couldn't let him crawl back into my life. I was on track with my fertility treatments and everything had been going well, until he came back. And now I couldn't find my laptop.

I shut the nightstand drawer, turned around, and startled. Hunter was standing in the bathroom door frame, drying his hair with a towel. Thankfully, he'd already put on a pair of joggers, and judging by the solid hang to the side, nothing else underneath. Again. The view of him sent warmth swirling through my veins, collecting everywhere it wasn't supposed to. I didn't know penises grew along with body mass. Hunter would gloat that it was due to experience. Was that why he was so large? Because he fucked so much?

"Are you just going to stand there and stare?" he asked.

My head flew up. "Ahem, no. I'm looking for my laptop. Have you seen it?"

He looked down. "It's not on my dick."

Right.

I covered my eyes with my hand. He was too distracting. "Do you have to parade around naked?"

The sound of thunder rolled in the distance, and rain splattered against the window.

"I'm dressed, Grace, and you'll get your laptop tomorrow. Gabe's adding security software."

I lowered my hands from my face. Hunter was wearing a t-shirt that did little to cover the bear underneath.

"Is Gabe going through my files?"

"No. He's reading code that has nothing to do with you. Trust me, it's boring stuff."

"I'm not boring." I followed him out of the bedroom and down the stairs, trotting along. The width of him took so much space, I could barely squeeze in beside him. He stopped at the bottom of the staircase, and I bumped into his hard arm.

"Sorry."

"You're not boring, Grace, but you are more feisty than I remember. I like a challenge."

He continued to the kitchen, and I quickened my pace. Challenge? I was a challenge? Frustration surged through my veins, heating my blood and surprisingly, awakening arousal with each step as my hormones hummed out of synch.

"I believe we've had enough challenges, Caveman."

He turned around at the counter. This time, I bumped into his chest, bouncing off.

"This is a unique challenge. I like this one."

"Okay, I'm confused. What challenge are we talking about?"

"Are you hungry?"

"Stop changing the subject, and no, I'm not hungry. I'm hormonal, frustrated, and…."

… and completely lost.

I hadn't been this lost since Hunter left. Lightning streaked across the night sky, and thunder echoed in the distance.

"Orgasms release frustration, and your toys are still in the same spot." He pointed upstairs, and I swatted at his hand.

"You looked through my drawers?"

"We both know your toys are not in a drawer." He leaned back on his elbows as his abs caught the kitchen light, shining like a beacon.

Fuck, Hunter.

I wasn't sure how long I'd last with him walking around like a bear and talking orgasms before I turned into a puddle.

"I don't need toys. What I need is a new phone."

And an orgasm.

"I already have one for you."

"You do?"

"Why are you so surprised?" His shoulders shook with a chuckle. "I'll do anything to help you get back on your feet."

I looked down and smirked before lifting my gaze back to his toned abs and semi-hard dick. "I didn't realize I'd fallen off my feet."

"Anything else you need, Grace?"

I needed *that thing* in his pants, that's what I needed, and none of my toys had what he had. Thunder crashed closer to the house, and I jumped. Hunter rose and drew his hand down my arm, sending my hormones awry. He gave me that look—like he knew what I needed better than I knew myself.

"Join me in the solarium?" He gestured to the open door beyond the kitchen, where fairy lights flickered through the plants and flowers. Over the years, he'd transformed my gardens into an oasis.

"Yes." A dry patch in my throat resisted my swallow. I sat down in one of the wicker chairs, and Hunter brought out the tea I'd brewed. He took his spot on the lounger and stretched out his bulky legs.

Long, lean, and strong.

I glanced sideways, wondering whether he was watching me, but his eyes were closed.

"I love this sound. It reminds me of home," he said.

"Home?"

"The rainstorms are crazy in Costa Rica. Palms bend underneath the winds, and water runs wild down the mountains. Streams cascade down cliffs and waterfalls, filling the rivers, and the next day, the sun shines and life grows."

"Sounds beautiful."

"Would be more beautiful with you there." He opened his eyes and turned sideways, his thick beard fluffy and shiny. I remained still as his voice curled through my body. "It was exactly what I needed after work."

I'd forgotten he'd actually been working there, and from my understanding, his job took balls the size of a bear's.

"Tell me about your work. What did you do in Costa Rica?"

"Jobs."

"Did you have to kill anyone?"

"Sometimes."

Goosebumps spread across my skin. His eyes darkened, reflecting a flicker of the fairy lights above us.

"Bad people?" I asked.

"Always."

"And you did that on your own?"

"We had a team, so no, I wasn't alone. And we were good at our job. We had each other's backs, and it kept us safe." He blinked and rose to sit up, swinging his legs over the lounger. I took a sip of the cooling tea, waiting for him to gather his thoughts.

"Do you feel safe?" he asked.

I smiled. "I do. I honestly don't understand all the security."

"Predicting a madman's plan is science."

Was I taking the threat too lightly? "Yeah, but they can't do anything. I mean, I want nothing to do with the Hartleys."

"I know that, and you know that, but they don't."

"So, let me tell them."

He burst out a laugh. "You're not getting anywhere near Chad."

"But if you cut the snake's head—"

"Another one may grow. Let me take care of this, Grace."

"How long will it take? Not that I mind you staying here. I appreciate the extra, um, unnecessary caution."

"Until we eliminate the threat and you're back on your feet. The salon will need renovations, which we'll do virtually, and by the time you go back to work, it will be all over."

"And after then? What will you do once I'm no longer a target?" I asked.

He drew in a lungful of air and released it with a whistle. "I don't know."

Rain pounded against the glass in tune with my heart, except I wasn't sure whether it synched with Hunter's. He had no idea what he wanted and no future plans. But he had space for me, and my time was running out. I finished my tea and stood up.

"I should go to sleep. I'll call Emma first thing in the morning to come over." If anyone could get me to the clinic, it was my best friend.

"All right."

"And I'd like an update on the Hartleys and who's telling them that I want anything to do with their estate."

"Of course." He nodded.

I went to bed confused, but refocused on the goal. Except somewhere deep in my dreams, that goal painted a picture of

Hunter pushing our son on a swing underneath the willow tree by the pond. They fed the koi fish and kicked a ball as I rubbed my swollen stomach. The sound of their laughter rose over the croaking of the toads.

The clatter of dishes forced my eyes open, rousing me from the quick dream. The sun was shining between the drapes and birds were chirping beyond the open window. I stretched, hopped out of bed, brushed my teeth, and changed out of my pajamas before dialing Emma's number.

"I need you here right now. It's an emergency."

Downstairs, Hunter had set out breakfast in the sunroom. The smell of coffee and croissants filled the house.

"You baked?" I asked.

"They were frozen. I just popped them in the oven. Good morning. Did you sleep well?"

I reset my glasses on my nose.

"Good morning. Yes. Emma should be here soon. What are your plans?"

"I wanted to swim in your pool, but it seems it has turned into a pond. Did you see the lilies and toads?" He popped a croissant in his mouth.

Yup. Five years of neglect turned pools into swamps.

"You're going to clean it?"

"I should be done by the evening, so it's nice of Emma to keep you company."

Perfect.

"Thanks. I appreciate it. Maybe we can go for a swim this evening?"

He looked at me but didn't ask a question, and I wanted to know what was passing through his mind. Was he thinking about all the times we'd splashed around only to end up fucking on the pool steps underneath the moon? Because I was.

He finished half his coffee, changed into his swim trunks, and gathered the tools from the pool house. Ten minutes later,

Emma drove past the front gate in her Jeep. I held the door open and hurried her inside.

"Where's the fire?"

"In my uterus. You should have warned me he's back."

"You wouldn't have seen him if I had. And isn't he the perfect solution for your burning uterus?"

I grabbed my purse. "I don't have time, Ems. Hunter's cleaning the pool. If he stays there, that will buy me the time I need."

"Let me guess. You're sneaking out. Did you know your neighborhood's having an annual pool party this weekend? I chatted with Bev on my way in."

Shit.

With Hunter's return, I'd forgotten about the girls down the street. While the party started at Bev's pool, it extended down her driveway and into the court, where she would set up a wet obstacle course. And I had signed up to bring buttered lobster rolls. I had to place an order with Oliver at the Marina.

"When Hunter finishes his work and comes inside, tell him I drew myself a bubble bath and I'm listening to an audiobook. That should buy me another hour."

"Maybe you should take the Hartley threat seriously. I should come with you."

"That's the investigator in you talking. What you should do is cover for me, Emma. It's what best friends do, and you owe me."

Her shoulders hunched forward. Emma wasn't the only one who got her way.

"All right. Just be safe. Can I know where you're going and how you're getting there?"

"I'm getting my eggs retrieved, and you're ordering me an Uber."

I sat on the plush couch in the clinic's waiting area, fidgeting like a fish out of water. A couple cuddled on the couch next to mine. He was older than she was by at least a decade, and she seemed young. Early twenties was a push. He was hiding behind a pair of aviator sunglasses and was dressed like Maverick. The man gripped the young woman's hand. Sadness squeezed my throat. I had wished to go on this journey with a partner, but Hunter was more concerned about lilies and toads. Across from me, the woman whispered in the man's ear, and his grip tightened. His possessive hold gave me the chills.

Single parenting for the win.

A few weeks from now, my life wouldn't be the only one on the line. Once I found a donor, I could be carrying a baby, and I would decide his or her path. Lorelei or Lucas, or both, would be my babies. Controlling men weren't my thing.

I checked my watch. We were fifteen minutes behind schedule. I'd called Dr. Riley and asked for an earlier appointment in the day. My egg retrieval would happen, and there was nothing Hunter could do to stop me. I'd left the phone he gave me in the bathroom so he couldn't track me.

My knees bounced and my heart beat so hard I could hear it in my ears. I fixed my gaze on the door, certain Hunter would walk through and ruin everything. Again.

"Nervous?" the man asked.

"A little."

"Implantation or…?"

"Retrieval. You?" I asked.

The woman shifted in her seat.

"Implantation."

"Congratulations." I smiled. "You must be thrilled."

"Hopefully, the embryo takes. It's still a long road ahead.

It's not our first time, but we want our baby strong and healthy. Doctor Riley is the best. He'll make sure our baby is… pure."

Pure?

"Good luck," I said.

The receptionist called out when I picked up a magazine. "Grace? Dr. Riley is ready for you."

I shot off the couch too fast, nearly tripping, and followed the nurse inside. Half an hour later, I was lying in a paper gown as Dr. Riley performed the ultrasound.

"Any new donors on the list?" I asked.

"Yes, a new list was uploaded to your account at the clinic this morning."

I hadn't had the time to check my account. I still didn't have my laptop, and I'd been too busy planning my escape.

"From your experience, Dr. Riley, do you think it's better to find your own donor or one from the clinic?"

"You can call me Stephen in here too, Grace."

Dr. Riley was dating—sort of dating—my Aunt Mary.

"If you're having second thoughts about the clinic's donor reputation—"

"No, I'm not. I'm just asking from your experience."

He moved the ultrasound, focusing on the screen.

"Looks like we shouldn't worry about that yet. I'm sorry, Grace, but there are too few follicles and no matured eggs. They're larger than the last cycle, but still not viable. You'll need to go through another IVF cycle, and we can try next month."

I sank into the hard mattress, dejected.

"Grace, the best thing you can do for yourself is relax. Pressure and stress can be detrimental to your health in different ways. Take time off work. I know you can. And do something fun for yourself. While you're doing that, see if you have a good friend willing to be a donor. Best friend."

"I know you know my history, Stephen, and I'm not asking Hunter."

"Why not? I heard he's back."

"It's complicated. Too complicated."

"Well, you know what's best for you, but don't get yourself down. And I'll see you at the neighborhood party."

"You're coming as my aunt's date?"

"Something like that." He winked.

Dr. Riley was one of the youngest and most brilliant fertility specialists in the state, and my twice-divorced Aunt Mary has been seeing him for the past ten years. She lived in my neighborhood, and although Stephen lived in her pool house, he was my aunt's steady boyfriend.

"Are you bringing someone?"

If Hunter agreed, I would have no choice but to bring him.

"Hunter. He insists on keeping me safe."

"The Hartley fiasco?"

I nodded. "I should go. I believe your next appointment is waiting."

His brows drew together. "I don't have another appointment until lunch because I'm not supposed to be here until lunch. That's why I could squeeze you in this morning. They're likely here for a different doctor."

"Thank you for all your help, and I'm sorry for taking up your morning."

"This will be your third cycle, Grace, and you know what they say—third time's a charm."

I dressed and left the clinic with an overwhelming tightening in my chest. Loss, even though I had lost little, consumed me. I crossed the street to the coffee shop, picked up a vanilla latte, and was walking to the bagel store when I felt someone's stare from across the street. A man stood in the sun's glare, the hood of his sweatshirt covering his head. He scrolled through his phone, occasionally checking the traffic.

I picked up my pace, sneaking a peek at the man from the storefront's reflection. The man crossed the street, nearly getting struck by a cab, and sped up his walk. I turned left into the first door and entered a business building. The corridor was empty, mostly. A stretch of offices ran along its length: insurance agency, real estate, lawyers. Unfortunately, no police, but a law office would do. I headed for Mercer & Williams' legal offices, secretly hoping one of my brothers would be there.

I glanced over my shoulder and breathed with some relief when I didn't see him anymore; but just then someone snagged my arm. A large man pulled me into a washroom corridor and clasped his gloved hand over my mouth.

Chapter 1

Hunter

"Where is she, Emma?" I'd dialed my cousin's number as soon as I'd realized Grace wasn't taking a bath.

If I'm too late, I'm going to kill Emma.

"Where's who?"

"I swear to God, Ems, if you don't tell me right now, I'll tell Julian you snuck out to see Eric Waters on his ranch."

"If you do that, I'm going to tell Grace you still love her."

"You won't be able to tell Grace anything if you're murdered. Where is she?"

Her breath rushed out with a grunt. "Fertility clinic. Her appointment should be over soon."

I dialed Scar's number next. He was closer to the clinic and could get to Grace quicker than I could. Fifteen minutes later, I pulled up to the curb by Mercer & Williams. Someone had parked an unmarked SUV across the street. I jumped out of the car and took the main entryway inside the building. Scar and Grace were standing in the main corridor, arguing.

"You could have said something instead of frightening me to death." Her arms were flying around in the air as she spoke.

"You were supposed to stay in the house, Grace. With Hunter. It's his job to protect you."

I hurried toward them.

"And it's your job to poke around my business and follow me?"

"I wasn't following you—"

"We stay here one more minute and they'll come inside," I interrupted. "You shouldn't have left, Grace. You're being followed."

She rolled her eyes.

"Yes, by my brother, and I don't understand why."

"I called Scar."

"And how did you track me?"

"Thankfully, your best friend knows what's right for you."

"Fucking Emma." She clenched her jaw, frustration pulsing through the veins along her neck. I grabbed her hand, and she yanked it away.

"Let me go, Hunter. No one's following me except you two fools."

I removed the handcuffs from my back pocket and locked a loop around her right wrist. Her head flew up. "What are you doing?"

I clicked the other loop around my wrist. "Making sure I don't lose you again. Scar, take my keys."

I threw the keys to my Bugatti his way. "There's a woman at the insurer, Grace's height and build. Why don't you give her a ride?"

Grace spun me around. "What are you doing?"

"Getting you out to safety." I removed my sweatshirt and threaded the garment over our hands to hide the cuffs. "Try to keep up."

Scar left, and we hurried in the other direction. I ordered an Uber around the corner and two blocks down the street. The

Cadillac was waiting by the time we reached the building's south exit. I slid into the backseat beside Grace.

She lifted her cuffed hand. "Now, can you take it off? As you can see, I'm not going anywhere."

"The cuffs are staying."

The driver snuck a peek in the rearview mirror, and I gave him a solid look to keep his eyes on the road.

"I want an update from my brothers today. Including Scar."

"They'll come over when there's an update to give. It's more important you see your mother. I invited her for dinner tonight."

"Wonderful, and how do you expect I'll cook with these on?" She shimmied her hand.

"You wouldn't have to worry about handcuffs it if you'd stayed home like I told you."

"If you'd allowed me to go to the clinic, I wouldn't have needed to sneak out. What is this? Babysitting mistake 101? I'm thirty-seven, for fuck's sake."

Grace and her occasionally dirty mouth weren't anything I hadn't handled before. I let out a frustrated breath and kept my eyes on the road, checking whether we were being followed. Grace laced her arms around herself, pulling my hand along her boob.

I turned toward her. "How did your appointment go?"

"Awful. My eggs didn't mature, and I have to start a new cycle of injections."

"I'm sorry."

"Are you sorry, Hunter? Because you've been standing in my way ever since you came back."

"I thought I was trying to save your life."

"Well, everything after that part."

"You're frustrated."

"We've established that already. Did you bring my phone? I should follow up on progress at the salon."

"Construction quotes are coming in today. I've scheduled a call in a couple of hours."

"Great! And I'm assuming you'll be there?" She yanked on my wrist again, pulling me onto herself. The same sweet scent of her that tortured me at the house hit me here, and I brushed the hair off her neck and nuzzled her ear.

"I'll be everywhere, Grace. I won't swim if you don't and I won't exercise if you don't. I will keep a constant watch over you, day and night."

She stiffened. I retreated and leaned back in the seat. If she thought I'd let her out of sight again, she was mistaken. We pulled up to her house, and Grace marched up the porch steps, pulling on my wrist.

"No need to be hasty. We've got time."

She stopped and turned around. "You mean, *you've* got time. I don't. My eggs are shriveling, and my uterus is getting more hostile every day." She stretched out her arm with the cuff. "Take these off. I'd like to freshen up."

"Fine, but step outside this house again without me knowing, and they're going back on."

I unlocked the cuffs and watched her ass sway back and forth as she walked upstairs, sending all the wrong signals to my dick. I heard the faucet turned on, and I dialed Scar's number. "Your mother's coming for dinner this evening to speak with Grace."

"Cancel it. She can't tell her the truth. Not yet. You know Grace. If she realizes how important a target she is, she'll freak."

"I don't think she's freaking out enough."

"Then it's your job to ensure she does. Chad gained access to Beth's medical records. It's a matter of time before he connects the dots."

"I think he's connected them already. I don't know how, but he already knows. Otherwise, the salon wouldn't have been attacked. I'd bet my balls on it. Did you get an ID on the unmarked SUV?"

"No. We're checking local surveillance for an ID on the driver. You just keep Grace out of the way. Oh, and do me a favor?"

"Yeah?"

"Get close to her. She'll need you once she learns the truth."

"Yeah. Talk soon." I spewed a breath out of my nose and hung up.

The shower continued upstairs and my stomach threatened to cave in. I opened the fridge and pantry and gathered the ingredients to make a vegetarian *casado*, a traditional Costa Rican dish I'd become fond of during my time there. I was setting the table in the solarium just as Grace walked in.

"Smells delicious."

"It's the sautéed veggies. I know you like avocado, beans, and, well, pretty much everything on that plate. Hope you're hungry."

She smiled widely. "Thank you. I'm starving."

"Good. Wine? Oh, I'm sorry. I forgot you don't drink anymore."

She straightened her frame. "You know what? I think I need a glass after this morning."

I poured her favorite sparkling rosé. She held the glass under her nose and closed her eyes. Her cheeks quickly took the wine's shade, and her shoulders relaxed. "It's been so long."

I lifted a brow. Her eyes flew open as if she'd just heard her hypocrisy. She was scarred, and I was the one who'd caused the pain. Grace had every right to question my drinking.

"This won't hurt my chances of maturing eggs, will it?"

"I don't know. I'm not a doctor."

She took a tiny sip, then another, instantly relaxing into the chair. "How did the pool cleaning go?"

"Good. A couple more days and we'll take a dip."

"You know, I could hire a company."

"Yet you haven't in five years."

She returned to her food.

The fresh scent of cilantro and lime wafted around my nose, but I set my fork aside and leaned forward on the table. "When couples struggle with infertility but take care of their mental health and their personal needs first, their chances of conceiving increase. They stop worrying about daily temperatures, cycles, positions, and PH balances. They enjoy the process and all the sex in the world, lose track of time and place, relax, and become pregnant. You should try it sometimes."

She took another sip. Her brows drew together and her mouth slowly lifted into a smirk. "Well, it's not like I can have sex with a turkey baster full of sperm three times a day."

We burst out laughing. She snorted, and I followed until my growling stomach reminded me about food.

"You know a lot about fertility." She stuck her fork into the avocado.

"What?"

"The temperatures, cycles, PH balances?"

I shrugged a shoulder. "I don't know. You learn these things. All I'm saying is, there was a woman in Costa Rica who adopted her deceased sister's baby. Sandra and her husband Tony tried to conceive for fifteen years. They got pregnant three months after they adopted their niece. Also, Abuela—the grandmother in the village—used a baster to get a pig pregnant. Not saying you're a pig, but I *am* saying you should relax and let nature take its course."

"I don't even have a baster, never mind the sperm." Her shoulders slumped, and I chuckled.

"You're overthinking this. Everything you need is in front of you. You're healthy, successful, and beautiful. Maybe your uterus isn't ready because of all the stressors in your life."

"But I had everything before the attack."

"Did you?"

She swallowed past the squeeze of her throat. I held her stare, desperate to read her brown eyes and certain she didn't have everything before the attack, because I wasn't here. The shadow of a passing cloud broke the wonder bouncing between us, and we returned to our food.

"We had some good times here, didn't we?" she asked.

"Good times, bad times. Everyone has them, just in different proportions."

"When did you get so smart?"

I showed her the smile reserved for defeat and rubbed my hands. "Unfortunately, a little too late."

I'd carry the regret of my past choices until I died. Leaving Grace had damaged us both and changed everything. Her lips parted, and she looked at me like she was really seeing me for the first time. I refocused on the *casado* and swallowed before filling my mouth.

"I ordered the lobster rolls from the Marina for the neighborhood barbecue."

"Thank you. I truly appreciate all your help. I do feel safer with you here."

"Of course." I nodded.

Grace finished her wine, and I refilled the glass. "Any update on the Hartleys? Can't you tell them they got it all wrong?"

I flicked both brows up. "Trying to reason with mafia kings?"

"Don't dismiss me, Hunter. I'm serious. You know, today was supposed to be a happy day, and it wasn't, so the least you can do is tell me the truth so I can let go of this stress."

I set my fork down again. At this rate, I wouldn't finish the lunch until tomorrow's breakfast of eggs Benedict, which had been calling my name for five long years.

"You don't want to be stressed? Take a stroll around the rose gardens. Sit in the jacuzzi. You've got all the surrounding amenities, but you never use them. Think of it as a mini vacation. And I promise, I'm not trying to dismiss you."

"All right." She set her fork down and pushed away from the table. "I'll use them. Jacuzzi, you say?"

She walked back three steps, staying in my view. Her eyes shimmered with mischief, and her lips lifted into a sly smile. She tugged at her shirt and opened the row of buttons, revealing a lacy bra. My gaze slid along her breast line, then was drawn to her sharp hand movements as she shrugged off the shirt and shimmied out of her shorts. My blood rushed south. Grace's lingerie wasn't an ordinary, off-the-rack ensemble. Her entire undergarment collection was from her Aunt Mary's luxurious Manhattan store, and the lacy garment she'd picked out showed everything that sang to my dick. The nude fabric hugged her skin, allowing for a glimpse of her pink nipples, which hardened by the second. Her diamond belly-ring sparkled in the sun, and her tanned inner thighs glistened.

I'd never seen a woman as sexy as Grace in my life. My dick throbbed, and the confinement in my pants was getting uncomfortable. Rapid-fire heartbeats drummed in my ears. I should have fucking kept her cuffed to my side.

"What are you doing, Grace?" A rumble rolled through my chest.

She turned around, showing off the g-string cutting into her ass. She moved her hips back and forth as she walked into the backyard.

The chair's legs squeaked over the hardwood floor as I pushed away, my chest tightening with panic.

"Relaxing in the Jacuzzi," she said. "Why don't you join me?"

There it was: her drunken offer to do all the wrong I wanted. She'd forgive me tomorrow, but I couldn't forgive myself. I couldn't lead her down the path of hope when there was none.

"Hunter? Are you going to join me?"

She tilted her hip to the side and beckoned me with her finger. My stomach sank in. I was starving, but not for food. The new menu in my head spelled out one word: *Grace*.

I stood up and removed my shirt, then looked down at my tenting joggers. My mustache twitched at the corner, hiding a smirk. I stepped away from the table and strode after her. Grace stepped into the jacuzzi in her barely-there bra and panties. I waited until she settled in the tub and looked at me, then lowered my pants. She bit her lip.

What the fuck am I doing?

The jets bubbled water, and the aroma from the wisteria hanging on the pergola overhead filled the air. I hadn't given Grace much romance when we were together, but she'd always had it figured out. Campfire nights, kayaking trips, secluded island getaways, the hammock naps underneath the willow tree and surprise picnics in her rose gardens—those were all Grace. She was more romantic, adventurous, and graceful than any woman I'd ever met.

I settled underneath the water, my dick hard and ready and my head spinning with all that could have been. Yet she was here, ready, willing, and with me.

"Help me let go of the stress, Hunter."

She scooted over to sit beside me, but I didn't expect her to straddle me. Her soft ass nestled over my lap as she trapped my dick between us. I smoothed my hand up her arm and cupped it around her neck. My fingers weaved into the hair at her nape.

"I don't want you to do anything you would regret." I pulled her in closer, my voice barely a whisper as I hovered my lips over hers. "What about your friendly neighborhood girlfriends? What will you tell them about us at the barbecue?"

Her breath flowed inside my lungs, reminding me she'd had wine tonight and overriding my thought. She shifted, raking her fingers through my hair.

"I'll tell them you're holding me against my will, demanding sexual favors and calling me dirty names."

Fuck, yeah.

"Is that what you'd like, Grace?"

"What I'd really like," she whispered, "is to borrow your turkey baster."

Chapter 8

grace

The sound of chirping birds stirred me awake. The sun's rays glowed behind my eyelids, and I covered my face with my hands, shifting. The sheets were tangled around my legs, and my head was ticking like a bomb.

"Argh…" I grumbled. I pulled the duvet aside and realized I was naked.

Fuck.

I slipped back underneath the covers and rose to my elbows, then reached for my glasses. The fog cleared from my eyes as I focused in on Hunter. He was sitting on the chair beside the balcony with a croissant in one hand and a steaming mug of coffee in the other. His joggers clung to his thick thighs, and his abs glowed in the morning light like he'd oiled himself.

"Good morning." His deep voice carried across the room and curled through me. My brain fogged and my head pounded.

"Morning? How is it morning already, and what happened to yesterday?" I pressed my fingers to my temples, and last night's dinner flashed through my mind. "Where are my clothes?"

I looked up as Hunter rose and paced my way. His firm

steps over the hardwood echoed in my brain. The croissant flopped in his hand as he passed me a mug of coffee. I took a sip, feeling instant caffeine relief.

"Last night, you stripped in the solarium before dipping into the hot tub."

My head flew up.

Oh, my God! The hot tub.

"Your panties and bra were soaked, so I took them off. They're hanging in the laundry room."

I remembered the wine, the gentle breeze, and the jetting stream between my thighs. The water bubbled; the sun fried my brain… and then Hunter joined me, naked. The memory of his firm dick pressing into my belly stirred my morning arousal.

My head flew up in time to see a coy smile stretch his mustache.

"I see the coffee's helping."

"What happened yesterday?"

"We had dinner, and you relaxed in the hot tub."

I clenched my teeth. "No, I mean, after I straddled you."

He pushed the last piece of croissant into his mouth. "You know what I miss most about Costa Rica?"

"Is it croissants?"

He finished chewing and swallowed. "Not just croissants. Pastries. All kinds of pastries. French sourdough, muffins, and home-made bread."

He was torturing me, but I indulged him.

"They don't have pastries in Costa Rica?" The sooner we were finished talking about food, the sooner I could find out what had happened yesterday.

"Just more difficult to get where I was at."

"What did you eat?"

"Fish, rice, and fruit. I'd get a juicy steak on the weekends down in the village."

Why did that sound so primitive in my head: Hunter chewing on meat, working his jaw muscles? A quiver tripped up my back.

"So, about yesterday—"

He slipped his hand underneath the covers and slid his palm over my thigh. His fingers skimmed upward, along the soft skin between my legs as he bent down to my ear.

"What about yesterday?" His steady voice unnerved me, or maybe it was the proximity of his fingers to my ache.

"Seriously, Hunter. What happened? Did we…" I trailed off because I couldn't ask him whether I'd fucked him. I knew I'd wanted to.

"Grace, you would have remembered if I fucked you." A current of his breath awakened all the hormones I'd injected in the past two months. My nipples hardened, and hot arousal flew through my veins.

"What if it was me fucking you?" I asked.

His beard tickled my neck. "Keep on dreaming."

My brows furrowed, and he pulled away.

"Where did you sleep last night?"

"Nearby."

"Why?"

"You were on the verge of puking your guts out." He paused. "And I feel better when you're safe."

Funny thing was, despite the attack, I did feel safe. Hunter was the one who was throwing me off balance and confusing me. Hunter and wine. I removed my glasses and cleared the fog off the lenses.

I checked the clock. "I slept long."

"Sleep is energy."

The vibrating hormones in my body were energizing me enough. I took a seat on the bed. "Put a shirt on, Hunter. Your abs are distracting."

His lips sloped into a grin before he grabbed a tank top and slipped it over his head. The skin-gripping fabric did little to hide the stacked muscles.

"Ibuprofen's on the nightstand, and breakfast is ready in the kitchen. You missed your call with the renovations team, which I rescheduled for today. And your mother."

"Shit. My mother."

"Just call her back and reschedule. The spare phone's in your office. Olivier will deliver the lobster rolls first thing tomorrow morning."

Where was the irresponsible man who considered party planning as showing up with a bottle of booze?

"Thank you. Did you say ibuprofen?" I glanced over at the nightstand and picked up the pill.

"It should help with the headache."

"How did you know I have a headache?"

"You always have one after you drink."

I'd thought it was because Hunter needed sobering after a night out, but when I thought about it, he hadn't been the only one with alcohol in his hand. He'd changed so much in five years. The boy who left had come back a man. A beefy man… whom I craved. Maybe it wasn't too late for the dream.

"Thanks," I said.

"I'll wait for you downstairs." His eyes crinkled with a smile.

I eyeballed the twisting muscles on his back as he walked away. My blood heated and my insides buzzed. I pulled myself together, and joined him at the dinette table where he was clicking away on a laptop.

"The smoothie's for you." He pointed to the green glass topped with a mint leaf. "It's hydrating."

I was parched, but not from a hangover. It was him. His presence, body, and alpha dominance over my life, had turned my mouth into a desert.

"I'm sorry I got drunk and stupid."

"You got tipsy and cute. That's all."

I sat down across the table. "What are you working on?"

"Catching up with my team back south, and setting up security for the barbecue. Scar is coming to the party."

"You invited him?"

"He's coming on business."

"You mean he's coming to babysit me."

"Since when are you two on bad terms?"

"We're not, but you're both hiding something. I'm not stupid."

He released a drawn-out breath. "You're not, Grace. You're vulnerable, and we're trying to protect you."

"What about the scars you'll leave after it's all over?"

"Scars?" He rubbed his chin.

"The ones on my heart." I looked him dead in the eye.

"I'm not trying to hurt you."

"Exactly. You're this perfect man strolling half-naked around my house, and I don't know where he came from. I don't understand why this couldn't have happened five years ago. I mean, we were happy at one point, right?"

He held my stare. His thick brows twitched, and regret flashed in his eyes.

"You're stressing again, Grace."

"I'm trying to understand."

"The only thing you need to understand right now is that you're in danger. Actual danger. How many people are coming to this party?"

Oh, no.

He wouldn't confine me to the house this weekend, would he? I needed my girls. I had to vent about all the heat Hunter was stirring in my body.

"We're not canceling, and I promise not to leave your side."

"How many people, Grace?"

"I don't know. Fifteen neighbors with about ten guests each, so 150, give or take."

"Give or take?"

"Some cancel and some replace the cancellations, but nobody keeps an exact count."

"Great. And you call that a small party?"

"I never called it a small party."

He cranked his neck sideways and dropped his shoulders. "Won't you be embarrassed in front of Bev and Susanne?"

What was there to be embarrassed about? "What? Why?"

"Because I'll be at your side the entire time, Grace."

"No, of course I won't be embarrassed. They know you, and… I'm sorry you feel that way. I… I didn't treat you right, and I'm sorry for that."

He tossed a couple of grapes in his mouth.

"You're not the only one at fault for our breakup. I was an asshole and I made terrible choices. If I could go back and do it all over again, I'd choose differently."

Sand scratched at my throat, and air stopped circulating. It felt like my heart took a pause, as well. Hunter stopped chewing and leaned forward on the table. His blue eyes softened, taking me back in time.

"I would have chosen you."

Why did that hurt so much? And why wouldn't he choose me now?

"I needed Costa Rica to grow up."

"It worked," I said, my words a mere push of air. "It truly worked."

He sat still, looking at me like he wanted to say more, but he didn't. What was I missing?

"I have a long day, and you have a call in fifteen with the renovations team."

"Right. Work. Got it. Thank you for the smoothie." I lifted the glass, stood and spun on my heel, retreating to my office. My mind raced, searching for answers I couldn't find. I drummed my fingers on the desk. They'd installed a new camera in the room's corner. The security system at my house seemed excessive, and I was beginning to think the police had gotten it wrong. The salon's attack had to have been random. Then again, I enjoyed having Hunter around.

After my call with the renovations team, I got in touch with Frankie and my staff, confirming their attendance for tomorrow. Cathy was still shaken up from the attack and was staying home, but I couldn't wait to see everyone else. Hunter sat at the dinette table for most of the day, munching on cookies, fruits, and vegetables all at once. In the afternoon, I made him his third coffee and called my mother.

"Hey, Mom. I'm sorry about yesterday."

"Hunter said you fell asleep, exhausted."

I snorted, and her forehead creased. "Yeah, something like that. Mom, why did you hire him?"

"To protect you from the Hartleys."

"No, I mean—why him?"

"You really need to hear it?"

"Yes, I do."

"I hired Hunter because someone who loves you will protect you best."

Wonderful.

My cheerleader would keep this up until I stood at the aisle with the caveman.

"We're over, and we're not getting back together. Now, what's going on with the Hartleys?"

"There was a mistake in the legal papers."

"What legal papers?"

"Grace, sweetheart, let your brothers take care of the paperwork. They're the lawyers."

I sighed. "And how's Dad feeling?"

"They've increased his dialysis to four times per week, and he still insists on working."

"He'll die in that office. Make him come home."

"We just moved his office back home, so he *is* home, and he's driving me crazy. I miss you, Grace. I'm sorry I can't come tomorrow, but I'll see you after the weekend. We need to speak in person."

"About the Hartleys?"

"Yes, about them as well."

"All right. I'll see you after the weekend, Mom. I love you."

We hung up, and I took my video call from the salon. The place was a mess, but Frankie took the lead, and the plan he'd laid out was drafted to perfection. My manager needed a promotion and a raise. After the call, I replied to emails and shopped for new store supplies online. My fertility app clicked on the screen for an update, and I slouched in my seat. What was the point of updating on nothing? I was getting my period in a few days and would return to the calendar then.

In the afternoon, I picked some roses from the garden and made four bouquets. Hunter moved his laptop and tray of nuts to the outside patio, from where he watched me. I made a margarita pizza, and Hunter devoured half before it cooled. By evening, I found him snoring on the living room couch. He stirred when I covered him with a blanket.

"Everything okay?"

"I'm sorry. I didn't mean to wake you," I said.

"What time is it?"

"Ten-thirty. I'm going to bed. Will you come upstairs?"

"Yeah, I'm coming."

He sat up and pulled the blanket aside. His joggers tented as he stood up, and I looked away. He followed me upstairs to the bedroom, turning off into the washroom. He shed his joggers before closing the door, and I stole a glimpse before slipping underneath the covers. I listened to the running shower and pictured the running water over his new body. We'd showered together so many times before, and I'd seem him naked countless times. Except, he had a different body now, and he was a different man. A man I could finally trust.

MUSIC BLASTED, and a hum of cheery conversation carried through the court. The organizers had set up a tent with rows of tables filled with food. My aunt's sexy manservants walked around in their tuxedos and shorts, carrying trays of drinks and hors d'oeuvres. Bev had ordered an inflatable water slide and a bunch of other water toys. By evening, we'd move the party to her backyard, and the replica of Hugh Hefner's pool.

I glanced over to the north corner, where my girlfriends were gathered by the tiki bar, and adjusted the leis around my neck.

"Are you nervous?" Hunter asked.

"No." My voice quivered. The moment I joined the conversation with my cougar friends, they'd dig their manicured claws into my bear.

He leaned into my ear. "Liar."

Shivers ran down my spine. "Okay, maybe I'm a little nervous. I need champagne."

His eyebrows jumped up.

"Oh, don't look at me that way. One glass of champagne won't hurt me."

"Champagne coming up." He snapped his fingers, and a manservant brought me a flute.

"Aren't you going to have one?" I asked.

"Not my favorite, and I'm on duty."

I turned in a circle, comically extending my arm. "Do you see any danger? Because all I see is a ton of horny women gossiping and having fun."

"It's the Housewives of Cougar Court." He snickered.

"They're not housewives, Hunter. My friends are successful business women—"

"Who enjoy your aunt's young servicemen."

"Manservants. And they're professional. Now stop teasing and go on the slide."

"I'm stuck to your side all day, Grace. I go wherever you go."

"Perfect. Slide it is." I looped my hand into his arm just as someone tapped my shoulder.

"Grace? There you are."

Emma hugged me hard, whispering in my ear. "I have so much to tell you. How do I get you away?"

She turned to Hunter. "Hey, cuz. Mind giving us a few minutes?'

"Sorry, Ems, but I'm not leaving Grace's side."

"Well, can you scooch over a few feet? Give us some privacy?"

Hunter scratched over his beard, grabbed a steaming pretzel off a table, and stepped aside. Emma pulled me further away.

"Did you see the new guy your aunt hired?"

"The one with the cowboy hat? Yes, I saw, but what the hell, Ems? Why did you tell Hunter I was at the clinic?"

"He blackmailed me. I had no choice! But it sounds like Scar found you just in time."

"How do you know?"

"It's all over Silver Securities. My brothers and cousins are all trying to keep a lid on it."

"Fucking Hartleys. No wonder their sister went crazy."

Simone Hartley had dated Emma's brother before he met his current wife, Allie. Then she snapped and tried to kill Allie, and was now serving a sentence in a mental health unit.

"What does Hunter have on you?"

"Eric Waters."

I sighed. She had a pass on that one. "All right. Can you help me tackle the cougars?" I nodded to the bar. "They're gonna rip Hunter to shreds."

"I'm ready when you are. Let's go and conquer."

Hunter followed us two steps behind. He grabbed a hot dog on the way and stuffed it into his mouth. We ordered two piña coladas and joined Lexie, Carly, and Susanne on the loungers. Hunter held back by the palm tree, scouring the area.

The girls hustled around me. "So? Who's the new man?"

"He's not new. It's Hunter."

"Hunter the pool boy?"

"Hunter the mechanic?"

"Hunter the gardener?"

The three of them asked all at once, lifting in their seats and lowering their glasses. They stared unapologetically until Hunter shifted in discomfort.

"Yup. That Hunter," I said.

"Delish."

"Hey, that's my cousin." Emma popped up. "But did you see *that* guy?" She pointed to one of the servers, but the girls paid her no attention.

"My new gardener said Hunter's living here." Lexie removed the silky throw from her shoulders, lifting her new implants.

"Hunter's here temporarily. You have a new gardener?"

"Pretty cute, but not as much muscle as Hunter. And he's older, so not my type. Hey Ems, you go for older guys, don't you? Maybe you should give Rick a try." Carly lifted a margarita in the air.

"Sorry, but I don't take seconds, Carly." Emma winked.

I glanced over at Hunter. He was pacing between the palm tree and the bar, talking on his phone. When he finished, he looked up my way and walked over.

"Grace, I need to steal you for a moment."

Carly cheered, and I rolled my eyes.

"What's the matter?" I asked.

"They caught the attackers," he whispered.

"Perfect."

"Scar's on his way, and I have a file at the house."

"So go get the file."

He pinched the bridge of his nose.

"I'll be fine. I'll wait here."

"Will you please stay with the girls and Emma right there?"

"Yes—relax, Hunter. They found the bad guys. That's good news." I drew my hand down his thick arm, wanting to ease his worry. "I'll be right there." I pointed to the loungers. Then I walked back to the girls. Hunter kept his gaze on me for as long as he could, walking backward.

"Is he obsessed?" Carly fanned her face. "He must be. You know what that means, Grace? He'd ravage you in bed."

Emma hopped off her seat. "Okay, this is my cousin we're talking about, so I'm going to step away. I'm starving. Let's get some of Olivier's lobster rolls." She grabbed my hand and pulled me off my seat, away from the group. "I thought you could use a break."

"Thanks. Hunter's going all bodyguard on me."

"It runs in the family."

I passed her a plate with a lobster roll and crunched on a celery stick. "Hunter's changed."

"You mean he grew up."

"No, I mean there's something different about him."

"Well, I'm sure the accident—"

"What accident?"

"Four years ago in Costa Rica, Hunter was shot and nearly burned alive, but that's all I know. That kind of shit can give you PTSD."

I remembered the scar on his thigh and abdomen from when I waxed him. "I can't believe he didn't tell me." The old Hunter would have bragged about bullet wounds.

Emma's phone rang with an *Achy Breaky Heart* tune, and her head flew up. "It's Eric."

"Eric Waters? You better take the call."

Her gaze flew from the phone to me and back to her phone again.

"Hurry, before he hangs up," I urged.

She picked up her phone and stepped away a few feet.

"These lobster rolls are the talk of the party." I turned around at the unfamiliar voice.

"Hi," I said. "They're Olivier's specialty."

"From the Marina?" he asked.

"Yes."

"I'm Rick. I'm Carly's new gardener."

"That's right. She mentioned you. How do you like the neighborhood?"

And where did I know him from?

"What's not to like? The air is clear, the drinks are flowing, and the women are hot."

I laughed.

He lifted his aviator sunglasses to the top of his head.

"Where do I know you from?" I asked.

"I believe we met at the fertility clinic."

Recognition set in.

"That's right. Is your wife with you?"

"No, she's visiting her sister in Chicago, so she couldn't join the party. I was stuck at home when Carly kindly invited me over. It'll be different once we have kids, you know? We'll do picnic trips, camping getaways, and Disney vacations."

It was everything I wanted. I set the empty piña colada glass on the table.

"May I ask if everything went well with your appointment?"

"Our embryos are now growing in a lab. Implantation next week."

"Congratulations. That's great news. And how long did it take?"

"Third cycle. My wife went through a homeopathic treatment before the last one, and it must have worked."

"Really?"

"You know, I think I have a pamphlet in my bag at Carly's, if you'd like to check it out. All natural and safe. Dr. Riley approved of the treatment. You can ask him yourself. I was pretty sure he'd be here today."

"I'd love to see the pamphlet, but I need a drink."

"I recommend the lemonade. It will quench the thirst."

Rick turned to the table and poured me a cup from the dispenser at the table.

"Thank you. Now tell me about this homeopathic treatment." I sipped on the lemonade.

We crossed the row of hydrangeas, and I followed him to the side entrance between Bev's and Carly's houses.

"My wife took the pills every day for a month. It's supposed to help the eggs mature, and it worked."

The sun beamed from above, and sweat dripped down my spine. I finished the lemonade and set the cup on a rock outside, feeling woozy.

"Are you all right?" Rick asked. "You look pale."

"I'm feeling a little lightheaded."

He took my hand and pulled me inside, a bit too forcefully. My knees softened and buckled underneath me, but Rick caught me by my arms and lowered me to the ground.

"What's going on?" I whispered. "I… I can't breathe."

"Just try to relax, Grace." He dragged his hand over my sweaty forehead. "That's a good girl. It will be all over soon."

"Grace! Grace!" I heard Hunter's voice in the distance, but my eyes closed before I could reply.

"Grace? Grace, wake up, baby." I skimmed my hand over her cheek. Her lips were blue and her skin translucent. "I'm so sorry. I shouldn't have left you."

Ambulance sirens blared as we sped to the hospital. The paramedic stuck an IV into her arm, but the doctors would need to pump her stomach.

Fucking Chad Hartley had been staking out Grace's house for weeks. I darted out of the house as soon as Silver Securities called me. Scar followed me, calling out for his sister. I screamed her name, searching through the crowd.

"Grace!"

My gaze caught Chad's head as he closed the side door to Carly's.

"Grace!"

I pushed my feet hard, my life flashing before my eyes, and burst through the door in time to see Chad dart out the back. Grace lay unconscious in the hallway, her body soaked in sweat. We had paramedics on standby at the party, but I'd never expected to use their services. They were at Grace's side a minute later.

"Is she gonna be okay?" I asked.

"Do you know what she took?"

"She was drugged, but it shouldn't be lethal."

"How do you know?"

"Because the fucker who did this wants her alive," I said under my breath. "And it's my fault he almost got her."

My phone rang with Scar's number, and I picked up.

"How is she?"

"Same as she was three minutes ago. Unconscious."

"I found a lemonade cup with residue and sent it to the lab. I'll get you the results asap."

"Thanks, Scar. Listen, I think once Grace is well, I'm gonna take off."

"You're gonna leave her?"

"No—I'm taking her with me. At least for a while, you know? I know he slipped up, but Chad's too close. He'll be furious he didn't get her. He'll try again, and I can't have her here for that."

"Got it. Just take care of her, will ya?"

"Scar?" I filled my lungs with air and took Grace's hand in mine. "I don't know what I'd do if I lost her."

"But you didn't."

"We were right there. How did he get through?" I asked.

"He posed as Carly's new gardener, so we're gonna widen our net. There's word he's now bragging about creating his pure race."

"Fuck his pure race. Once we leave the country, we're not coming back until he's eliminated."

"Anything to keep her out of the bastard's hands. Keep me updated on her condition."

I hung up and took her hand in mine.

Grace's family hovered at the hospital for the next twenty-four hours. Security stood at her door, and we screened every nurse and doctor. They pumped Grace's stomach and flushed it with charcoal and gave her fluids, but she didn't regain consciousness. After many scans and tests, the doctor said that Grace was simply sleeping.

"You're saying she's in a coma?"

"No. I'm saying everything is fine with Grace, but the stress and the drugs are keeping her asleep. Continued fluids will flush out her system, and she'll wake up."

"Make it happen, Dr. Simmons."

Twenty-four hours later, Grace squeezed my hand, and I lifted my head off her bed. She opened her eyes.

"Hey, beautiful. You snore like a bear."

"I do not." She smiled, looking around. "Why am I at the hospital?"

"Chad Hartley drugged you at the party."

She blinked repeatedly, and her forehead furrowed.

"Don't think right now. Just rest. We're flying out as soon as you're strong enough."

She lifted her head, and I gently pushed on her shoulder to make her lie back down.

"Flying out? Where are we going?"

"As far away from that bastard as possible."

"Hunter..." she breathed, and closed her eyes. I took her small hand in mine. He'd gotten so close to her. Too close, and it was my fault. I honestly didn't know what I'd do if I lost her.

She drifted off to sleep within minutes.

A day later, Grace was discharged from the hospital. I drove her from there straight to the airport.

"Is this really necessary?" she asked.

"Yes. I wish you could remember being drugged. Maybe you'd take it more seriously."

"I *am* taking it seriously. It's just hard to believe what you're saying. Why would I follow him to Carly's?"

"He got himself hired as Carly's gardener, drugged you, and lured you inside her house. He slipped GHB in your lemonade.

Look, it doesn't matter why you went, but you did, which means I need to keep a better eye on you, that's all."

"I'm sorry."

I parked my Bugatti on the tarmac near my jet.

"Where are we going?"

"Costa Rica."

THE PATH AHEAD NARROWED. We'd taken a double scooter from the airport, and Grace could barely keep her eyes open. The flight might have been exhausting, but it wasn't until I showed her a picture of Chad Hartley while we crossed the sky ten thousand feet in the air that awareness set in. She knew him from somewhere before, but she couldn't remember. Scar said the bastard had been stalking her for weeks. My mistake nearly cost her life. I should have shown her a picture long ago.

She clung to me like a monkey from the back, her arms wrapped around my torso and her front glued to my spine. Night had set in just as we arrived, covering the ground with darkness. I'd have to wait until tomorrow to show Grace the rainforest. She gripped her fingers around my arm.

"You live in a jungle?" she asked.

"It's a rainforest, and I live in an eco-house." I took her hand and pushed through the overgrown foliage. Mateo hadn't cut it since I left, but I wasn't supposed to return so soon. A week away from home made this place unrecognizable. "It must have rained, because everything grew."

"Is that how you grew? Guzzling rainforest water?"

"No." I choked out a laugh. "I believe it was the food."

We stopped by the tree trunk, a web of roots braided and tied into pretzels, all invisible in the night.

"Okay, Grace. You're gonna have to let me go, and you'll have to trust me."

"I don't like this. I can't see anything."

"I'll fix that in a moment, but for now, just trust me, okay? My home is up in a tree."

"I thought you were kidding."

"I wasn't. There's a rope and pulley system. I'll drop a ladder in the morning so it will be easier. Come on—step this way." I guided her to the twelve-inch platform. "There's a rope in the middle. Hug the rope between your feet and hold on. I'll let you know when to step off."

I set her onto the plank and made sure she was holding the knot in the rope before I pulled. The platform wobbled as it rose.

"Oh, my God! Hunter! Hunter!"

"It's okay. Five more, four"—I pulled on the rope with each count—"three, two, one. Step off. Doesn't matter in which direction, but make sure the step is wide."

A moment later, she called out. "Got it."

I yanked the pulley, bringing down the platform, and used the same rope to climb up the tree house. I lit a few candles, then the oil lantern, and got the generator going. Grace stood in the middle of the room, watching me.

"I don't think I'm tired anymore. Are we really staying in a tree house?"

"I prefer eco-house."

"And this is where you lived?"

"Yes. For five years. It looks better in the daylight. There's a full bathroom in another section and a shower down below, but it's useless at night with all the bugs and snakes. I prefer the waterfall and filled up a bowl of water over there, and if you—"

"Hunter, stop. I'm fine. I'm a little thirsty and tired, but I'm fine. You can show me around in the morning."

I grabbed the bag I'd stuffed with soft drinks at the airport and popped open a can of Coke.

"Enjoy. We won't get these down in the village. Water is pretty much all you get here to hydrate."

She took a sip. "And how long are we staying here? How long will it take to catch Chad?"

"Already getting bored? Come—the bed's on the second floor."

"There's a second floor?"

I laughed. "Yes, with a better view. It doesn't look like much at night, but I promise, it's beautiful in the day." I showed her to the ladder. She set the can of Coke aside and climbed up. I carried the lantern behind her and hung it on a branch hook, where it cast a soft glow over the bed. The mattress end hugged the back wall and stretched the full width of the space. White netting flowed around its perimeter. Grace paced around the bedroom and stopped at the window. Moonlight peeked through the clouds and lit up the forest's canopy. She swiveled on her heel, eyes wide. The lantern's flicker brightened the excitement filling her orbs. I expected her to run up to me, but she stood in her spot, shivering.

"Are you cold?"

"No, I just… it feels like we're in the middle of nowhere."

We were.

"I'll stay close by. You're safe here."

She eyed the bed.

"Are we both sleeping here?" Her mouth twitched, containing a smile.

"No. I'll be up there." I pointed to the net above head, and she looked up.

"I feel bad taking your bed."

"Don't worry, it's sturdy, so I won't fall on top of you. Besides, you never felt bad about taking my bed before. Enjoy the night, and I'll see you in the morning."

I turned to the ladder and climbed the first three steps, stopping at the sound of her voice.

"Hunter?"

"Yes?" I looked back over my shoulder.

"Thank you. For everything."

"Of course." I nodded. "Zip up the net behind you, or the mosquitos will eat you alive."

"Will do. Good night."

"Night."

I scaled the ladder and crawled out onto the netting. The ropes gave a bounce when I lay down. Clouds cleared beyond the sky window, and the moon came out around midnight. Grace slept in the light below me. She turned on her side and stretched her long legs across the sheets. Her lips parted, and a hitch of a smile curled her lip.

My mustache twitched. I must have fallen asleep staring at her, because when I woke up and she wasn't there, I shot up. My big toe caught in the net, nearly ripping off as I scrambled.

"Grace?" I called out.

The smell of coffee reached me, and I froze.

"Grace?" I jumped into my boxers and climbed down the tree, but she wasn't anywhere near. A small fire pit puffed smoke and a pot of boiled water was set up by the rock. Two steaming cups of coffee stood on a tree stump. I pushed past the foliage to the riverbank where I saw Grace bathing underneath the waterfall. I cupped my hands around my mouth to make a bullhorn and called out, "Grace!"

She turned around and cleared the water off her eyes. Her t-shirt clung to her chest, outlining her breasts and nipples, and her lace thong may as well not have been there.

"Did you see the anaconda?" I called out to her.

"Anaconda?"

She flatted her back against the cliff-side, avoiding the

water's edge, and shuffled her feet sideways until she reached me at the shore. I wrapped a towel around her.

"You could have warned me."

"You can't sneak out like that on your own. It's too dangerous. I'm kidding about the anaconda, but you must tell me when you leave."

"How can some place so beautiful be dangerous?"

Looking at her standing in front of me with soaking hair, wet lashes, and pouty lips, I asked myself the same question. For the five years I'd lived here, I'd never imagined Grace coming to Costa Rica with me. Yet here she was, fitting in like she'd been raised by the Swiss Family Robinson.

She clutched the towel in front of her and looked up. "I don't have a bathing suit." Water dripped off her soaked lashes.

"There's nobody around for miles."

"So, it's just you and me?"

"Plus a few monkeys, jaguars, and cougars."

"No bears?"

I kept my stern gaze on hers and dipped my chin.

"You're serious?"

"Yes. I'll show you around, but stay close. Always. There's a sonic sound barrier fencing the perimeter, but animals can slip through."

"All right. I promise to stay close if you give me a tour of this paradise. Let me guess—no wifi?"

I laughed. "No. We'll need to hike up the mountain to get a signal."

"You have a phone?"

"Not yet."

"Can I call Frankie when you do?"

"I told Frankie we were going on a vacation before we left. He has explicit instructions not to disturb you, and I made him responsible for the salon's re-opening upon our return."

"Wow. Thank you. And… when are we going back?"

"Scar and my brothers are on Chad's tail. Ace and Axel are working on the legal papers."

"What legal papers? I still don't understand why Chad's after me. Why did he drug me? What does he want from me?"

"Don't panic when I tell you this, but we believe he wants you to give him a child."

"*What?*"

"I know. It's sick."

Her face fell ashen and her lips turned purple. "Oh, my God. It was him."

"Who?"

"You call him Chad, but I know him as Rick. We met at the clinic, and we talked. That's why I felt comfortable with him at the party. He went to get a pamphlet about naturopathic medicine his wife was taking—"

"He doesn't have a wife. He lured you in."

Her knees bent and she bent down to sit on the stone, shivering. "Why me?"

"His father's dying wish was for an heir."

"And he chose me? What the fuck? Was he gonna rape me back at Carly's?"

I didn't reply. She shuddered and pulled the towel tighter around her body.

"You have nothing to worry about now. He'll never find you, and he'll be behind bars by the time we return for the Gracie's grand re-opening."

"You make it all sound so easy, when I feel like my life is a complete mess."

"It's not a complete mess." I took her hand and helped her off the rock. "You're here with me, so that's perfect. Now, tell me, Jane, how did you make coffee?"

She snickered. "I lit a fire and boiled water."

"No, I mean, how did you light the fire? We have no matches."

"Oh, that. With my glasses. I used them as a magnifying lens, and once the sun hit the paper and dry leaves, it was quick."

Crafty.

"We have electricity. I just didn't turn on the generators last night. This eco-lodge is solar powered and totally off the grid."

"I don't know what that means, but if it's the new name for Tarzan's home, then it works for me."

"So I'm Tarzan now?"

"If I'm Jane, then you're Tarzan."

I shrugged a shoulder. "We'll take the scooters down the village after you dress to pick up some matches and supplies. We can have breakfast there, because I'm starving."

"Hunter, I'm gonna need tampons soon."

"That may be a problem."

"No, no, no. I must have tampons, or pads, at least."

"Relax, Grace. I'm not gonna let you free-bleed, although that's exactly what most women in the village do."

"Maybe you should have chosen a different destination?"

"Don't worry. We'll make it work. Get dressed."

I tidied the place and dressed as Grace changed into a pair of shorts and a tank. The black coffee she'd brewed tasted like home. We took the scooter down to the village, where I parked by the bakery.

Paula greeted us at the front of Abuela's bakery.

"*Cariño!*" Her arms flew up in the air and swung around my neck. She kissed me on each cheek. "*Dónde has estado? Te he echado de menos.*"

"*Buenos días*, Abuela. I missed you as well."

Paula, one of Abuela's granddaughters, stepped outside. "*Buenos días, cariño.* You come back to take your wife?" she asked in her sexy Spanish accent.

"What?" Grace's head flew up, and I gave Paula a warning look—which she ignored.

"I give you memories here"—she touched my lip and lowered her hand to my crotch—"and give memories here, but you leave."

I caught Grace's snicker and removed Paula's hand from my dick.

"What happen to hair?" She raked her fingers through my shorter cut.

"Ahem, I cleaned up a bit. Listen, *querida. Puedes traer agua, por favor?*"

"*Cualquier cosa por ti, cariño.*"

Paula and her grandmother went inside while we sat at the only dusted table by the bakery.

"Are you hungry?" I asked.

"A little."

"I'll get fish going for dinner back home, but I'm sure Abuela is in the back kitchen, making breakfast."

"Oh, I didn't realize we'd ordered."

I laughed. "We didn't, but she knows we arrived late, and that's enough. Abuela is the chief of this village."

"A grandma?"

"Who better to protect all the women and girls than a fierce lioness? Her husband died protecting the girls, and she was the one who found me and dragged my ass over here."

"She found you?"

"Drowning my sorrows at a bar in San José. Poor Abuela. I threw up most of my way from there to the coast."

"That's gross."

"She's a determined woman."

Paula came outside with a tray and two empty glasses. She walked across the street, pushed a lever on a pump three times, and filled them.

"Oh, my God. Is that for us?" Grace watched Paula carry the glasses back to our table. I was parched.

"Straight from a spring. It runs off the river where you swam."

Paula set the glasses on the table, winked my way, and turned back to the kitchen. The smell of eggs, corn pancakes, and fried plantains drifted in the air. I lifted the glass, but Grace caught my arm.

"Wait. I have to tell you something."

"What?"

"You can't drink that. I peed in the waterfall."

I chuckled. "Okay."

"So you're going to drink contaminated water?"

This time, I laughed louder.

"The spring water is deep underground, so whatever pee the river carried down the stream is long gone and nowhere near the source. Drink the water and get used to it. It's the only source of hydration here."

She took a cautious sip, then another, until she'd gulped half a glass. "Hunter, I don't see a supply store for anything."

I let out a deep-chested laugh.

"Come on, Grace. We have work to do."

Chapter 10

grace

Heat nipped at my neck, and I covered myself with a shawl gifted from Abuela. After breakfast, we stopped by the local school, where Hunter played soccer with the kids for a bit. I sat on a bench watching them as a line of locals formed in front of me. The first older gentleman held a pair of scissors in his hands.

"*Corte*," he said.

"Hunter! What does *corte* mean?"

But he couldn't hear me. The gentleman snapped the scissors between his fingers and pulled on his hair with the other hand.

"Cut?" I asked, and he nodded.

More locals joined the line. I stood up. Someone had set a chair in front of me and I smiled. "All right. Sit, *por favor.*"

I clipped away, losing count after the fourteenth head, while the boys took Hunter across the street to a hut filled with scooters. He fiddled with the bikes, fixing them and starting up one after the other. Two hours later, he came back all greasy and sweaty. I'd styled eight women, including Paula's younger sister, who, from what I gathered, was getting married within days. Hunter pulled his greasy hands through his hair. Sweat dripped down his chest. His arms bulged, and God, did he ever look hot. Paula brought out a tray of pineapple empanadas and stuck one into his mouth. Jesus, was she ever sexy.

"*Come, mi amor.*"

He took a bite, she cleared the crumbs off his beard, and I decided I wanted to learn Spanish. Jealousy tickled in my stomach.

"Paula, *ven!*" Abuela called out, and Paula retreated. I finished the second to last cut and set the scissors aside, cracking my fingers.

"Where does she want you to go?" I asked him. "She said, *come mi amor.*"

"*Come* in Spanish means eat. She wanted me to eat."

The jealousy in the pit of my stomach gained potency, leaking into my veins. Why was I so jealous of this woman?

"Oh, well, now I see how you fed all those muscles over the years. I mean, Paula fed them."

"Paula, Maria, Rosetta…" His mustache lifted into a cocky pattern, and I rolled my eyes. Was he doing this on purpose?

"I thought you said they had no pastries, yet here is Paula, stuffing your mouth with muffins, cookies, and pineapple empanadas all day. And God knows what else."

"Would you rather stuff my mouth?"

Yes.

And just like that, my jealousy morphed into arousal. Heat swooshed through my body, sending sweat to my pores. I removed the scarf and fanned myself.

"I'm gonna wash up in the river, and then we're riding up the mountain to get a wifi signal."

Yes!

I did an imaginary fist pump. Frankie was the first on my list to call, then Emma and Carly. I'd check in with Bev as well.

"Grace? Are you listening?"

"Yeah, I am," I lied.

"I shouldn't be long, and it looks like you're on your last client." He pointed a little girl sitting on the chair.

"All right. I'll see you soon," I said.

Hunter left, and Paula, along with a young boy, packed two bags on our scooter, one on each side and brought a container full of coconut buns.

"*El favorito de Hunter,*" she said.

"*Gracias.*"

"*De nada.*"

I sat on the scooter behind Hunter with my arms wrapped around him. As we pulled away, kids waved, running along to the village limits. He weaved between trees and bushes, ferns slapping at his arms, until he turned onto a path leading up the mountain.

"You've got a GPS in your head?" I called out.

"I do." My body shook along with his laughter.

We passed ageless trees and ferns the size of two men. A family of monkeys followed our path for a while before retreating into the rainforest. About a half hour later, we reached what looked like a peak. He set the scooter by a tree and turned on his phone. Humidity hung thick in the air. Droplets clung to my skin. My heart drummed, waiting for the beep of technology as the phone caught a signal.

"Make yourself comfortable. It will be a while," he said.

I sat at the edge of a cliff overlooking a valley. The white of a river's rapids foamed at the bottom. Higher, the green land-scape stretched out as far as I could see. The tree-topped horizon resembled military camouflage in all shades of green. The afternoon sun was sinking in the sky. A flock of macaws flew by. A pair broke off from the group and landed on a branch. They watched me watch them, and I just couldn't stop smiling. I closed my eyes and listened to the ruffling leaves, chirping birds, and every so often, an animal noise I didn't recognize. God, this was exactly what I needed. The soothing sounds forced the thoughts of heavy traffic, complaining clients, and constant sirens to the back my mind. And Hunter's protective presence brought back the freedom I never knew I needed. It finally felt like I could breathe again.

"Grace?"

I jumped up and pressed my hand to my chest.

"Holy shit, you almost gave me a heart attack." I took his offered hand and pulled myself up. "How did the call go?"

"Good. They questioned everyone from the party. Chad kept a low profile, and Cindy hadn't introduced him to anyone."

"I bet the court is a beehive of gossip. What else?"

"They have a lead on Chad, but that's all I know. Either way, we're staying here until he's caught. We can go back once he's behind bars."

What would that look like once Chad was out of the picture —our lives? Would Hunter stay? Would he leave? Did I want him to? I didn't know what life without Hunter would look like. Strike that—I did know because I'd spent the last five years without him. Despite my success, they were the most miserable years of my life, and I didn't want to be alone any longer. Was this our chance?

"Can you dial Emma for me? I have to speak with Frankie, too."

"Sorry, but I can't do that."

"Why not?"

"Because there's only one number I call from here, and it's scrambled to stay off the grid."

"You're doing this on purpose."

"I'm not, Grace. We can't risk being traced."

I pouted.

"If it makes you feel any better, my brother James followed up with Frankie about the salon, and everything's going well. Now, come on—we need to make it home before the sun sets."

He restarted the scooter, and I sat behind him. My limbs were aching, and the day's heat was getting to my head. I held on tight and rested my head on his back. He stopped at a suspended bridge and turned around.

"I need you to close your eyes for this."

"Wait—we're going over that?" I pointed to the row of planks tied by rope.

"Yes."

"It's not gonna hold."

"It's held more. Now, close your eyes, don't let go, and don't sway. Got it?"

If it was so safe, why was he giving me all those instructions?

"Got it."

I tightened my grip and shut my eyes. He revved up the engine, accelerating. The footing underneath changed from soil to plank and air. My body shook with his as he rode over the bridge. The sound of loose planks clattered in my ears. The wind blew stronger through the valley, pushing on our right.

What if we fell? What if we lost our chance? What if I lost him?

We returned to steady ground, and the vibrations stopped, but my body was still trembling. Hunter let go of the steering with one hand and smoothed it over mine as I gripped at his chest. The lower the sun dipped, the faster Hunter rode, and by the time we arrived, the sun's orange orb was just touching the mountain tips.

"We're gonna miss the sunset," I said.

"Not if we hurry. Come on."

He set the scooter in its spot, looped the two bags over his arms, and took my hand, leading me through the foliage and up the rocky hill. Fairy lights flickered around the trunk of the tree, and I looked up to the canopy, where thousands more were looped through the branches.

"Hunter, this is beautiful."

"It's solar-powered, but should last until morning. Let's go. It's almost time."

He helped me up the rope lift, and I ran to the bedroom's ledge, cautiously climbing onto the net below.

"Hunter, hurry."

"This isn't the spot, Grace. We need to climb higher. Come on."

I followed him to the netting up near the ceiling. He pushed open a latch and pulled down a ladder, then reached out for my hand. "You go first. I'll guide you and spot you. Just don't look down."

"Okay."

I climbed one rung at a time, looking up into the canopy. Fairy lights twinkled around us, and I caught the sun between the foliage.

"The view through the leaves is beautiful. I can't wait to see it from above," I said.

"Doesn't look so bad from below, either."

I stopped and looked down at Hunter's smug smile—except when I did, I also realized how high we'd climbed. My knees softened and my belly swirled.

"Whoa."

Hunter pushed up on my ass. "Don't look down. Keep going, Grace."

God, I didn't even want to know how we'd make our way back down. I took the last five steps, passing through the canopy, and stepped onto a wooden platform. My knees wobbled and my heart pounded. I crouched, touching my hands to the floor.

"Don't worry. It's sturdy." Hunter jumped up and down.

"Stop that! Please."

He touched my shoulders and gently spun me around to face the view.

"Oh, my God."

The sun touched the horizon, its glow catching the rain-forest as far as I could see. Pink and orange tones drifted across the sky. I sat down, stretching my legs to the front, and closed my eyes, listening to the chirping birds and swaying trees. Hunter sat beside me, his shoulder touching mine.

"Beautiful, isn't it?"

"I think I've been missing out on life."

"What are you talking about? You seized life. You took control and built a successful beauty empire. It's everything you wanted."

"Almost everything."

He breathed out calmly through the nose. "I know things have been stressful, Grace, but you can still have a baby," he whispered.

Me? Not we?

"Yeah... I, ahem, I'll start the new fertility cycle as soon as we return."

"See, you've got a plan, and that's more than most people have."

But I had Hunter, didn't I? He came back to protect *me*, and I could feel there was something still there between us. I pulled my knees to my chest, wrapped my arms around them, and glanced his way, my eyes begging for a hint of emotion, but he kept focused on the horizon. His face and beard held the sun's glow, and though he was sitting next to me, it felt like he was on the other side of the world. I wished he'd look at me.

"What happened to us, Hunter?"

"I don't know." He followed a flock of macaws with his gaze. The birds disappeared, the sun hid behind the tree line, and he finally turned my way.

"That's a lie. I know exactly what happened. I was an asshole."

I took hold of his large hand with both of mine, turning

him my way. "Let's be honest—you were a twenty-one-year-old boy who could get pussy on call."

He burst out in laughter. "Is that what you thought I was after?"

"No. I just wanted you to look at me."

"I *am* looking, Grace."

Why couldn't I read past the clouds in his beautiful blue eyes? "Why don't you want to be with me?"

"That's the furthest thing from the truth."

"So, you do want to be with me?"

He gave a long, slow exhalation before pulling his fingers through his hair. "As much as I want you, I can't give you what you need."

"And how do you know what I need?" I asked in a hush.

"Because I know you."

The sky was darkening, and his eyes brightened again. I reached for his beard and swept my hand over the growth, then higher to his cheekbone. He sat still, like a statue, but the haze slowly cleared in his eyes.

"I'm gonna kiss you, Hunter." I leaned in and took his hesitant lips. His mustache tickled and carried the forest's scent.

He pulled away. "Grace—"

"You don't want me. Oh, God, this is so embarrassing. Here I am throwing myself at you and thinking we could—"

"Grace, stop. I just need you to look up for a second."

"What?"

"Look up."

I followed his finger to the night sky and the bazillion of stars forming streams of light. A meteor shower splashed across the sky. My mouth opened wide, and I lay back on the platform. Hunter snugged in beside me and named constellations and stars. I only half listened because the breathing in my chest overpowered his voice. I didn't want the magic to end. He finally fell quiet, easing the chaos in my head. A shooting star streamed across the night sky, and I made an unrealistic wish.

"Did you make a wish?" His voice faded into a wisp, and we turned our heads inward.

"Yes. Would you like to help make it come true?"

His body tensed and his eyes darkened. The heat of him wrapped itself around my limbs, coaxing desire in my groin. He brushed his hand up my arm to my cheek, the rough pads of his fingers tracing heat over my skin.

"I'll do my best."

His throaty voice sent shivers down my spine.

"But I should go down. I mean, *we* should go downstairs before the bugs come out." He shuddered, like he hated the thought of bugs, and the moment was gone.

"You live in a rainforest, and you're afraid of bugs?" I asked.

"Ask me again when a giant tarantula gets up your shorts."

The blood drained from my face.

"Or a beetle, but that's not as bad as a wood scorpion."

"Scorpion?"

Now I understood the need for all the mesh around the house.

"The sting isn't fatal, but you'll feel it for days."

I shot up to my feet. "Let's go downstairs."

I didn't wait for Hunter to tell me about all the other critters, and hurried down the ladder without missing a step. I was getting better at this climbing thing. He closed the latch on the roof and met me in the main room, where an oval bed with a canopy mesh was set across from the darkening rainforest view. Lights twinkled around the home's perimeter, and crickets chirped.

"Go shower. I'll make something to eat and meet you in the kitchen."

"Shower in the waterfall?"

"No, in the washroom."

"What?"

"Shower in the washroom."

"You have a washroom?"

He laughed. "I'm surprised you haven't asked about it. Wait —did you think I pooped in the bushes and bathed in the river?"

"Of course that's what I thought. You bathed in the river in the village. I... I don't know what to think about you anymore, Hunter Silver. You've turned into a caveman, a bear, and Tarzan all at the same time."

"Tarzan? I thought you'd peg me for John Robinson."

The patriarch of the Swiss Family Robinson? Why would he have mentioned a family man?

"Then... then why did you let me bathe in the waterfall?"

"If you recall, I was sleeping, and you ventured out on your own."

I expelled a breath through my nostrils. He stood in front of me grinning, his bright eyes focused on mine.

"So, are you going to show me the washroom, or do I need to bathe in the waterfall underneath the moon?"

"Sounds... intriguing."

"And dangerous. Washroom?"

He took my hand. Instant heat flew through my veins. "This way."

The enormous eco-house wrapped around the tree's trunk. Sleek drapes floated over the mesh windows. I followed him past the kitchen and through a partition to a space larger than the sitting area and bedroom. Lights twinkled everywhere. His enormous feet flapped against the polished wood to the tune of my pulsing ovaries. I felt like I was living a romantic fairytale, beautiful man included.

"That's another bedroom?" I stopped, pulling on his hand and pointed to the bed beyond a white curtain.

"Yes."

"Why did you sleep on the net above me last night?"

"Because it was your first night here. I didn't want you alone or afraid."

It had made me feel better knowing he was near, watching over me.

"Thank you. So you'll sleep here tonight?"

"We'll see."

Was that a wink? What did that mean?

He flicked open a mesh partition to the outside. The magnets closed the seal behind us, and we scaled up a small suspended bridge covered with more mesh. Feeling the sway underneath us, I tightened my grip on his hand. We stepped on another platform, through another partition, and into an oval washroom.

My mouth dropped open. "Hunter... this is... this is incredible."

Wood covered the entire space, with branches waving along the walls. More fairy lights twinkled around the perimeter, giving the space a warm glow. A cabinet stood near the main branch, with two sinks. On the other side, near the mesh window, were two open showers. I paced forward, taking in the natural decor and beauty.

"Why do you have two showers?" I asked.

"When I built this place, I was thinking about you."

I turned around and found him right behind me.

"Hunter..."

His hands slowly drew up my arms to my shoulders. He towered over me and slowly wrapped me into his bear-like body. My head rose and then lowered to his chest until he kissed the top of my head and breathed out. "Grace... my queen."

I pulled away and looked up. There he was. My Hunter. My over-protective best friend, lover, and bodyguard. He cupped my face in his hands and drew his thumbs over my cheeks.

"I… I still love you, Hunter. I never stopped loving you, and I'm not sure I ever can." My heart pattered against my ribcage. Was I getting this wrong? Because it felt very right. "Hunter, please say something."

Instead, his mouth covered mine, drawing out a sensual kiss and messing with my head. His tongue slipped between my lips, and my arms fell to the sides, limp and unresponsive.

When he pulled away, he braced his forehead against mine, breathing hard.

"I never stopped loving you either, Grace."

"Please don't say *but*—"

"But we're both starving."

Yes. Yes, we were. Except I was starving for him.

He kissed me again, ever so gently, and backed away, pulling a white shirt over his head. It was just him and me… and thousands of twinkling lights in the middle of nowhere.

"And I need a shower."

He stepped out of his shorts, springing free, and turned on both shower heads. My belly did a somersault, and my ovaries nearly burst with emotional overload, thumping through my pelvis. I watched him submerge beneath the stream and tilt his head back. He pulled his fingers through his hair and turned around with a sly grin. "Be a good girl and wash up before the water runs cold."

There it was. Two words that turned the flaming desire in my chest into an inferno.

Good girl.

Fine. Two could play this game.

Chapter 11

Hunter

She stripped out of her clothes in slow motion, and I froze, holding her dreamy gaze. First went the tank top, then the shorts, bra, and panties. Grace stood there bare, watching my dick rise into a full salute. I scanned her body, drinking in her curves and tanned flesh. Memories of her soft skin flooded my head. All the lonely nights I'd spent here, stroking my cock to the dreams of this moment, seemed like a waste. I should have done this before. I should have brought her here long ago.

She came forward and brushed her arm against mine before ducking under the showerhead. I shut my eyes and stepped underneath my own stream. Was this a mistake? Was I leading her on to a future that would never make her happy?

I jumped up at the touch of her hands over my back.

"Relax, Hunter. I'm just giving this bear back a scrub."

Her hands stroked over my skin, her nails gently scraping down the neglected area and driving me mad. My blood rushed south. As her hands traveled lower, the shivers crawling up my spine made a U-turn and followed the path of her torturous touch. The long forgotten strokes circled over my skin and awakened a desire I fought to suppress. My balls zapped with urgency and my dick throbbed. She removed her hand, robbing me of her touch, but I could feel her still standing behind me. I turned around and faced her. It was just her and me, and thousands of lost moments I regretted.

A roar sounded from the outside, and Grace jumped into my arms, trapping my dick between us. Her soaked, soft body clung to my skin, testing my patience.

"What was that?" She shook in my arms.

"Likely a cougar."

"Like a wild one?"

"No, they're all trained from the zoo." I snickered.

She slapped her hand against my arm and backed away, reading my eyes. "I'm serious. Has one ever broken in?"

"Yes, before I properly secured the home."

She stepped closer, nearly touching me again.

"Did it attack you?"

"Did you not see the scar on my chest?" I pressed my palm over my heart, and she immediately removed my hand, searching for the wound. That was a mistake on my part. Her fingers raked through my trimmed chest hair, inflaming my arousal. Did she not notice she was rubbing up against me? I gripped her wrist, and she looked up.

"I'm kidding. I had a flare gun, and it left. No harm done." I turned off my faucet. "Your water's getting lukewarm. Better hurry."

She cleared her throat and returned to her shower.

"Right—no harm done."

I awkwardly turned the shower back on and washed in haste, finishing before she did. I wrapped a towel around my hips and scooped our clothes into the hamper. As Grace washed her hair, I set out the towels.

"I'll wait for you on the bridge."

She swept the water off her face. "Yeah, okay."

On a night alone, the rainforest sang with chirping crickets and croaking toads. It helped me sleep. But how could I sleep when she was offering herself to me? Why did I kiss her? Why did I need her, and why was I leading her on?

I shifted forward and braced my hands on the rope. The bridge swayed but held. It had supported much more than me at one point: a cougar and me. That one wasn't friendly, and my best friend, Kali, had saved my life. I got lucky that night. The next morning, I secured the area, and bought weapons and flare guns.

"Hunter?" I jumped up at her voice. She was waiting at the end of the bridge, wrapped in a towel. "Are you all right?"

I reached for her and took her hand. "Come. We need to eat."

We crossed the bridge back to the main house. I left her in the bedroom with a backpack full of clothes her mother had packed and set up the food Abuela and Paula had prepared for tonight. Tomorrow, I'd take Grace fishing, and we'd pick fruits and vegetables near the river. I'd do anything to keep my mind off her curvy hips and soft skin.

"Hunter?"

I startled for the second time at her voice tonight and turned around. She was standing there in a black silky top and shorts. The fabric outlined her breasts and nipples, and my effort to suppress my need for her failed.

"You keep sneaking up on me," I said.

"You're just not used to living with someone again. You keep forgetting I'm here."

"Quite the opposite, Grace. You never leave my mind."

She smiled and strolled to the dining table. My gaze followed her swaying hips. I swear to God she was doing that on purpose. She slid into the seat on the wooden bench and picked up a fork.

"Sit down, Hunter. You'll need your strength." She winked.

And patience. She forgot to add patience.

"One sec. I have something for you." I extracted a bottle of blush wine from behind the counter and I poured her a glass.

"It's not rosé, but my choices were limited."

She licked her lips, drawing my attention to her tempting mouth. "Are you trying to get me drunk?" she asked.

"No, Grace. I definitely don't want you drunk."

"Relaxed?" She tilted her head.

"Do you need to relax?"

She thought for a moment. "All right. Maybe relaxed is not the right word. How about being satisfied? The last time a man satisfied me—"

"I don't want to know, Grace."

She laughed and scooped a forkful of rice and beans, stuffing her mouth. "It was you."

My head flew up.

"Why are you so surprised?"

"Honestly, I thought you'd find someone who would give you a baby."

She sipped on her wine and cleared her throat. "The thing is, Hunter, I already found someone to father my baby. Sperm donor 43874 is a mature engineer. He's athletic, with blue eyes and curly hair. Best of all, I don't have to argue with him over baby names or stalking ex-girlfriends. I don't have time to look for a man I can trust. I trust you and the sperm bank, so those are my only options."

She was so wrong.

"But I get the feeling you don't want to talk about babies."

I shrugged a shoulder.

"What I don't get is why you're so opposed to kids since you definitely know how to play soccer with them—"

I laughed. "You think I'd be a good father because I can play soccer?"

"No. I think you'd be a good father because you're protective, caring, helpful, loving, giving, and hot."

"Looks don't make a good father."

"But they make a sexy one. We don't have to talk about babies. I just want to enjoy your company and this adventure in the rainforest with... my personal Tarzan." She winked. "I needed this, so thank you."

I snorted through a laugh. *Tarzan.* "You're welcome. I'm happy to see you relaxed."

She stood up, slid out of her seat, and walked around the table to my side. I pushed away from the table and watched her saunter toward me. Her hips swayed in a hypnotizing motion. She lowered her lips to my ear, breasts spilling forward, and murmured. "Don't you want to satisfy me?"

Fuck.

The scent of her sent a flood of memories rushing to my head. Specifically, ones of my dick deep inside her thoroughly licked pussy. She parted her legs and straddled my lap. Her crotch rubbed over my straining dick. I weaved my fingers into her damp hair, bringing her face in front of mine.

"I wouldn't satisfy you, Grace." My lips buzzed against hers. "I would obliterate you."

"That would work." Her mouth trembled and body gave in the way I liked.

"Oh, Grace—" I pressed my nose in the nook between her neck and shoulders, breathing her in.

"Why are you holding back, Hunter?"

"I don't want to disappoint you."

She laughed, and I lifted my head. Where did that hope in her eyes come from? She caressed my cheek with her hand.

"Well, that's silly. I don't know what you've done over the past five years, but you've added a good three dozen muscles on top of the ones I remember, and that's definitely not disappointing."

"So, what you're saying is you like muscled men?"

"No, I like *a man* built by hard work. And…" She shifted on my lap, grinding against my dick.

"And what?" I whispered.

"I love you."

Her ass slid forward on my lap with a sweeter temptation. My stiff cock ached with her movements.

"And I want you, even if it's just for one night. No expectations. Make love to me, Hunter, one more time, here in this jungle. Or… I mean, if you prefer to fuck me—"

I secured my hands underneath her ass and stood up, lifting her. She squealed in my hold and wrapped her legs around my waist. I gently removed the glasses off her nose and set them on the table.

"How will I see you?"

I kissed her, taking my time with her mouth while walking across the room. "You won't see me, my Queen. You will feel me."

I carried her to the oval bed, pushed past the canopy, and lowered her to the sheets, hovering above her. The moon shone from beyond the mesh wall opening like it was meant for the two of us.

She touched my cheek and drew her fingers down my beard, pulling on my facial hair until my breath connected with hers.

"I've been wanting to do that since you walked into the salon." She panted, her chest swelling beneath me.

I seized her willing mouth and parted her lips with my tongue, swallowing her soft moan. Her body yielded to mine, writhing underneath me. She drew her hands up my arms to my head, raking her fingers through my hair. Her delicate tongue swept against mine with a moan, and my hips settled between her legs. The head of my dick popped out from the waistband, rubbing over the crevice underneath her silky shorts. I held her face between my palms, concentrating on the lips and moans I'd missed, kissing her over and over. When we pulled apart, her eyes were large and her hair wild. She leaned back on the bed, and her feet flew up to my waist. A smirk caught the corner of her mouth as she hooked her toes on my shorts and dragged them down. I shimmied out of the fabric and lowered my mouth to hers.

The kiss hardened, and I sealed my mouth around hers, drawing on her every breath and whimper. Her swollen breasts lifted, silently pleading for my touch. I pulled my mouth away from hers and traced my lips down her jaw and neck. Her skin turned a fervent hot pink.

She squirmed as I sat up. Her legs were parted, shorts wedged into her pussy, and her breasts partially spilled out of her top. Her hair scattered wildly over the pillow, and her cheeks were tinted like rosé wine. She lay on my bed, in my home, in the middle of the rainforest, waiting.

Who would have thought?

If there was anything I'd learned over the past five years, it was seizing the moment, because opportunities didn't knock twice.

I arched an eyebrow. "My turn."

She bit her lip and lifted her legs high in the air, resting them on my chest.

"Perfect." I pulled her shorts off her hips and up her legs, flinging them across the bed.

She laughed, and I crawled higher, removing her top. I sat back up, taking in her glistening skin. Her arms lay spread out to the sides, and her hands gripped the sheets. Her stomach sank in and her swollen breasts rose, spilling to the sides. I dragged my gaze down her tanned body, over the aquamarine belly button ring I'd convinced her to get for my nineteenth birthday. She bent at the knees and parted her legs. Her pussy glistened.

I felt my smile twist, and I looked up. "We won't be getting much sleep tonight."

I kissed around her navel and up to the valley between her breasts. She arched her back, and I took her hard nipple into my mouth, stretching out its length.

"Hunter…" she breathed out into the night, lifting her hips and dragging her soaked pussy down my abs. My cock leaked, and I grunted, tending to her other breast. I locked my lips around her stone-hard nipple and squeezed to where the pain became pleasure, and then pulled up. The flesh sprang back to her breast. I centered over her chest, my mouth on a downward path to the heat between her thighs. I lay on the bed between her legs with the perfect moonlit view of her heated body. Her ribcage lifted and stomach hollowed as I kissed over her navel. The honey-coconut scent of her skin filled my lungs.

I slid my tongue through her flesh, and the sweet taste of her arousal sailed through my mouth. God, I was right. She was the best fucking thing on the menu. I kissed through her lips, enjoying the impatience as she centered herself under my mouth. Her pussy swelled, pulsing between my lips. I then looked up, watching her mouth part as I slid three fingers inside her.

"Ahh." Her eyes flew open.

"You've neglected your toys, Grace."

I pumped in and out her tight pussy while her hips gyrated to the rhythm. She squeezed around my fingers, gripping and holding their length deep inside her. The sound of her essence squishing between her and my hand echoed in my brain, and the smell of her potent need made my mouth water. My dick felt like it was on fire, waiting for its turn as I closed over her pulsing clit. Oh God, she tasted like heaven. Her legs shot straight out, stiffening. I sucked on the tender nub, pushing my fingers and getting her ready. The first spasm flew through her body, and she clenched so hard around my hand I could no longer move it. Her clit pulsed in my mouth until she let go, screaming my name.

"Hunter!"

Her legs released my hand, but I flicked my tongue harder. She gripped the sheets and thrashed underneath me. I sucked on her until she flopped on the sheets, completely spent.

"Hunter…"

I crawled up to her moonlit face. Sweat beaded down her forehead, and the fairy lights flickered in her brown eyes. I tenderly kissed her hot mouth into a drawn-out smile. I didn't realize how much I'd missed her until I had her again.

"You were right. You obliterated me," she said against my lips.

I rose to my hands, the tip of my cock ready at her drenched opening. "Baby, I'm just starting."

Her mouth fell open as I slowly pushed inside her, then withdrew.

"Fuck, you're larger than I remember."

"Should have used those dildos from your secret kitchen cupboard," I said.

She burst out a laugh, and I pushed in again, this time deeper, launching her body higher on the bed. She closed her eyes and urged with her hips for more. I worked in and out of her pussy until she took me to her depth, and I lowered myself to her body, connecting skin to skin. Her cheek pressed against my chest, and she moved her hands to my ass. I took her hair into my fists, filled my lungs with her essence, and thrust harder. She nipped at my nipple and I jerked back as the arousal in my groin burst with a zap. My eyes flew open.

"You like that?" She grinned.

"Yes. If you're trying to make me come…" I reached back for her hands and gripped her tiny wrists, pinning them over her head.

"Wear a condom, if that's what you think I'm doing. Otherwise, shut up and fuck me."

I skimmed my lips over hers "You're gonna come before I do so again."

"Again?"

"Don't you want to come again, Grace?"

She blinked repeatedly, a thousand questions swimming in her eyes and I wanted to erase them all away.

"I do."

"Good girl."

I slammed into her pussy, her breasts bouncing high. She moved her body with mine, but I needed more of her... of me... and us, together. I stopped, withdrew, flipped us over, and sat up, lifting her onto my lap. She wrapped her arms around my neck and bent her legs at the knees, sinking onto my dick. My cock stayed deep inside her, pulsing. She rolled her hips like she owned me, and I loved every minute of her control. I gave into her lead, supporting her in my arms. The intimate sway of our shadow in the moonlight tightened the grip she had around my heart.

I fucking loved her so much it hurt. I wanted her. All of her. But would she want a broken man?

Her movements shortened, and my need heightened. The first shot of cum jerked out of my dick before I realized I couldn't hold it anymore. I let her do what she wanted: ride me and milk my last drops with her pussy. A cloud passed by and covered the moon as I settled inside her.

Chapter 12

grace

His arms wound tight around me and mine around him as he emptied himself and then settled. Skin to skin and heart to heart, we sat in the middle of the bed, breathing in tandem. He traced his lips over my shoulder, audibly inhaling the smell of my hair and skin before moving onto my neck. I tilted back my head, his lips brushed over my throat, and I wanted to do it all over again. I raked my fingers through his beard, releasing its wild scent, and the past hour flashed in my mind. My inner thighs tingled from the gentle scratch. I gripped the sheets and held back as long as I could, getting lost to the sound of his lapping tongue, but Hunter's vicious mouth won. My arousal flourished to the tune of his tongue strokes. His thorough licks sent fiery blood surging through my veins as he brought me to the point of no return. Point was, he had a talented mouth. A man's mouth… no… a beast's.

I grazed my fingers down his back, and he gave a grateful grunt, easing his possessive hold to an intimate one. Thousands of fairy lights shone above us. The magically moonlit night was more than I'd ever expected. It felt like we were the only two people in the world. Plus a cougar.

My heart beat against his and my head spun, while my ovaries radiated with hope. If his sperm was as healthy as his body, and if by some miracle, Dr. Riley had missed a mature egg on the ultrasound, it was the perfect time to make a baby. Maybe a little late and just before my period, but not impossible.

I looked out into the night. The moonlit view of the rainforest hid behind a cloud before drifting away.

Hunter tilted forward, lowered us to the bed, and slowly withdrew. A leak trickled down my inner thigh and I had the urge to lift my legs high in the air, but he spooned me from behind and nuzzled his nose in my neck, breathing me in. "I missed you."

"I missed you too," I said.

His large hand slid over my tummy and up to my breast. He felt its full weight and curved his palm around the soft flesh. I relaxed into the comfort of his cuddly body. His semi-hard dick rested against my ass cheek, and I wiggled my behind.

"It feels like you're ready for more."

"I hope you realize you're not sleeping until I get enough."

"Sign me up, Hunter Silver. I may be older, but I can keep up."

"We'll see, because I don't think I'll ever get enough of you."

Was that commitment? I had no time to think because he kissed my shoulder and rose to his knees, pulling me to my feet.

"Get up."

"What are you doing? We just lay down." I balanced on the mattress and then followed him off the bed.

"We need to wash up, and it's the best time to see the waterfall."

"What about the cougars?"

"I think I'm doing fine with you here." He winked.

I shuddered, trying to sweep the goosebumps off my arms.

"That was supposed to be a joke. You think I would let anything to happen to you?"

He wouldn't, would he? But I was sure the cougar wouldn't listen to logic, just like none of my girlfriends did when they preyed on younger men. I swallowed past the lump in my throat.

"No. You wouldn't."

He chuckled and passed me a towel.

"We're going naked?"

"No. We're wearing shoes."

Fuck. He's serious.

I held the towel against my chest, watching him move through the room, collecting a few items into a backpack. He went to the kitchen freezer, grabbed a giant piece of meat, and packed that as well.

"What's that for?"

"If I leave it out for the cougar, it will leave us alone."

"I'm not going."

"Grace—"

"You're being irrational, Hunter."

"I'm asking you to trust me. You can come, or you can stay here on your own."

"You wouldn't leave me."

He tied the towel around his hips, flung the backpack over his shoulder, and pushed down the ladder into the hole.

"Come on, gorgeous. Where's your sense of adventure?"

"Stuck in hell with my courage."

He laughed, waiting. I secured the towel around my body and took his offered hand. We climbed down the ladder into the forest's abyss. Hunter turned on the flashlight and led me to the river's edge, where we followed the moonlit path to the waterfall. The river's surface reflected the moon, and the hum of the falling water grew louder. We set the towels and the backpack on a rock and treaded along the cliff side until we were underneath the waterfall. Droplets rose in the air, condensing over my skin. Water trickled from a hole in the caved in cliff, like a shower, and more cascaded from behind us, sealing us in between the cliff and the shimmering curtain.

"I can't believe we're doing this," I screamed over the water's roar and stepped underneath the stream, pushing back my soaked hair.

"You mean this?"

He spun me into his arms and crushed his mouth to mine, sealing my breath. His fervent tongue swept over my gums like he was trying to make up for lost time. I melted into his body, yielding to his roaming hands and taking pleasure in finding new paths in between his packed muscles. His back was so wide, I couldn't wrap my arms around him, so I slid my hands to his tight ass, digging my fingers into his skin. He groaned into my mouth, pressing his hard dick against my belly.

I reached to his front and wrapped my fingers around his thick cock, pumping. His kiss tightened and his hand found my breast. I pushed my chest into his manipulating fingers, losing concentration as a new swell built between my legs.

He pinched my nipple. The painful ache turned into pleasure as it took the path to my pussy. His hand slid across to my other breast, down to my hip and over my flat stomach. Arousal buzzed in my groin. I got drunk on the tantalizing touch of his fingers. Anticipating the trajectory of his hand, I opened my legs and was rewarded with his fingers, spreading my wet pussy lips. Starving for a breath, I broke our kiss, and Hunter dropped to his knees.

"Oh, no." I breathed out.

I wasn't sure whether he heard me, but it was already too late. His mouth locked over my clit, and the voice in my head screamed out *Yes*. I shut my eyes and dug my fingers into his shoulders. He held my lips open and flicked his tongue over my swell. My ass clenched and my breasts ached for more, but his devious mouth won. The first orgasmic jolt zapped through my limbs, and my eyes flew open. I looked up. The waterfall blurred the darkness behind its flow, and the stars shimmered like diamonds. He pushed his fingers deeper inside me and sucked on my flesh, pushing me over the edge.

"Hunter!"

My toes curled, and stars flashed behind my eyes. The orgasm shot through my limbs, shooting through my core over and over. His tongue lapped and his mouth sucked until I couldn't hold myself up anymore. I physically pushed him away, sucking in air. He kissed his way up my body, grazing his beard over the heated path. He licked over my nipple and rose to his feet. The moon shone behind him and water hit his back.

"I need to cool off." I stepped underneath the water's stream.

"You're not going anywhere." He hooked my arm and spun me back to my spot, pinning my front against the stone. My cheek pressed to the wall as his beautiful body, along with his hard dick, seized me from behind, trapping me. The escarpment cooled my body from the front while Hunter's front heated my back. He stretched my arms out and secured his fingers around my wrists.

"Cool enough for you?" he murmured into my ear and tapped his foot on the inside of my ankles. I stepped further apart, giving him access.

"Because I'm not done with you." His hand slid down my ass crack to between my legs, fingers circling my opening. He dragged them up through the crevice and rubbed my clit, stimulating me all over again.

Not again.

My head fell back, and he pulled his lips along my ear, touching me there like he owned me.

"I asked you a question, Grace. Is this cool enough, or do you want me to stop?"

"I don't want you to stop." My voice was lost to the water's hum.

He withdrew his hand from my pussy and lined himself up behind me, thrusting hard without a warning.

Fuck.

My body flew up the wall. I braced my hands on the rock's surface as he advanced the second time, hitting deeper and harder. Air leaked out of my lungs. He took hold of my hips and pumped quicker and harder. My eyes grew wider with every thrust, and hot arousal flooded my veins. I tilted my ass higher and looked back over my shoulder. The moonlight behind the backdrop of the waterfall outlined Hunter's tensed body. His eyes held steady over my ass, and his jaw clenched as he focused on where we connected. I pushed back, opening for him. His right hand slipped forward, over my belly and down to my pussy, while his left cupped my breast. My back pressed against his chest, and he slowed the momentum, caging me within his arms, staying deep inside me. We rolled our hips in tandem, his fingers rubbing over my clit in delicious circles. I looked back and kissed him as he rolled my nipple.

I didn't know which hand to concentrate on, and then his tongue slid through my mouth like a viper. I nearly bit my lip. He groaned into my mouth, and I lost it. The orgasm's current tore through me, surging through my veins as he pushed in once more. My legs shook underneath me and my knees buckled. Hunter caught my weight and held me against his body as his fingers finished me off. His strokes eased, and my climax settled. Except it didn't, because he kept rubbing and reviving the pleasure until it tingled everywhere, and I couldn't breathe.

"Hunter." I pulled his hand away. "I… I can't…anymore."

He kissed the side of my temple. "Are you all right?"

"Just spent. Fuck, Hunter."

"I thought we just did that. Hold on."

He slowly withdrew, holding me steady, and I shut my legs tight.

"Are you trying to keep my sperm inside you?"

I shrugged a shoulder. "Maybe it'll work."

He shook his head and stepped underneath the waterfall again, pulling me along with him. The cold water soothed my burning body but did little to stop the constant ache for this man. We washed up and headed back to the towels and the tree house.

"Where's the slab of meat you left?" I asked.

"In a cougar's tummy."

"You're kidding."

"No, I'm not. I wasn't lying earlier."

I whipped my head toward the tree house. "Are we going back now?"

He let out a chesty chuckle. "Yes, we're going back."

I hurried ahead with the flashlight and climbed the ladder like I was next on the cougar's menu.

"What time is it?" I asked as I slipped on a nightshirt and shorts.

"Not time to get dressed." He winked. "Take off that shirt."

"Hunter—"

"I need to feel your body." He pulled the sheets aside. "Take off the shirt and hop in."

I shed my clothes and climbed up on the bed. He slipped in naked underneath the covers and lay down beside me. I settled at his side, resting my head over his arm and chest.

Clouds covered the moon, and Hunter turned off all of the lights. It was just us and darkness.

"Why can't life be simple and we stay here?" I whispered.

"We could. I've lived here for five years."

"What would we do?"

"I can think of a few things to keep you busy." He tickled my ribcage, and I squirmed.

"I mean, what would we do for work?" I asked.

"If my account was empty, I would work. But it's not, so we could retire."

"Here?"

"Why not?"

"What would I do?"

"Me."

"Seriously, Hunter."

"Wait—are you serious about this? You'd leave Long Island and the salon behind?"

"Let's not get carried away. This is only hypothetical."

He repositioned himself, and I took a deep breath in, filling my lungs with his wild scent. "Hypothetically, if you wanted to work, you could open a salon in the village. They love you down there."

"You know, a baby would keep me busy in the beginning."

"I guess we could adopt."

"Adopt? You wouldn't want kids of your own?"

"I don't think that's in the plan for me."

"Why not?"

"Grace… Just… I don't want you to get your hopes up. What about your fertility treatments?"

"I… I haven't thought about it much since coming here. You've kept me busy."

"Because if we moved here, you'd be likely giving that up too, and I never want you to give up on your dream."

"We could make it work, Hunter, because I'll never give up on you again."

I woke to the sound of macaws squawking nearby. I swept my hand over the pillow beside me and found the spot empty.

"Hunter?" I sat up.

Bright sun shone through the wall opening, and the smell of coffee pushed my eyes wide open. I hurried out of bed. A French coffee press with steaming java was waiting on the kitchen counter, along with a heap of bananas, mangoes, and two coconuts. I dressed, poured myself a cup, and stepped onto the viewing platform by the kitchen.

The rainforest swayed to the wind's push. Down in the valley, Hunter was sitting on a rock, fishing by the river. His wide back hunched forward as he rested his arms on his knees. God, the man was a beast. Our little adventure was messing with my head. How could I even consider living in a jungle?

Something moved in the bushes behind him, and I set my coffee on the table, focusing on the area. A beige coat snuck in between the foliage, advancing toward Hunter.

Oh, my God.

"Hunter!" I screamed, but he couldn't hear me over the rushing water.

I grabbed Hunter's flare gun from the backpack, jumped into my runners, and swung down the tree rope like Jane, a little surprised I stuck the landing. I ran down the path, pushing through the bushes. Leaves and branches slapped against my arms as I screamed, "Hunter, there's a cougar behind you!"

A loud splash echoed from the river. I reached the rock where Hunter had been sitting earlier, but he was gone. He surfaced to my right, along with a cougar. The cat leaped into the air and landed on top of Hunter.

Oh, my God.

I fumbled with the flare gun, frustrated that it kept slipping from my grip.

"What are you doing here, Grace? Go back to the house."

I looked up, waving the flare gun in my hand. "Not letting it kill you."

"Put down the gun and go back to the house, Grace. Now." His command struck my body like lightning. The cougar surfaced and turned to the shore, focusing on me.

I backed away in slow motion and turned on my heel as soon as I was out of view. On my way back, a branch cut my arm and a giant leaf that looked like Swiss cheese slapped my face red. I was pretty fit, but by the time I got to the tree house and climbed up the fifth step, the wild roar behind me sent me shooting to the top in a blink. I hurried to pull up the ladder as the cougar circled underneath the opening.

"Kali, stop that. There's no need to scare her." Hunter came up to the cat, and the animal brushed against his leg. "Drop the ladder. It's fine." He waved.

"Fine? There's a cougar beside you."

"And one up there." He pointed to me. "I promise you'll be okay. I planned on introducing you two anyway."

"You want to *introduce* me to a cougar? Are you crazy?"

"Kali's been interested in you since the day you arrived."

"Well, that makes me feel better." I rolled my eyes. "I think I'd rather spend time with Chad Hartley."

"Spit that out, Grace. Kali won't hurt you. She knows you're mine."

The cougar roared.

"I call bullshit on that."

"She's not like other cats. I found her orphaned after poachers killed her mother, and I raised her. If she wanted to come inside the house, she already would have. She may be wild, but she's loyal and trained. You wouldn't be alive if she wasn't. You're safe. Come down."

"I can't."

"Sure you can."

"It's not happening. Use the rope."

I kicked down the loop near my foot, and Hunter's shoulders slumped.

"Kali, leave. We'll play later."

The cougar disappeared into the jungle, and Hunter pulled himself up the rope without effort. His biceps bunched and the wet shorts clung to his skin. I shut the latch as soon as he entered and backed away from the exit. Water dripped down his legs, collecting on the floor. He gripped the waistband of his shorts, removed them, and walked past me. I followed him all the way to the washroom, watching his naked ass strain and tighten with each step. He hung the shorts on a rope between the two showers and turned around. My body flushed with heat.

"I was wrong about you. You're not a caveman or a bear. You're definitely Tarzan."

Chapter 13

Hunter

Bongo drums boomed and maracas shook as we arrived in the village. Mister G, the bride's uncle, joined in, strumming his guitar. Grace hopped off the scooter and unwound the dress Abuela had left for her to wear.

"I look like Big Bird." She swept her hands over the fabric. Her brown hair spilled out in waves over her chest. She hadn't mentioned a hair dryer once, and the natural look brought out her eyes. For a split second, I could see the resemblance to the Hartleys, but then she smiled, and she was my Grace again.

"You look like a sunflower," I said. "Absolutely gorgeous. And no one here knows who Big Bird is."

"My arms are itchy."

I smoothed my hands over the scratches Grace carried from the forest. Running through a jungle was never a good idea. Prey ran every day—and died.

"Abuela has an ointment. She'll paste it over your arms, and it will heal by morning."

"I'm still like a beacon for Kali."

She looked back, glancing up, and I kissed her. "She protects the territory around our home. Also, my cougar is coming into heat and likely sticking her ass out to a stalking mate. A sunflower is the last thing on Kali's mind."

Her breath caught, and I inhaled her scent, tracing my fingers over her pulsing jugular. The sweet coconut and jungle aroma took me back to the tree house, arousing the urge to hitch up that yellow dress and fuck her again. My blood flow turned south, and I rubbed myself against her hip.

She moaned, taking my mouth again in a sensual kiss. Grace was in heat, just like Kali. Her breasts swelled, her nipples tinted, and her pussy leaked at my touch. She'd strad-dled me on the bed before we changed for the wedding, forcing us to skip breakfast. I rested my head against the pillow and watched her fuck me. She rolled over my dick like Aphrodite, squeezing her breasts and pinching her nipples. I came hard and fast, spilling inside her, and watched her mouth stretch into a satisfied smile. Guilt filled my chest every time I fucking orgasmed. Was I betraying her?

Someone whistled from near the house, and we pulled apart.

"Are you going to walk around with a hard on?" she asked.

"Yes. It won't go down until after I come inside you again."

She rose up on her toes and kissed me again. "We'll just have to sneak away later on."

"I'll ensure we do. We should go. Abuela made you break-fast, and Paula's sister needs help with her hair."

"Right. She's the one getting married. Did I cut everyone's hair for the wedding?"

"Wedding aside, you gave every person their first profes-sional cut. Four new couples went out on a date that evening."

"So I'm like Cupid."

I kissed the tip of her nose. "You're more than Cupid."

My stomach growled, and I took a good whiff. The smell of homemade food filled the air. I rubbed my stomach. "Today's gonna be great."

Grace chuckled. I took her hand and led her down the path to the village. They'd decorated the street with palm branches and flowers and everyone was running around with last-minute chores like there was a fire. Men carried extra chairs to the outdoor venue. More food was carried inside the hall, and kids roamed around the streets everywhere. The chaos brought satisfaction to my face. We stopped in front of Abuela's bakery.

"It's so busy." Grace turned to the window. "Oh, my God. Look at that cake."

Paula was just setting the marzipan bride and groom on the top tier.

"Where did they get all this?"

"I managed a small shipment in here last night."

"A small shipment?" She flicked her brows up, and I shrugged.

"Listen, I have to go help with some lights, but I believe someone needs you." I pointed to the kitchen window.

"*Venir. El cabello de mi hermana es un desastre,*" Paula called out.

"Her sister's hair is a mess. She needs your help." I took her lips once more. "I'll have someone bring you breakfast, and I'll see you soon."

I grabbed a sweet coconut bun off a window shelf, stuffed it into my mouth, and waved to Paula. "*Gracias.*"

I hurried to the river, where the men had set up the wooden dance floor. They scattered a mess of string lights in the middle. I got the boys working on four different corners, and three hours later, we were ready to hang them on the trees overhead. I helped carry the buckets of roses I had delivered, setting them around the perimeter. Then came the pots of food, sitting benches, the canopy, and torches.

Over the last two days, the men had built a pizza oven, and they waited for me to fire it up. I circled the stone structure and checked the solid construction. I bent down to the ground and took out my matches. The kindling was stuck deep underneath the oven. I stretched forward, crawling inside until I reached the wood. The smell of kerosene wafted around me. I removed my matches, ignited a flame, and aimed underneath the teepee of twigs. Sparks flickered onto my face, and the blaze spread quicker than I expected. By the time I pushed out from within the oven, my beard had caught on fire. I swept my hands over my flaming facial hair when a bucket of water was splashed onto my face. The fire sizzled and died as the stench of burnt hair filled my lungs.

I shook off the water and touched my face. "Shit."

Everyone burst out in laughter.

"Fuck. Mateo," I called out to the boy. "*Maquinilla de afeitar, jabón,* and a mirror."

I turned to Juan Carlos. "How do you say mirror?"

"*Espejo.*" The man waved at Mateo. Three minutes later, the boy brought a razor, soap, a tub with water, and a five-inch shaving mirror.

"*Gracias.*" I splashed the water over my charcoaled hair growth and soaped up. Grace would hate this, but I couldn't go to the wedding with a charred face. I hurried with the shave and washed up in the river. Mateo went to get me clean clothes. By the time I was dressed, everyone from the village had gathered near the bamboo gazebo. The groom stood in front of Abuela, who would perform the ceremony. I searched through the crowd of colorful dresses for my Big Bird.

She was standing by the wine barrels, perched on her toes for a glimpse of the bride behind a rooted ficus tree. Her hair held a crown of pinned flowers and floated over her shoulders. A red shade tinted her cheeks from a fresh sunburn, but she truly looked like a queen.

I stood still, watching her chest rise and fall. Her skin glowed and eyes shone, and for a split second, I saw myself waiting for Grace in front of Abuela. The wind blew, and

Grace's gaze shifted. She scanned the crowd until she found me near the back row. Her mouth dropped open and her hand flew up to cover her surprise. I felt a slight tug at my lip. She sidestepped through the crowd and darted toward me once she reached the edge.

The music started, the crowd turned, and she slowed her run to a reserved walk. She stopped in front of me and lifted her hand to my face.

"What did you do?"

"A small fire. I had no choice."

"Are you all right?"

"Alive and standing. You preferred the beard?"

She torqued her lips into a smug smile. "I liked the way it scratched between my thighs."

"That's because you can't remember my full face in your pussy," I whispered in her ear.

She shivered and nudged me in the ribcage. I refocused on the bride, but with Grace standing next to me, the only thing I could really focus on was the access underneath her dress. She leaned into my side, her soft arm resting against mine. The bride approached the front, and the music stopped.

"I can't wait until you remind me."

I couldn't wait either. I wasn't sure how much time we had left in Costa Rica, but I'd draw out every second I could. The team of contractors at Grace's salon had been working around the clock, and they'd be done within days. If Silver Securities got it right, Chad Hartley would be behind bars before they finished. Reality was knocking too fast, and I expected news before the night's end. Rachel was supposed to arrive this morning with a satellite phone, but I hadn't seen her.

"I can't believe you did all this for the village."

Grace watched the bride and groom twirl on the dance floor.

"It makes me feel better than saving pool frogs." I shrugged my shoulders.

"I loved having you save those toads." She snuggled in closer, and I wrapped my arm around her shoulder, bringing her to my body.

The intimate ceremony, filled with customs and dances passed through generations, was the eighth wedding I'd attended in this village, but I wanted to make this one special. Once we returned to the States, who knew when I could come back? The case against Chad could drag for years.

The couple was pronounced wed, blessed by Abuela, and they kissed. Grace looked up, and I looked down, sharing her sentimental smile. Hot pizzas were removed from the oven, and the party shifted to underneath a tent, where I enjoyed a crispy crust.

I had just stuffed the third jalapeño empanada into my mouth when Grace passed me a glass of guaro.

"What are you doing?"

"What's it taste like?"

"More like vodka than rum, and it burns."

"Have one with me?"

"I thought you didn't want me drinking."

"We're at a wedding in a tribal village decorated like it's Paris Hilton's wedding. I think this occasion is special enough."

"All right. Dip your lips first. It will evaporate before it gets to your tongue." I passed her back the glass.

"Just on my lips?"

"Yeah. Gently. The way I like to taste you."

She bit her lip, gave me a self-conscious look, and tilted the glass at her lips. One, two, three... I stopped the count as she emptied the glass and shook her head. Shudders flew through her body. She stomped her feet on the ground like she was getting ready for a takeoff, and I laughed.

"I said, your tongue only."

"I heard you."

She grabbed a bottle of guaro off a table and shoved it into my hand. "Your turn."

I set the bottle back on the table, popped a fried sweet potato in my mouth, and spun her in a circle. Grace laughed, forgetting all about the alcohol, likely because she already had a glassful flowing through her veins. The stars came out, and we moved onto the dance floor. Grace had learned a traditional dance and gyrated to the drum's beat. The tune slowed, and I took her into my arms. She slid her hand along my face.

"It's gonna take time to get used to this smooth face."

"How about you get used to it?"

I took her plump lips between mine. She tasted like guaro and smelled like sunflower. After the third song, the rhythm sped up again. I spun her around. Her hair flew wild and her head tilted back. She laughed freely, and happiness danced in her eyes. Guilt squeezed my insides.

Mateo, the little boy, grabbed Grace's hand and pulled her into the middle of the dance floor. I laughed to myself, stepped off the platform, and went to get snacks. Grace joined me after I had chewed through the third fish stick.

"I've never had this much fun," she said as I passed her a glass of water.

"It's nice to see you like this."

She hooked her arm through mine, and we walked down the torch-lit path. Her breathing slowed to match our pace.

"Can I ask you a personal question?" Her hold on my arm tightened.

"Okay."

"You tell me kids aren't an option for you, but you're so good with them at the village."

"I'm just glad to help out."

She stopped and turned to face me. Her brown eyes clouded over.

"What is it?" I asked her.

"Why do you come freely inside me?"

"Do you not like it?"

"Of course, I do. I'm just confused." She tilted her head and pursed her lips.

"What's there to be confused about?"

"What if I get pregnant? What if Lorelei or Lucas is born, but you say kids aren't in the cards for you—"

"You picked out your kid's names?"

"I picked out *our* kid's names."

I cupped my hand over her cheek. "I came inside you because you're before your period, which means your ovulation days passed, and..." I swept my finger over her opening mouth. "You already told me your appointment didn't go well. There are no viable eggs this cycle."

Her forehead creased. "Right, but there's still a chance," she said.

No, there wasn't.

"There's my boyfriend."

We pulled apart and turned toward the familiar voice. Rachel was striding toward us in a purple dress. My eyes opened wide. I'd never seen her in a dress before.

"You were supposed to arrive this morning."

"Traffic in the jungle. I'm here now. You can bitch about it or give me a hug."

I took her up into my arms, spun her in a circle, and held her tight.

"Glad to see you again."

"Me too."

She slid down my body, and we turned to a stunned Grace. I cleared my throat.

"Rachel, this is Grace. Grace, Rachel. My old partner."

"And girlfriend?" Grace lifted a brow.

Rachel laughed. "No, no. It's an inside joke. Hunter's like a brother to me, and my wife would be upset."

If Rachel was trying to ease Grace's worry, it worked. I gave her a quick kiss where the pink shade covered her glowing cheek.

"Did you get it?" I asked Rachel.

"Yeah. I got it." She passed me the phone.

"Do you mind keeping Grace busy?"

"I can definitely do that." She winked.

"Not that busy. Hands off."

"Are you going up the mountain in the middle of the night?" Grace asked.

"No." I lifted the phone. "This baby works from here."

Her eyes sparkled.

"And I promise to get an update on the salon."

"Thank you."

I left them to chat and dialed Scar's number. He picked up on the second ring.

"I've been expecting your call."

"Does that mean you have good news?"

"Chad's in custody, and the salon's ready. My mother wants to talk to Grace as soon as she gets back, and your jet will be ready in the morning."

Morning.

It felt too soon for the adventure to end. I wanted Grace here. I wanted us here.

"Got it. We'll see you soon."

I hung up and walked back. Grace and Rachel were sitting on a bench underneath the rooted tree. Grace's shoulders were slouched forward, and I stopped before reaching them.

Grace lifted her head. Tears streamed down her face and her body shook visibly. I tightened my hands into fists.

"Rachel, what did you say?" The tendons in my neck strained.

"I'm sorry," Rachel whispered. "I didn't know."

Grace stood up and looked me dead in the eyes.

"Is it true? You're sterile?"

Chapter 14

grace

We flew home from Costa Rica the next morning, and Hunter refused to answer any of my questions. I called Emma and found out that Chad was awaiting trial, and my salon was ready for its reopening. Hunter sat in his seat with earbuds in, unaware that I knew his phone was turned off. Rachel had told me about his accident: four years ago, a trafficker shot Hunter during a rescue. He and Rachel saved the girls, but one of the bullets cut through Hunter's pelvis. He'd lost a lot of blood and had nearly died. The internal injury to his groin was irreparable.

I hated and admired him at the same time. He'd risked his life to save those girls, and as a result, had lost so much. Or was it me who'd lost? Was that why my blood boiled with anger? The picture of the beautiful family I'd dreamed of was gone, but what hurt more were his lies. He knew what making love to him meant to me. He made me feel stupid, and the betrayal made me sick to my stomach. I was nauseous all the way home and threw up in a trashcan as soon as I crossed my home's threshold.

"Are you all right?" He passed me a tissue, and I wiped my mouth.

"Now you wanna talk?"

"I never meant to hurt you or give you hope."

"What did you think coming inside me would give me? A miracle baby?" Because that was exactly what I'd hoped for. A miracle baby without viable eggs… but I didn't know I had no viable sperm. "You knew what making love to you meant to me—"

"Yeah, a baby. You've been very clear on that, Grace. I'm just a sperm donor for your baby. Although I thought we'd already established you weren't ovulating and had no viable eggs. So why was all the hope placed on me?"

My face heated and my hand flew to his face.

"Fuck you, Hunter."

The slap stuck and stung my palm. He barely moved. Tears welled in my eyes, and my throat seized. I hurried up the stairs, gathered a change of clothes, and slammed the washroom door behind me. The echo shook through my bones. I locked the door and twisted the shower knob.

The flow of the water did little to ease the tension in my neck, and I tilted back my head. It felt like I'd woken up from a dream and plunged headfirst into a nightmare. I didn't know what I saw in that stupid jungle…and the stupid beautiful eco-lodge…and the stupid waterfall. This here, was so much better. Water on demand, washing away the stress and sorrow. Truth was, it barely washed anything away. Maybe the tears, but they'd come back. How could they not? My dreams were gone, and it was his fault.

A loud knock on the door startled me, and I nearly slipped.

"Grace, are you all right?"

"Yes, I'm fine."

I regained my footing and turned off the shower. Hunter must have gone downstairs because I didn't hear him anymore. I got myself ready, grabbed my purse, and hurried downstairs, heading for the front door. He was leaning against the wall with his foot propped up and his arms crossed.

"Where are you going?"

"To see my mother."

"I'm coming with you."

"Chad's in custody. I believe I no longer need a chaperone. "

He set his hands on his hips, and his mouth formed into a straight line. "I'm staying here until the trial is over," he said.

"Whatever, Hunter. I've got things to do. Now, if you'll excuse me."

I pushed past him. The light brush of his arm sent a feverish chill down my skin, reminding me of everything I'd had and lost. He stood in the doorway as I drove off. I watched his silhouette disappear in the rear-view mirror before I called my parents. My mother must have sensed the torment in my voice because she urged me to come over right away.

"It's so good to see you." She took me into her embrace and held me for a good few minutes, squeezing out the sorrow. "Come—we're in the back."

My father was sitting in a lounge by the pool. He set his beer aside and stood up.

"Grace. Finally! I've missed you, girl."

I hugged him tightly, holding on for stability. God, it was so good to be in his arms. When Hunter took me to Costa Rica, everything had been clear; but now it was a mess. I didn't know where to start or what to say.

"Hi, Dad. It's good to see you too."

I sat down, and my mother brought out some lemonade.

"So, how was Costa Rica?" she asked.

"It was nice to get away, but I'm glad to be back, and even more happy that Chad's in custody."

My parents exchanged a knowing look. My father stood up and kissed me on my cheek. "I'll let you two catch up."

"Love you, Dad."

"Love you too, sweetheart."

My mother poured the lemonade and passed me a glass. "You look stressed. I thought you'd be relaxed after your vacation."

"It wasn't a vacation."

Sort of.

"I know, I know. I thought if you got together—"

"We got together, but I don't think it's gonna work out."

"Oh, stop that nonsense right now, Grace. Hunter Silver has loved you since the day he turned eighteen, and there's nothing he wouldn't do for you. He came back to keep you safe."

"Right. He did."

"But you're not happy?"

"I am. It's just that… Did you know he had an accident in Costa Rica?"

"I may have heard something. Was it serious?"

"He was injured, Mom. He can't have children."

"Oh… I… I'm sorry. But you know, there are many ways to form a family."

"Like adoption?" I slouched.

"Where else are those babies supposed to go?"

I lowered my head, feeling like an asshole. "I don't know. I always thought we'd create our own family. One with his genes and mine."

My mother took my hands into hers and squeezed hard. She took a deep breath and exhaled in a long whoosh. "Genes are overrated."

I looked up and connected my gaze with hers. Lines of worry firmed her forehead, and uneasiness swam in her eyes.

"Mom?"

"Grace, I need to tell you something, but I don't know how."

I moved to the edge of the chair. "What is it?"

"It's about Chad and the Hartleys."

"Chad's going away to prison."

"It's still a long fight to make sure he stays there permanently."

"Aren't my brothers working on the case? Why was he after me, anyway?"

My mother released a strangled breath. "Before Jeff Hartley died in the plane accident, he directed his oldest son to carry on his legacy and business."

"Mafia business."

"I don't presume it's a legal operation. But before his death, Jeff asked Chad to create a pure Hartley race."

My forehead creased, and my heart picked up its beat. My mother stood up and started pacing between the table and the pool.

"Jeff wanted a Hartley grandchild. A grandchild from his son and daughter."

"That's sick." I pushed away from the table and stood up, setting my hands on my hips. "Oh, my God—Simone? He wanted Chad to procreate with his *sister*, Simone?"

My mother gently touched me on the shoulder, guiding me back to my seat. That was when I noticed my knees had started shaking.

"No. Not Simone, because she's ill. Jeff wanted Chad to impregnate his other daughter. You."

"What?"

I closed my eyes and waited for the nightmare to pass. It had to be a nightmare because the only other reasonable explanation was that I'd misheard her. I opened my eyes.

"What did you just say?"

My mother stared at me in silence as I made sense of her words. Humid air collected on my skin. My heart stopped and my lungs collapsed.

"Oh, my God. I'm not your daughter?"

She passed me the glass of lemonade, but my hands were

shaking too much to grip it. Was she saying I wasn't a Wagner, and she wasn't my mother?

"You're still my daughter, but biologically, you share Jeff Hartley and Candice Watson's DNA."

I wasn't her daughter, and Scar wasn't my twin brother. I braced my elbows on my knees and lowered my head into my hands, gripping my hair. This wasn't happening. Yet I knew the nightmare was just beginning. I looked up again.

"I'm a Hartley? How is that even possible? Did you adopt me?"

My mother took a moment to compose herself. "I ran into Candice Watson at my obstetrician's appointment."

"Jeff Hartley's ex-wife?"

"They had already separated. We knew one another from different social circles, but I didn't know she was expecting. One conversation led to the next, and I… I couldn't say no."

"Couldn't say no to what?"

"She already had a daughter—Simone."

"Tristan's ex. The one that's ill."

"That's right, and Jeff Hartley drove her to that state. But even before then, he'd told Candice of his plans. She wanted to protect her other babies. She was expecting a boy and a girl."

"Twins? Just like you. But how did I end up in your belly?"

"I was expecting only one child, a boy. I had Scar, and Candice had Chad and you. I'm not your biological mother, and Scar is not your twin. Candice gave birth to you and Chad the same day I birthed Scar. We'd made the arrangement months earlier, after she told me about her husband's dangerous affairs. She had asked for my help to protect her second daughter. You. We bought out our doctor, had our medical records switched, and we thought we were success-ful...until Jeff found out. I don't know how he found out, but he did."

"Oh, my God." My gaze unfocused and I lowered my glasses, looking over their rims.

"Was anyone ever going to tell me the truth?"

She didn't say anything.

"If Scar is not my twin, then Axel, Ace, and Cash aren't my brothers?"

"Not biological ones, but they're still your brothers, and we're still a family. That will never change."

I stared at her, my mouth opening and closing, then shook my head in a slow, back-and-forth sweep of denial. It made sense now that I didn't look like my brothers and had taken a creative path, but… they still *felt* like my brothers.

My mother touched my hand. "I'm sorry you had to find out this way. I never meant for any of this to come this far."

Did Hunter know? Did it matter? *What else have they kept from me?*

"Grace, talk to me."

I gulped down a steadying breath. "I don't know, Mom. Everything I thought was stable in my life is falling apart. Do I still call you Mom?"

"Of course, you do."

My phone rang with an alarm, and I reached inside my purse and shut it off.

"I… I don't know what to make of this. I need time to think. I'm sorry I can't stay any longer, but I have an appointment I can't miss. I want to talk more about this. I'd like to speak with Candice as well."

"Of course." My mother stood up and took me into her arms for a heartfelt hug. "I'll let her know."

"I love you, Mom."

Her breath eased out of her lungs, and I tightened my hold around her. How could I not love her? She'd raised me, supported me, and given me a life many would dream of. I had a loving family and a wonderful upbringing. She'd sacrificed her life for me, and kept me away from a monster. God knew where I'd be if I'd stayed a Hartley. She'd always be my mother, regardless of DNA.

"I love you too, Grace." She kissed the top of my head. "Come back to chat soon. I'm sure Candice would love to see you."

"I will."

I didn't know how to sort out my life. It was changing with every beat of my heart. I hopped in the car and drove to the nearest park where I sat at on a hill away from the swings.

I lay back for no longer than three minutes when the sound of approaching footsteps brought me up to my elbows.

"I thought you'd fallen asleep."

I squinted at my brother's voice and sat up, wiping my hands over my jeans as Scar walked up. He reached out for my hand and pulled me to my feet.

"Are you following me?" I asked.

"Yes. Mom called after you left, and she was concerned."

We sat on a nearby bench. A family of ducks wobbled by, the ducklings following their mother to the shore.

"Are you all right? I know Mom told you about Candice Watson."

"I'll be fine as long as we still claim you're the older twin." I bumped my shoulder into his.

"Technically—"

"Come on, Scar, you've got to give me something."

"Fine. I'm older. By a few minutes." He wrapped his arm around me. "I know it's a lot to take in, but it doesn't change the fact you're my twin sister."

"Really?"

"Fuck, yeah. Are you kidding? I'll never forget the time you tried to punch me and stuck your finger up my nose instead. I bled like a motherfucker, and we didn't want to upset Mom, so we made up a story about a heat wave striking my head."

I laughed, remembering the moment.

"We share more than a genetic connection can give. We share experiences that will last for life."

"Thank you. I needed that." I leaned my head on his shoulder. "How are my nephews doing? How's Jules?"

I wasn't the only one with Hartley troubles. It seemed like that family had something for our family because Chad's brother, Brad, had nearly killed my sister-in-law. But he was dead now, sharing his space in hell with his father.

"The boys are at the clingy stage, and Jules is delighted to be back at work."

I laughed. My sister-in-law was a doctor at the emergency department and found work less hectic than their twin boys. Hopefully, one day it would be me running around the yard, chasing little ones running after the dog.

"And you're as madly in love with her as the day Brad Hartley croaked?"

He laughed.

"I need his brother to join Brad in hell." I said.

"We're working on it, but I need you to stay close to Hunter in the meantime."

"Why?"

"Chad's bail hearing is coming up."

"And you think they'll let him go?"

"There are things we can control in court, and there are things we can't. What we can control is your safety, and that won't happen until the jury reads the verdict and he's put away."

I slumped. "Sounds like it will take some time."

"Hey, maybe you want to release some tension on a pole?"

"You and my brothers can keep your strip club business to yourselves. I'm not that talented."

"You work out. You'd be surprised what you can do."

"Not stripping. I want want a family and I don't want to do it alone. I want Hunter there, you know?"

"Hunter loves you. I know it's been hard, but you rarely find a partner who would die for you."

"The way Jules risked her life for you?"

"For me, her sister, and many more. You should come over sometime to see your nephews. They're growing up fast."

My stomach grumbled. "Only if you promise to make my favorite barbecued ribs." Truth was, I'd come over to watch cartoons with the boys any day.

Scar walked me to my car. We said our goodbyes, and I drove to a café near my aunt's boutique. I picked up a granola bar and a sandwich to go, snacking on the way to my aunt's store.

Aunt Mary hugged me hard and immediately moved onto her new lingerie collection. "I set that special one aside for you. I also sent a box with every item from the collection to your house."

"Thank you. These are gorgeous."

"You're welcome, but I hope you didn't need them in Costa Rica."

I tried to dismiss the query with a smile. "Wouldn't you like to know?"

"I would, actually."

My cheeks heated.

"We had a great time, but I have to get ready for my reopening. I need to hire your staff again."

"Frankie already hired some of my men. I'll make sure there are enough."

"Thank you."

"Would you like a glass of water or orange juice? Grace, you look pale."

I fanned my face and sat on a cushioned seat in the middle of the room. "It's humid outside, and..." I stopped, searching for the right words. Maybe it was better to just spit it out?

"What's the matter?"

"My mother just told me I'm not a Wagner."

She touched her fingers to her parted lips.

"You knew?"

My aunt sat in the chair next to mine and unfastened the top button of her shirt. "We're sisters-in-law. Of course, I knew. It was a difficult time...a different time. And the Hartleys—"

I touched her hand. "I know; I understand."

"Grace, this doesn't change how much I love and admire you."

"I feel the same way, Aunt Mary."

I wiped the sweat off my forehead, and she touched the back of her hand to my cheek.

"What did that boy do to you down in Costa Rica? You're burning up."

"It's just the humidity."

"It's air-conditioned in here. Was Costa Rica dangerous? Exciting?"

I smiled. Costa Rica was amazing, and though it had only been days, it felt like eons ago. I missed the eco-lodge, the rain forest, the waterfall... And most of all, I missed Hunter. Our connection was one you found once in a lifetime, and I couldn't imagine spending the rest of my years without him. He just should have told me he was injured.

"Did you know he nearly died four years ago?" she asked.

I caught her gaze.

"Yes. Where did you hear that?"

"At your salon. Teresa Silver told me Hunter had an accident, and she feared for his life because of the incompetent doctors."

"Incompetent? How incompetent?"

One of the staff brought out a tray with two frosted glasses of cold water, and I took a sip.

"Incompetent enough that the Silvers sent a private medical team into the rainforest."

"He didn't want to leave?"

"He couldn't leave because of complications."

"Oh."

Was it possible Hunter's diagnosis was a mistake? The doctors must have missed something because deep inside, I could see our future so clearly, with a family of blue-eyed Hunter clones playing in the backyard.

"Thank you for the chat, Aunt Mary, and thank you for the gifts. "

"You're welcome. I have a few ideas we can go over after the re-opening. We must collaborate after my vacation."

"And how are things going with Dr. Riley?"

"Stephen and I complement each other, like salt and pepper, and that's what matters."

"How long has it been? Twelve years?"

"Fifteen, but who's counting?" She winked. "The great thing about younger men is they're full of stamina, strength, and adventure. They appreciate your experience."

"And he doesn't want a family one day?"

"You'd be surprised how many men don't want children."

"Why didn't you have any kids? I'm sorry... Is that too forward?"

"No, Grace. It's all right. At first I thought I didn't want kids because I couldn't find a partner. I come from a large family of siblings who have kids, so I babysat nieces and nephews, and they were always enough. Being an aunt made me really enjoy spoiling them all. I won't lie—not having children gave me more time for myself. It may sound selfish, but before I knew it, my clock had run out, and after a few tearful nights, I realized I had exactly what I wanted. A career, a partner, and a family full of children who loved their Aunt Mary."

I smiled. "It's not selfish. We each have one life, and nobody can tell us how to live it. Kids, no kids, single, divorced… A woman will be judged no matter what path she takes, so fuck it. Live the life you desire. It's yours, and we only get one of those."

"Exactly. And what do you desire, Grace?"

My heart drummed hard in my chest. I finished my glass of water and set it on the table. "I don't want my clock to run out. I want a family with Hunter."

"Keep going with your treatments, then. Miracles happen."

"Thank you." I hugged her and took my gifts.

If miracles were going to happen, it would be wise to use my aunt's new collection tonight.

Chapter 15

Hunter

I marched inside the Wagner office full of arguing lawyers and slammed my hand on the table. I'd received a call from Axel Wagner, Grace's oldest brother, soon after she left. He didn't have good news. The room fell quiet, and a wave of heads turned my way.

"What's the problem now?"

I grabbed a turkey sandwich off a platter, pulled back a chair, and sat down.

Axel cleared his throat. "Chad bought out the judge. The chance he'll make bail on Monday is no longer a chance but reality. The judge will add an ankle monitor, but it won't stop Chad from fleeing—"

"Or from coming after Grace. What are our options?"

Silence and tension spread through the room. They had no solution; and if Chad walked on Monday, Grace couldn't be here. I opened a bottle of water and washed down the sandwich. "I don't think she'll want to leave the country again. How quickly can they start the trial? How long do we have?"

"Chad's team is ready to drag this out for as long as they can."

I drummed my fingers on the desk. There was no doubt

Chad would go after Grace the moment he smelled freedom, and I wasn't sure she'd let me take her away again.

"Where's Grace now?" Axel asked.

"With your parents, learning that she's not your sister. Where's Scar?"

"He's still tracking Grace, so he's likely nearby. Until that bastard is transferred to ADX, we sleep with our eyes open."

My head flew up. "What about a transfer before the bail hearing? Different county, different judge… But you'd have to work fast. We only have six days to the hearing."

"That could work. Judge Harris is going on a vacation right after. But we'd need a reason for transfer."

"He's in Nassau County?"

Axel nodded and typed something into his phone.

"I have someone on the inside," I said.

"I'll arrange to have Chad transferred as soon as you confirm." Axel stood up and pulled the chair away from the table. I did the same.

"She'll need every single one of us to win," he said.

They nodded in unison, and Axel walked across the room toward me.

"Blood or not, she's our sister, and she's one of us. We're bringing your team from Silver Securities on this."

I left with a more hope than I'd had when I arrived, and I headed for the shopping mall. If I had a chance of winning back Grace's trust, it would have to start with a good bribe and a ton of flowers. I dialed a friend's number, and she picked up on the second ring.

"*Hola, cariño.*"

"Rachel, I need a favor."

"Aww, I would love to be a godmother to your child. You're so sweet."

"Cut the crap out. This is serious."

"So is this. A little bird told me that Dr. Grios made a few surgical errors before he died—ones specifically related to pelvic injuries. He had some agenda to populate the world with handsome little babies and told eight of his previous patients they were sterile when they weren't; and they ended up with a dozen pregnant women. There's a lawsuit in place."

"What the fuck are you talking about?"

"I'm saying Dr. Grios told eight other patients I interviewed they were sterile, and they weren't. You could be the ninth."

"Why the fuck did you interview them?"

"I felt bad after Costa Rica. I know Grace was upset, and I wanted to fix things. Also, we're looking into having babies, so we're searching for a sperm donor. Hey, are you interested? Your genes and our genes would make beautiful babies."

"I'm sterile, Rachel."

"So said the guys I interviewed. Anyway, you needed a favor?"

Fucking Rachel. "Yes, thank you. Do you know anyone in Nassau County?"

"Do I know anyone? I know everyone. What's the job?"

"I need a prisoner hurt enough to be transferred to ADX Florence."

"That's quite a few counties away."

"Can you pull it off?"

"Can you make babies?"

I tightened my grip on the steering wheel and merged onto the interstate, praying the answer to both was a yes. But she was wrong. If I could have babies, I would already have had a bunch running around the village in Costa Rica. After Grace dumped me, I thought I had nothing to lose, and Paula was there to unwind. But I was wrong. I had a lot to lose. I didn't want to lose Grace now that she was mine again.

"You're delirious, Rach. Listen, if you won't do it, I'll find someone else."

"Okay, I'll do it. Relax, Hunter. Jesus, you sound like your balls are on fire."

She wasn't wrong. "I need it done before Monday. He can't show up for bail. I'll send you the details."

"Monday. Got it. Consider it done. So, about the godmother thing—"

"Fine." I pulled my fingers through my hair and made a turn. "I promise you're first in line to be my kid's godmother."

"Yes!"

I imagined her punching through the air.

"Are you around this weekend? Grace is reopening her salon. It would be great to see you."

"Any more secrets I shouldn't speak of?"

"Paula."

"Got it. You know, maybe the doctor didn't lie to you after all, because the number of times you fucked that woman, you two should have had a little army of blue-eyed monsters."

Aside from her four sisters, Paula had nine younger brothers, and all of them were pesky little devils.

"Thanks for being the sunshine in my life." I said.

"I heard the sarcasm."

"Good. See you this weekend?"

"See you."

We hung up at the same time, and I made the last turn into a shopping center. I picked up a box full of rose-scented candles and Grace's favorite wine before heading to our local bakery for fresh baguettes. At the marina, Olivier prepared a box full of ingredients, along with instructions. I wasn't the best chef, but I was sure I could manage Grace's favorite vegetarian dishes. When I pulled into Cougar Court, Grace's car was still missing.

I brought the groceries inside, rolled up my sleeves, washed my hands, and gathered the dishes and utensils. Soon enough, fresh pasta was boiled and the tomato herb sauce had reduced.

I set up the candles underneath the pergola while fish steamed over apple bark on the barbecue. A delicious aroma filled the house. I set the food in the warming drawer, picked the brightest clumps of roses from Grace's garden, and arranged three vases on the table. I lit torches around the perimeter and saved three toads from their never-ending pool laps. The first sound of crickets echoed as twilight neared. I lit the firepit in the backyard and sat down on a lounger, stretching my legs.

I took a whiff. The stench of sweat wafted from underneath my arms. I shed my clothes and hopped underneath the shower in the pool house. I dried myself, combed my fingers through my hair, and knocked a stick off a shelf. When I realized the piece of plastic was a pregnancy test, I almost dropped it. But it was negative.

Grace wasn't pregnant. Of course, she wasn't. I was sterile.

The oven timer went off. I set the stick back on the shelf and went back to the kitchen in time to remove the crème brûlée from the oven. The sun disappeared below the horizon, and I was worrying about Grace. Scar had promised to monitor her until her return, but what if Scar was in trouble? I didn't look when I grabbed the glassware without a towel, burning my hand.

"Fuck!" I screamed.

My skin sizzled red, and I turned on the faucet.

"Mother fucking hot water!" I withdrew my hand from underneath the stream.

My skin shriveled before forming bubbles, which grew with every blink and sweat drop.

A tumble of footsteps sounded from the upstairs. I kept my focus on the kitchen entry and changed the water flow to cold. Grace ran into the kitchen, cheeks flushed, hair wild, and large breasts bouncing in a new, lacy bra. The white fabric clung to her body and hid nothing. Beautiful pink nipples winked my way.

Hello.

Her full breasts stole all of my attention.

"Hunter? Are you okay? What the hell happened?"

My head flew up to meet her gaze. She froze midway to the kitchen and slowly drew her robe from the sides, tying its belt at the front. It still did little to hide her body, and by then, my blood had already drained south. White was officially my favorite color.

She sniffed the air. "Are you cooking?"

Cooking?

My hand seared with pain.

"I burned my hand." I wiggled my fingers.

"Jesus, what the hell?"

"More like an accident, but it definitely burns like hell. I grabbed a hot crème brûlée dish."

"Crème brûlée?" She licked her lips while filling a bowl of water to which she added ice. "Soak it here. It should help. Since when do you cook?"

"Since I lived like Tarzan in a jungle. But you're forgetting I've lived here as well. I picked up the ingredients from Olivier at the Marina."

She nodded. Her attention was drawn to the glow outside. She eyed the table set beneath the pergola, where soft candle-light illuminated the space. "Impressive."

"Glad you like it. I hope you're hungry."

She rubbed her stomach. "Actually, I am. Looks beautiful outside. What's the occasion?"

"Me, begging for forgiveness."

"Hunter—"

"I'm serious."

"No, Hunter. Let me see your hand before that blister gets any larger. You need burn cream."

"We have burn cream?"

"Yes we do, Tarzan. A very useful item in a first-aid kit.

Keep it under water for now."

She grabbed a kitchen stool and hopped up, reaching to the cabinet above the fridge. Her silky robe rose, exposing the ribbon of lace cutting through her ass cheeks. My dick hardened. Her seed-shaped pussy swell peeked through her panties as she rose to her toes. I'd do anything to watch her shiver underneath my touch as I ran my fingers over the heated mound.

"What are you looking at?"

I tilted my head higher, guilty and unashamed. "Your beautiful ass is rounder than I remember."

"You saw my naked ass two nights ago. How can it be rounder?"

"I don't know. Feels like it's been longer. Maybe that's why I can't remember."

She stepped down the ladder and returned to the counter. "That makes little sense. Let me see your hand."

I lifted my bright red palm, and she secured a towel underneath my hand.

"Does it hurt?"

"Feels frozen, but nothing a little pussy juice can't cure."

She snorted through a laugh. "Is that your way of hitting on me?"

"I was hoping the dinner, candles, and soft lighting might do it."

She giggled, and I tugged on her silk robe.

"Is this from your aunt's collection?"

She bit her lip. Hesitant sparkles danced in her eyes. "Yes," she whispered. Then her face fell sad, and tears came to the verge of spilling.

"What's the matter?" I asked.

"I'm a Hartley. My parents aren't my parents, my brothers aren't my brothers, and I... I just feel like I'm losing everything."

They told her.

"Hey, hey. You're not losing everything. I'm not going anywhere, and neither is your family."

"I… I can't think. I don't want to think."

I brought her hand to my lips. "I'm so sorry for your pain. I'm so sorry for everything."

She stepped closer, and our breaths met. Her gorgeous thighs and heavy breasts pressed against my skin, their coolness burning over my body. I lowered my head until my lips hovered above hers. My mouth skimmed her earlobe, my lips tracing up the outer rim, and she trembled. Her body molded into mine, and I secured my hold around her. Her soft skin firmed underneath my touch. One handed, I grazed over her delicate curves and took a long whiff. She smelled so good.

Her sniffle stopped me mid-breath, and I pulled away. A trail of tears stained my shirt.

"What's the matter?" I lifted her chin with my finger. She blinked, releasing a fresh wave. I reached for a tissue and wiped the tears away.

"I don't know who I am anymore."

"You're Grace. The same beautiful woman I've loved since I was fifteen."

She pulled in another sniffle before blowing her nose. "Fifteen? Not after you fixed my Harley?"

A shrug rolled over my shoulder. "I was already madly in love with you by then. I had a crush on you before I let you fuck me."

"You let me fuck you?"

"Yes, and then I let you teach me about every arousing spot on your body." I nipped at her. "Do you remember all the spots, Grace?" I swept my fingers underneath her knee, and she closed her eyes. I went for the inner thigh next, drawing to her apex until she opened her legs.

"Hunter…your hand."

"I can't feel my hand when I touch you." I kissed her down her neck, heading south for her swollen breasts and pebbled nipples. My unscathed hand drew up her inner thigh, and she opened her legs, letting me feel along the soaked fabric of her panties.

"Good girl." I bit on her nipple through her bra and tugged the panties aside, drawing my fingers along her wet pussy lips. She writhed in my hold until burning pain reached my scorched palm, and I winced in pain.

"Fuck. I need meds."

"You need cream," she murmured.

"That's what she said."

She choked with a cute snort. "The pain's getting to your head, and if we don't go to the hospital in the next five minutes, you'll turn into a total asshole. Let me put on the cream and drive you to the ER."

"And here I was, ready to make love to you."

"We can do that when we come back. Right here, on this counter."

"Kitchen?"

"Everywhere," she grinned. "I want you everywhere."

"I can't give you what you want, Grace. I can't give you babies."

"All I want is you. I... I just want to be with you."

"And kids?"

"You said you'd be open to adoption, but we can talk about that after your hand heals."

I took her lips and got lost in her delicate mouth. Her body eased back into mine, diminishing my pain. God, how much I wanted to give her everything she deserved: safety, a family, and a baby...or babies.

What if Rachel was right?

Chapter 16

grace

Hunter's hand healed like wild Tarzan's: unexpectedly fast. His skin regrew like he was immune to the injury. We changed the dressing daily, and he hid the pain searing through his arm every time I applied the prescribed ointment. Thank God there was a doctor in the family. I followed Jules' strict rules for three days, and I didn't let him touch me. He tried many times, but I was afraid I'd hurt him.

Sheets were twisted around my right side, and Hunter's skin burned against mine on the left. His left hand drew up my thigh, and a soft moan escaped my mouth. The sun had risen a few hours ago, and we'd slept in. Hunter's hair held a messy morning look that set my ovaries on full alert. I stood up, but he grabbed me by my wrist.

"Come on. You couldn't get enough of me in Costa Rica."

"You weren't injured in Costa Rica."

His free hand pushed through my inner thighs, and my legs parted, allowing him access.

"I swear, the things I'm gonna do to you once you let me," he growled, and his words, coated with a throaty voice, set my skin ablaze.

He pulled his fingers over my soaked panties, and my resistance plunged.

"What about the things I can do to you?" I hitched my eyebrows and watched the corner of his mouth lift.

"Oh, yeah? Like what?"

I pushed on his shoulder. He lay flat on his back and waited as I climbed on top of him. I stood up and set my feet at his hips, then stripped from my panties and négligée. His dick rose to a mast, tenting the sheet. I grasped the cover's edge with my toes and dragged it down his thighs. His hard cock popped out from underneath. I licked my lips, and he groaned again.

"I fucking hope you're not just teasing."

My lip tweaked to the side. "I have one rule."

"What rule?"

"You can't touch me."

"What?"

"I promise to make it worth your patience."

I bent to my knees at his side and wrapped my fingers around his thick cock. I couldn't connect them, but felt him expand at my touch. The steel-hard muscle underneath his soft skin stood tall. A drop of pre-cum collected near the tip, and I lowered my lips to his hot crown. I licked underneath the hot rim, waiting for our temperatures to meet. Another fresh drop spewed from his cock, and I couldn't help myself. I licked off the pearl and wrapped my lips around his crown, taking him slowly to the back of my throat. The thick veins along his cock pulsed against my lips, and he tasted like pure man. His hips rocked up and down, and I stroked him to their motion, keeping my mouth near the top.

When I drew my spare hand beneath his balls, his free one flew to my behind. He popped out of my mouth.

"Hey, I said, no touching."

"That's not fair. You're getting me off too fast. Sit on me."

"What?"

"Sit on me. I want to come inside you."

"You can come in my mouth." I placed my lips back over his cap.

"No, Grace. I need to come inside you."

His commanding tone pushed me to my feet, and I straddled him. He lined himself at my opening and I slid down his cock, watching his mouth open wider with each sinking inch I lowered. Air leaked from his lungs in a lingering stream. His eyes flew open, and he anchored his naughty gaze to mine.

"Now, fuck me."

His words struck the center of my libido. It zapped through my body with a force, awakening fresh desire for a vulnerable man who resembled a caveman, a bear, and Tarzan. I rolled my hips, tightening around him as he hit my depth, rubbing myself along his pelvic bone. He gripped the sheets with his free hand, and his jaw tensed. I cupped my breasts in my hands and pinched my nipples, pulling them out. He jerked higher, thrusting inside me. I braced myself on his stiff abs and used them to balance as I rode him quicker and quicker. The sound of slapping skin echoed through the room, and the smell of him and me, and sex filled my lungs. I lowered myself to his front, connecting skin to skin, and he lost control. My breasts grazed over his muscles, and I slid my hand to where we connected, drawing the sleek moisture to my clit. I rubbed myself in tight circles, and his eyes opened wide.

"Fuck, Grace."

He rose, grabbing the back of my neck with his hand, pulling my mouth to his, and bringing us both back down to the sheets. His lips crushed mine, and his tongue dove possessively deep. He stilled and spilled himself inside me with a low grunt. I could have sworn I heard choirs singing in the background. I remained on his chest with his cock nestled inside me. His heartbeat underneath my ear, settling with each breath.

"You are my world, Grace Wagner. You are my Queen, and

I'll never love another the way I love you." His whisper carried down my body, awakening shivers over my skin. "Once the case is over, I'm going to see a doctor."

I lifted my head. "For what? What's wrong?"

"Nothing's wrong, but maybe they can check out the damage and reverse it? There's nothing more in the world I would love than to see you carry my child and have you be his mother."

"His?"

"Or her. It doesn't matter. But if there is a chance..." He trailed off.

I slowly rose off of him and shimmied higher. My mouth took his in a lingering kiss, breathing gratefulness into his lungs. When I pulled away, I skimmed my nose over his.

"I love you, Hunter Silver, and I'll love you no matter what the outcome."

He kissed me again.

"I should shower and go. I'm meeting up with Frankie at the salon for final touches, and I promised I'd let him give me the official tour."

"No seconds?" He grasped my behind and squeezed it. "Because my hand is feeling better, and it's my turn to fuck you."

I left a promising kiss on his lips. "Later tonight. Kitchen counter?"

"You're a vixen, Grace Wagner. Give Frankie my best, and tell him the place looks amazing. Also, tell him not to keep you long."

I laughed. "You've seen my salon?"

"I had to ensure it was up to your standards, and I'm happy to say you'll love it."

"Thank you for taking care of me. Now, if you'll excuse me, I have to shower." I slid off of him and off the bed.

"Since when do you shower alone?" He hopped out of bed

and ran after me to the washroom, catching up midway. I wrapped his injured hand in a bag and washed him up before I took care of myself.

I dressed to go out. We shared a quick breakfast, and I kissed him with longing at the door. Frankie was seeing me in three hours, but Dr. Riley had me booked in less than thirty minutes. My period was delayed, and I wasn't sure when I could start my injections—because if Hunter agreed to donor insemination, maybe we'd have our family after all. Or maybe his damage could be reversed? It felt like my options were multiplying by the minute, and I couldn't wait to see Dr. Riley.

I grabbed a banana on my way out the door and hopped in the car. Thirty minutes later, I was at the clinic, lying down in a paper gown on a paper-covered cold table and counting spots on the ceiling. Dr. Riley aimed the warm gel on my belly. A nurse had drawn my blood, and I lowered my gaze to his guiding hand across my skin.

"Any viable eggs, Dr. Riley?"

"We'll do an internal ultrasound for those, but I want to check for something else first. You say you've been feeling nauseous?"

"Yes, but I've also been under a lot of stress."

"I thought you went to Costa Rica on a vacation." He pulled his gaze away from the screen and apologized with his eyes. "Sorry to intrude. Your Aunt Mary told me."

He refocused on the screen and shifted his hand, angling over a spot off the center.

"It's all right. I can't lie. Costa Rica was fun, but returning home wasn't."

He laughed. "That's what usually happens after a vacation. Nobody wants to return to reality."

"I think you're right. In Costa Rica, I lost a sense of reality, and it felt so good." I beamed. "The nature and the people were amazing. It was a different world, and the few days we spent there felt like months."

It also felt like the time spent there was absolutely not enough. I missed the rainforest.

Dr. Riley cleared his throat. His brows narrowed as he focused on the screen, then he gently nodded to himself as if he knew exactly what he was looking at. He removed the monitor from my belly and passed me a towel to clear the gel.

"Grace, I'd like to present you with a new reality, because it looks like you're pregnant."

"What?" My heart nearly stopped, and I pushed up to my elbows

"That's impossible."

"You've had sex?"

"Yes, but you said I had no viable eggs."

"It's also possible I missed an egg."

I shook my head as he took the towel and cleared the gel off for me. "You don't understand. It's not possible because the guy I was with is sterile."

His tablet chimed, and he swept his finger across the screen. "Blood results are back, and your hCG level is elevated. Congratulations, Grace. It's early, around day twenty-four, but you're definitely pregnant, and your guy is not sterile."

Oh, my God.

My hand flew to my belly. I drew my palm over my uterus, tears welling in my eyes. "I'm pregnant?"

He nodded, and I couldn't hear anything afterward. I walked out of the clinic in a daze and didn't notice when I ended up in a park. I crossed the playground and walked to the shore of a pond, where the frogs were performing a croaking symphony from the tops of lily pads. Their throaty bellows echoed across the pond. I stepped to the shoreline and crouched, checking the tepid water with my hands. A toad jumped in the water.

I stepped higher on the hill and sat down, then lay back on the grass. Marshmallow clouds drifted across the bright blue sky. Hunter's eyes held the same shade, and I hoped our baby would as well. Would Hunter be happy to be a father? It was still early, and I wasn't sure how to share the news. I'd waited my entire life to hear the words Dr. Riley spoke. But what if I told Hunter, raised his hopes, and then lost the pregnancy? The first trimester was delicate.

A range of emotions buzzed through my body, and hormones messed with my head. I'd just found out I wasn't blood-related to my family, and I was pregnant with Hunter's child.

He's not sterile.

I relaxed my shoulders, enjoying the soft breeze blowing my hair across my face. I swept the strands aside and watched the shimmering leaves above my head. When it calmed, the sound of footsteps in the distance drew my head sideways.

"Hey, Grace. Are you all right?" Scar plopped down on the grass beside me.

"You're following me again." I rose to sit.

"What can I say? This job can be hazardous sometimes. They're prepping Chad's transfer."

"Is that good?"

"Means he won't make bail, so yes. It's very good. Are you all right?"

"Yes. So, if I'm all safe, why are you checking up on me?"

"Because I love you like a twin, and I care. Jules is asking about Hunter's hand, and it's been a while since you've seen the boys. Come to a barbecue."

I smiled. "I'm sorry. I'll fix that. You name the date and time, and we'll be there."

"You and Hunter?"

"Yeah." I smiled. "Me and Hunter."

"Finally." He let go of an exasperated breath, and I laughed.

"And thank you for caring so much. Even though I'm a Hartley."

"Nah, you'll always be a Wagner to me. Are you heading home?"

"I was going to see Frankie, but yes, I need to go home. I have to go see Hunter."

"I'll walk you to your car."

"Thank you. Will you be at the re-opening tomorrow?"

"I wouldn't miss it for the world."

On my way home, I bought two bottles of water and drank them both before arriving. I ran inside and to the bathroom upstairs to pee on the three spare pregnancy sticks underneath the sink cupboard. I set the tests aside and washed my hands. The smell of burning wood drew my attention out the window. The fire pit had been lit near the pond. Hunter was sitting on a chair with his legs stretched out front.

I quickly changed into an outfit from Aunt Mary's collection, the skimpy white ensemble. Five minutes later, I lowered my gaze to the counter, not surprised by the positive pregnancy tests. I looked out the window. Orange flames danced over Hunter's face. It was time to tell him we were expecting.

BUTTERFLIES FLAPPED IN MY BELLY, and sweat dripped down my back. Silver, pearl white, and gleaming black balloons floated through the salon. Lights twinkled, music hummed, and the smell of lavender aromatherapy filled the air. I stood at the front door greeting and welcoming guests. Hunter went to use the restroom, and Emma adjusted my dress in the back.

"You look stunning, Grace." She checked my cleavage and dabbed a cotton pad over my glistening forehead. "You're glowing."

"In a good way, I hope."

"In a very weird way. I guess I'd be glowing too if they renovated my salon."

"You have an office on the thirty-third floor of Silver Securities instead. No other woman in Manhattan can claim that."

"True. I can't complain about the view, but my brothers are keeping me away from a case."

"A good one?" I fanned my face, feeling the first wave of lowered air conditioning.

"I'll give you a hint: Eric Waters."

"That sounds more than good… Is *delicious* the right word?"

"Yes, as soon as he realizes I exist."

"You're Emma Silver. Everyone knows you exist."

"Except my brother's best friend, Eric Waters."

"Then do something about it. What's taking Hunter so long?"

I turned to the salon as someone tapped me on my shoulder, bringing my attention back to the front. A handsome, chiseled face with gorgeous whiskey eyes stared back at mine.

"Xavier, hello. Thank you for coming."

"I'm sorry I rejected the job offer for tonight, but I thought it for the best, given what happened last time."

"Thank you for understanding, and thank you for coming."

"I didn't want to miss this. My friends at the company are big fans of the spa."

"Thank you."

My aunt's manservant business was also one of our largest corporate clients.

"Please, make yourself comfortable inside."

"Champagne?" Emma passed him a flute.

He grasped the glass, tilted his head forward, and went inside.

"I don't think boiling hot is hot enough." Emma fanned her face.

"What is it with you and older men?"

"What is it with you and younger ones?"

"Come on, you can't deny Xavier's—"

"Hotter than Eric Waters? Impossible." She shook her head vigorously, and I laughed.

"You were asking about Hunter, and I saw him chatting with Scar by the bar."

"The bar?"

"Not drinking. Ahem, there's Mrs. McCormick. I should go. I'll see you inside."

The widow strolled through the front door in true McCormick fashion: fashionably late and pimped out like a twenty-eight-year-old. Aunt Mary's best friend had lost her billionaire husband six months earlier, and she was a regular client at Gracie's. According to Frankie, the salon booked up six months in advance within a day.

I greeted Mrs. McCormick with a glass of champagne, and Emma showed her inside, where my family and staff had settled in.

"You look ravishing," Hunter's voice murmured from behind. He snaked his hands over my hips to my belly, like he was comforting our child. He nipped at my neck. Warmth spread through my veins.

"Not now, baby. Everyone's looking."

Baby.

Tonight was the night I'd tell him I was pregnant. It hadn't worked out when I'd tried before, because Hunter couldn't keep his uninjured hand off of me. He took me three times that night, and I couldn't reject the kisses, fondling, and fucking. My hormones got the best of me, and I lost time to his mouth and his constant hard-on. It was incredible. We were incredible, and I couldn't wait to tell him tonight, after the party. He kissed my cheek. The smell of his fresh aftershave messed with my head.

"I can't blame them for looking. You're the most beautiful woman here, my Queen."

A loud bang sounded, and I jumped. "Oh, my God."

"It's okay, Grace. It's only champagne."

"Are you sure? It sounded like a gun."

"I'm sure."

"How much longer do I have to stand here?"

"I believe Mrs. McCormick was our last guest, so it's time for the official tour."

"And I don't need to make a speech?"

"Frankie will thank all the guests and make sure everyone leaves with a goodie bag."

I looped my hand through his hooked arm. We walked through the curtain of streamers, and everyone cheered. My family, neighbors, employees, and loyal clients waved silly pom-poms and whistled. Someone passed me a champagne glass, and while I didn't want to make a speech, the moment felt too perfect.

"Thank you, everyone, for coming. Thank you for your support, for your love, support, and loyalty. I have the best team there is, and these renovations couldn't have happened without you. I'm very grateful to Silver Securities for the safety upgrades. Frankie, you'll forever be my right hand. None of this could have been possible without you. Now, I promised myself not to make a long speech, so I won't. With that, please eat, drink, and have fun. Cheers!"

"Cheers!" the crowd chimed, and someone turned the music up.

I touched my mouth to the flute. The champagne barely skimmed my lips. "Okay, what's this surprise I know you've been keeping?"

"Come. I hope you like it." His breath smelled of a stronger alcohol than champagne.

"Were you drinking?"

"Just the champagne." He lifted his glass.

Maybe it was just me.

We walked to the back of the salon and took the staircase to the lower floor with the main spa. A soft glow from a dozen candles kissed the air as we stepped into what I liked to call a rainforest.

"It's a combination of Costa Rica and your gardens," he said.

I paced along the silicone floor. Further in, the shade turned greener, reminding me of my gardens. I stepped over the silicone floor. Underneath, koi fish swam through a flowing stream, surrounded by lily pads and toads. The walls housed fresh plants, and the new waterfall feature near the showers flowed into the floor and underground.

"Was this your idea?"

"I can't take all the credit. I had some input, but this is mostly Frankie's doing."

As if on cue, my partner in crime peeked out from behind a wall. "Do you like it?"

"This is beautiful, Frankie."

I hugged my best friend hard as Hunter's phone chimed.

He looked at the screen and frowned. "I gotta go."

"Everything okay?"

"Yes, I'll see you upstairs." He turned on his heel and headed to the main floor, skipping every second step.

"Would you like to go?"

"No. Definitely not. You've worked hard on this, so show me around."

"The spa's on Hunter. He designed most of it. I don't know what the guy has for toads, but he specifically asked for a few dozen. Don't even get me started on the toilets."

I laughed. "I love it. Thank you for everything, Frankie. I was wondering if I could ask for another favor?"

"Anything."

"Would you like to join me as Gracie's new managing partner?"

"Are you kidding me?"

"I'm very serious. Gracie's wouldn't exist without you. It's well-earned and deserved. We'll need a few new hands on deck—"

"Already done. I invited four potential employees, and they're eager to meet you upstairs."

"Were you anticipating this?"

"What I wasn't anticipating was how busy it would get. We're booked months in advance. Heads up, one of them is expecting, so she'll be on maternity leave soon, but she has the fingers of an angel, and I told her she could bring the baby to work."

"You did?"

"This was before I knew you didn't get the unit next door, but we've made space and we're adding a daycare to the salon. Moms can leave their kids to play while they get themselves glammed up."

"Oh, Frankie. I can't believe you did all this. Thank you. I'd love to meet them right after I find Hunter. There's something I've been meaning to tell him, and it can't wait."

He hugged me once more, and we went back upstairs to the party. Music blasted, lights flashed, and fake fog spewed from the corner. I spotted Hunter across the room by the coloring station, talking to Scar.

My brother's quick hand movements kept my attention; he seemed to be explaining something to Hunter, who was holding what looked like a drink in his hand. He lifted the glass to his lips and took a long swig, finishing the contents. He shivered as the alcohol passed through his throat.

Someone tapped me on my shoulder.

"Grace?"

I turned around to face a beautiful woman: Candice Watson.

"Hi! Thank you for coming."

I looked over her shoulder and thought I saw someone familiar. A chilly breeze swept down my back. I didn't know everyone I'd invited, but I'd greeted every single guest at the door—except for the man who disappeared to the washrooms.

"Thank you for inviting me." Candice brought my attention back to the room.

"Of course, I've been meaning to talk to you—"

"I'm sorry," she blurted.

"For what?"

"I'm sorry I gave you up."

I shook my head and took her hand in mine. "You saved me, Mom. God knows what would have happened if they'd found me earlier."

"Chad won't give up easily. He'll still try to... Beth, your mother, told me she told you about his plans."

I squeezed her shaking hand. "You have nothing to worry about."

"I know, because they transferred him to the most secure prison in the country this morning."

"Also because he can't get me pregnant. I'm expecting with Hunter."

Her eyes grew wide.

"Nobody knows yet, but I thought you'd like to know."

She gripped my hand, squeezing hard. "Grace, you're in more danger than before."

"Why?"

"What do you think my deranged son will do when he finds out you're carrying another man's child?"

My hand flew to my belly, like I could protect it. "I'm not planning for him to find out. Besides, you just said he was transferred to the most secure prison in the country. "

From the corner of my eye, I saw Hunter arguing with Scar again. What the hell was going on with those two today?

"Will you excuse me?" I left Candice and walked up to the bar station. I touched Hunter's shoulder, and he flinched.

"You all right?" I asked.

"Scar just told me you went to the clinic." His raised voice drew in the attention from around us.

"What the hell, Scar?"

"I was doing my job."

I pinned my arms over my chest. "And I thought you were my brother." I turned on my heel and pulled Hunter aside. "What the hell are you drinking?"

"It started with gin, then it was vodka, and now rum."

His breath smelled like a half-digested sanitizing station.

"Hunter? What's going on?"

He swayed on his feet, and I had a déjà vu moment.

"You went to the clinic after our conversation? You made this decision without me?" His voice rose, and I could feel the people within earshot turn our way.

"Yes, I went to the clinic, but—"

"I found the pregnancy tests, Grace. How could you fucking do this to me?"

By then, I felt like we were the center of the room. "Hunter, you're drunk."

He poured himself a fresh glass of an orange-tinted alcohol and swung his hand up, spilling half the contents.

"You go get yourself impregnated at the clinic because my steel cum is not enough," he yelled, emptying the last of the liquor into his glass.

My insides twisted and my face burned with heat. "You have no right," I whispered.

"What rights do I have, Grace? I'll never be enough for you, will I?"

"Hunter—"

My brothers took him away by the elbow. The DJ turned up the music, and I scurried to the back, away from everyone. I took the metal staircase in the alley up to the rooftop, ripping my dress mid-thigh. I lay down on the warm asphalt and looked at the stars, which were barely visible amidst the high-rises.

Fucking Hunter.

How could he embarrass me like that—tonight, of all nights? The smell of his toxic breath lingered in my mind. He broke his promise, but there was a reason for the saying that you can't teach an old dog new tricks. Except Hunter wasn't old, and he definitely knew some tricks; but the drinking was unacceptable. Not when we were creating a family. Not ever. I drew my hands over my belly in comforting circles, waiting for a shooting star, but there were none.

I stayed on the rooftop a while, but regretted the decision the moment I heard the sound of long, heavy footsteps.

Chapter 17

Hunter

The sun beamed in my eyes, and I rolled in the bed, away from the window. A heaviness hung in the air, and I swept my hand across the empty pillow beside me.

"Grace?"

I rose up. The hard pounding in my head and the spinning room reminded me of the high alcohol level in my veins. I flopped down to the bed and pulled my fingers through my hair, groaning.

Where the fuck was Grace?

I sat up again, this time more slowly. The room continued spinning, and I reached for the bottle of water on the night-stand, knocking the half-empty bottle of guaro to the floor. The cushioned rug saved it from breaking. I opened the cap and emptied the water bottle, which barely quenched my thirst. My bladder pulsed with urgency. I lowered my legs over the bed and shuffled my feet to the bathroom. The piss drained at the same rate as my energy. I flushed the toilet, washed my hands, and checked Grace's toothbrush. It was dry.

What the fuck happened last night? I had the first drink after I saw Xavier stroll through the front door and greet

Grace, like Zeus. I whisked her away to the basement spa, and had the second drink after Scar told me about her visit to the clinic. I lost count of my drinks afterward. We fought… She slapped me… And I couldn't remember much after that.

I picked up my phone and called Emma. She answered on the second ring.

"You better have a good explanation for yourself."

"Hey, Ems, is Grace with you?"

"No. She texted me last night after your fight that she went home. Thanks for ruining the night, asshole."

Fuck.

"I… I don't remember much. "

"You were an asshole, and that pretty much sums it up. Grace deserves better than an asshole."

"She does. I'm sorry… I know there's no excuse, but I was upset."

Upset was an understatement because I so badly wanted that baby to be mine, it hurt. Grace had gone to the clinic behind my back. The moment I was comfortable, considering a future with her, thinking she'd loop me in on the decisions partners made, she deceived me.

"Do you know where she would have gone?" I asked.

"My place, but she isn't here now, so I'd check with her parents. And if she's not there, a hotel room."

I leaned forward and lowered my elbows to the sink counter. The room was still spinning.

"All right, Ems. Thanks. I have to go. Let me know if you hear from her."

We hung up, and I dialed Scar's number before spreading panic through the Wagner household.

"Hey, it's me," I said.

"Yeah, I can hear that. What the fuck is wrong with you?"

"I'm drunk."

"I know. I got your sorry ass home last night."

"So Grace wasn't here when we got here?"

"No. I went back to the salon, but Grace was gone by then, and Emma told me she got a text that Grace went home. I assumed we missed each other on the road. Are you surprised she's not home?"

I wasn't. "Listen, can you make some calls to see if Grace is in a hotel somewhere?" I rose from my elbows, but lost my balance and stumbled to the floor with a grunt.

"Are you okay?"

I recovered my breath. "Yeah, I'm fine."

"I doubt you're in any shape to look for Grace. I'll get the search going and be over in fifteen minutes."

I braced myself on my hands as my eyes fogged. "I just need some water."

"Then get some fucking water, and I'll be over soon."

He hung up, and I dragged myself to the shower where the water dripped in what felt like slow motion. By the time I finished, the front gate buzzed, and Scar drove through with his wife, Julia. I jumped into a pair of jeans and a shirt before going downstairs to open the door.

"You look like hell."

This hangover would hold for days. I shut my eyes, willing the pain away. It didn't work. "I had no time to shave. Any word about Grace?"

Julia, a doctor, set her medical kit on the table and removed an IV bag of fluids from within.

"Nothing from Grace. Silver Securities is calling around and searching."

"Damn it! Why would she do this to me?"

"Because you stink like a distillery," Julia said.

"I need to find her." I moved to the door, but Scar grabbed me by the arm and pulled me to a chair.

"Sit the fuck down. The search team is out already, and you

can join them after you're done with the IV. It's only two hours."

"She could be dead in two hours."

"Chad's behind bars. He won't kill her."

"Like rape is better? I'm gonna fucking kill that bastard."

I stood up and Scar pushed me down again.

"I said, sit down. I'll cuff you to the chair if I have to. You can't help her if you're drunk and delusional. Chad's been transferred, and he's nowhere near Grace. She's probably in a hotel room. We'll call around and find her."

My phone buzzed on the table from the other side of the hall.

"Maybe it's her." I jolted, but Julia held my stretched arm in place. She cleaned the skin with an alcohol pad and tied an elastic around my bicep.

"I'll get it."

Scar brought my phone. It was another call from Rachel, so I set it aside. I had no time or patience for her conspiracy theories.

"Not important?" Scar asked.

"It's Rachel. She's bugging me about getting checked... You know, to see if I can have kids. She has a conspiracy theory about Dr. Grios down in Costa Rica. Said he had an agenda to fill the world with pretty babies."

Julia stuck the needle in my arm. I barely felt the pinch. "You should get checked, though, just in case. For yourself and for Grace."

She set a pillow underneath my arm and adjusted the IV flow. "And since when do you not believe in crazy? Haven't we all seen our share of it? People have done worse than Grios."

"She's pregnant," I said.

"What?"

"What?"

They chimed at the same time. Julia pulled a chair away

from the table and sat across from me. I turned my head to Scar. "You told me she went to the clinic. I found a pregnancy test, which means Dr. Riley fertilized her egg. "

"So, not yours?"

"I'm sterile."

"If Dr. Grios isn't a mad scientist." Julia tilted her head. She had that look on her face she reserved for Scar when he re-coated furniture—a hobby no one understood— and didn't warn the family about drying paint.

"Jules, you're a doctor. Since when do you believe in conspiracy theories?" I asked.

She leaned forward. "I work at a hospital. Trust me, I've seen my share of unbelievable. It's worth checking out, and it's possible—"

My front gate buzzed, then buzzed again with insistency. Whoever was there was stabbing their finger vigorously on the button.

I checked my phone and let Rachel in through the gate. Moments later, she stormed through the front door like hurricane.

"Why the hell aren't you answering my calls?"

"I'm a little busy right now."

"It's fucking important."

"Can't you text?"

"Since when do you text?" She gestured to the IV. "What the fuck is all this? Did you get drunk?"

"Yes. Grace is pregnant."

"I knew it! You're gonna have a baby."

"It's not my baby. She got it in vitro."

Julia stood up and set her hands on her hips. "Do you know anything about in vitro?"

We all turned her way.

"It's a process. Even if she just got the embryo transfer done a few days ago, it takes time for the blastocyst to hatch, come out of its shell, and attach itself to the uterus."

We all stared at her like she was speaking in tongues.

"What I'm trying to say is that if Grace saw Dr. Riley a few days ago, she couldn't get a positive pregnancy test this fast. She was pregnant before."

I grabbed my phone off the table and fumbled before dialing the clinic's number. An answering machine turned on.

"Fuck. He's on vacation."

I dialed Dr. Riley's private number next. It might have been out of line, but he was Grace's aunt's boyfriend, and this matter was personal. I waited for the beep after his recording.

"Hi, Dr. Riley. It's Hunter Silver. I'm sorry to call you on this number while you're on vacation, but this is urgent. It's about Grace. Please call me back as soon as you can."

I hung up.

The sound of my heart drummed over my thoughts, and I shut my eyes, desperate to concentrate. Grace's breasts were fuller, and her appetite had changed. She was horny, but that was nothing new. But she was also on hormone shots, which could explain the symptoms...

Or she was pregnant. With my child. The room was silent for what felt like forever, but lasted only seconds. Rachel touched my arm, and I flinched.

"We've got a bigger problem now. Chad's transfer failed. He escaped."

And just that fast, I sobered, shooting to my feet. The IV line tugged at my arm.

"Sit down." Julia pressed on my shoulder, putting me back in the chair.

"Why are we discussing in vitro?" I asked.

"I'm not the one who brought it up. Now, are you just going to sit with an IV like a pussy, or are you going to do something about Chad?"

"I'm not fucking sitting." I ripped the needle out of my arm. Because if the bastard was out, the chances he was after Grace was one hundred and fifty percent. And I didn't want to think about the possibility he already had her.

Julia quickly pressed a cotton pad to my bleeding arm.

"Stay still for a moment or you'll bleed out before you find Grace. Put pressure on this for two minutes."

Scar's phone chimed. "I have an update from Silver Securities. It may not be anything, but an alarm was just triggered in the unit beside Grace's salon. All cameras are clear except one."

"Grace?"

I opened the salon's security cameras as Scar read out the group message.

"Part of her face was identified as she tried to open the connecting door, but then jerked back, and the door was shut."

"He got her at the party?" Rachel asked.

"Impossible. We were there, and we screened everybody," Scar replied

"Yes, but that side door was somehow open, and it shouldn't have been. He didn't get in through the front door; he got in through there. It's the property Grace wanted to buy. Find out who bought that property. I know it was up for sale a couple of weeks ago." Scar tapped on his phone screen.

I pulled my fingers through my hair, pacing the room.

He has her.

"When was the alarm triggered?"

"An hour ago."

I held my arm bent and grabbed my car keys. Rachel and Scar followed me to the door.

"Get me in on the group chat. We need a solid plan, and I don't want to hear any objections that I'm too close to Grace to get involved. We've been involved since I was eighteen, and… She may be carrying my child. I can't let anything happen to them."

Saying so out loud made Grace's pregnancy a reality, and regardless of the DNA, I was going to be a father.

Rachel grabbed the keys from my hand. "Let's go, Tarzan. You're lost in space, and we both know I'm the better driver."

I followed her out the door to her Mercedes. Scar and Julia packed up their car. Scar was meeting up with the Silver team at the head office, but we were heading elsewhere. I didn't even ask Rachel where, because the great thing about awesome partners was they could read your mind. And the great thing about Rachel was her instinct.

She gripped the steering wheel and focused on the road. Thirty minutes later, we crossed the city limits and pulled to the side of the road. It was already late afternoon, and I worried about how much time I'd lost sleeping while Chad had Grace.

My phone dinged with a notification. "Interstate cameras picked up Chad driving west. The Silvers identified five possible properties he could be heading to from there. They're sending a location map." I opened the image and showed Rachel.

"That one. We'll take that one."

"You sure?"

She nodded with a coy smile. "Are you gonna be a father?"

Fucking Rachel.

I quickly typed a message to the group chat: *Gearing up and heading to the northeast location. Dispatch units to all other locations and have medical on standby.*

Rachel was already driving by the time I finished the text. Fifteen minutes later, we pulled into the driveway of a secluded home in the forest. I followed her inside the safehouse and we changed, geared up, and went back out on the road without saying a word.

It wasn't until we parked a mile away and started a hike

through the woods that she spoke. "Whatever happens, you're not going in alone."

I cranked my neck sideways, releasing pressure. The night I didn't listen to her flashed in my mind. Gunshots, fire, screaming girls... I wouldn't make the same mistake again.

"I'm not going in alone, but I'm not holding back either."

I set my night vision on. She adjusted her goggles, and we scoped the little cabin in the woods. "One car, barred windows, turning on heat sensor... and there he is. They're alone in the back corner bedroom, and no one else is visible around the perimeter."

"Got it."

I confirmed her visual and prepped my gun.

"Going lethal tonight?" she asked.

"I'm not taking any chances. Just have my back."

I focused my binoculars on the bedroom window and zoomed in. Grace was lying flat on the bed with her arms above head and legs apart, likely tied to the bedposts.

"I'm gonna kill that bastard." My jaw ached from clenching.

"We can't wait for backup. Are you sure you can do this?"

I don't deserve fatherhood if I can't.

"She's my world." *She's my Queen.*

My phone rang with Dr. Riley's number. I pressed the button on my earpiece.

"Hello? Dr. Riley, thanks for calling me back, but I can't talk. Grace is in danger. I know she's pregnant, but did she choose a sperm donor? Did you implant her?"

Was that even the right way to ask?

"Grace came in for a check up and new IVF treatment earlier this week, but we did an ultrasound and there was no need to continue. She was already pregnant. Grace got pregnant on her own, Hunter."

"That's impossible. I'm sterile."

"I'd get that checked out because if you're the only man

she's been intimate with, then you know how she got pregnant. Is she in real danger?"

I held the binoculars firmly against my eyes and focused in as Chad knelt in the middle of a bed. He lifted his arm and jabbed something between her legs.

"Yes, she is. Thanks, Dr. Riley. I gotta go."

I hung up.

Chapter 18

grace

I woke on my side in an awkwardly uncomfortable position with the sound of my brain expanding and my head pounding. Somewhere in the distance, the rush of flowing water reminded me of a waterfall, but I wasn't in the rainforest. And I wasn't tucked safely in Hunter's arms. I was somewhere cold and dark, without a source of light. My limbs ached, and my mouth felt like a giant cotton ball. A dull pain throbbed at the side of my head, but when I tried to bring my fingertips to the source of the pain, I realized my wrists were bound and tied behind my back. My breath hitched.

"What the hell?"

I swung my legs over the mattress but my feet were bound as well and I nearly fell off. The smell of mold and mildew filled the space. A distinct stench of urine hung in the air. I stopped moving and listened for outside noises, but I heard nothing. It was dead silent.

"Where am I?" I whispered, trying to remember the events from the night before.

After my argument with Hunter, I'd gone up to the rooftop, lain back, and watched the stars. They weren't as bright in the city, but the quiet up there was better than listening to Hunter slur obscenities. I texted Emma and Frankie that I went home, but I spent the rest of the evening on the rooftop. Guests left, the party settled, and then long, striding footsteps along the tarred rooftop drew shivers up my spine. I hoped it was Hunter, but I couldn't see the man approach in the night. And he spared no extra breath when he covered my face with a chloroformed cloth.

Fuck.

My glasses were gone, and while my eyes were adjusting to the darkness, it was nearly impossible to see anything in the room. I rolled to my side and slowly inched my feet off the mattress. The ground was concrete and cold.

"Hello? Is anyone here?"

The sound of my voice was lost in the room. I stood up and shuffled to the wall, where soft foam covered the surface. The room was soundproof.

Heavy footsteps sounded, and my head flew up.

Maybe not completely soundproof.

I hopped back to the mattress. Something cracked underneath my sole, and I banged my shin on the bedframe. A door clicked open, then shut. Another door squeaked and closed. By the time a key twisted in the lock, I didn't know whether to hide or attack, and I chose the latter.

A light switch flicked on, and I launched myself at a man, bringing him to the ground.

"Ahhh!"

He fell with a grunt, and I kneed him in his crotch. He groaned in pain, and I kicked my legs like a seal, thrashing in his hold. His thick fingers gripped my arm, digging in until it hurt.

"Stop kicking and calm down, Grace. "

The familiar voice sent a wave of fear through my body. "Let me go!" I bit into his forearm.

He pushed me aside. I rolled to the concrete floor and

flopped like a fish. The zip ties around my wrists further cut into my flesh, burning.

"Help me! Somebody help me!" I bellowed from the back of my throat. He stood up, removed a switchblade from his pocket, and set it against my neck. I froze mid-swallow.

"I said fucking shut up, or I'll make you shut up."

My body went into shock as I stopped breathing and moving.

"Are you gonna be quiet?"

My gaze flew to his, and I blinked past the fear, meeting my biological twin brother's eyes. They were identical to mine, yet devoid of emotion. He withdrew the blade, lifted me by my arm, and set me down on the mattress.

"It's good to see you again, Grace."

"You're not Rick."

He stepped closer, and I shrank back against the wall.

"Don't worry, Grace. I won't hurt you. You're very important to me." He tilted his head to the left. "I don't believe we've been formally introduced."

I eyed his extended hand and the dirt underneath his fingernails.

"Chad Wagner, your twin."

I rolled my eyes and twisted sideways to show him my tied hands.

"Right, I'll get that off as soon as we leave."

"Why don't you save yourself the trouble and let me go before Hunter finds you?"

He laughed. "Your boy-toy doesn't have a clue you're missing, sweetheart. He doesn't know I'm free, and we'll be long gone before he realizes you're not coming back."

Fuck.

How did this happen? How did Chad get out of prison? Hunter was upset last night, but it wasn't about Chad, and as much as I wish we hadn't fought about his stupid assumption that I'd gotten myself pregnant, reasoning with a drunk was impossible.

I looked around the padded room.

"Where are we?"

"There was a unit for sale next door to your salon, so I bought it."

"*You* were my competing offer?"

"Don't worry, Gracie. As long as you're with me, it'll stay in the family."

My stomach tightened into a knot, then released. I pushed back the bile coming up my throat. Sooner or later, someone would come by, and they'd hear me and they'd catch this lunatic, wouldn't they?

"You said we'll be long gone. Where are we going?"

"We're leaving for our cabin before nightfall. Get some rest. It's a long trip."

Fuck.

"Wait—what do you want from me?"

He looked at me like I should have already known the answer. And I did. My throat seized, locking my breath. The thing was, part of me didn't want to hear what I already knew to be the truth.

"Get some sleep," he barked, and I flinched.

He turned to the door.

"Wait. I can't sleep with these on." I showed him the zip ties again.

"Then you're not tired enough. And don't bother screaming. The room is soundproof."

He left, shut the door, and locked it. The light flickered. I pushed my shoulders back and cracked my neck, releasing uncomfortable tension. I turned my head in a circle, stretching my neck muscles. My ribs ached from the fall, and my lower back pinched a nerve. I twisted my spine. It cracked, the sound lost within the walls.

I carefully made my way to the steel bed and sat on the filthy mattress. My stomach rumbled with hunger, and I looked down at my belly. "How you doing in there, peanut? You're more like a poppy seed. Let's hope you've got your daddy's strong genes, but we'll get through this. Just settle in and hold on."

As time ticked away, my discomfort grew, and I switched to my side. Where was Hunter and what was he doing? Was he aware Chad was free? When I left him last night, he was pissed drunk and likely passed out somewhere. What the hell did Scar tell him? Why would he assume I'd gone to the clinic behind his back? I went for a check-up and found out I was pregnant. I was about to tell him we were going to have a baby.

"I miss you, Hunter. Argh!"

I kicked my feet into the mattress with a groan. The blood boiled in my veins. I should have never allowed Scar to follow me around like a dog—although if he'd done a better job, I wouldn't be here. And if I'd listened to my gut at the party, I could have avoided Chad altogether. I had a feeling something was off, and it wasn't Hunter's drinking. We should have stayed in Costa Rica. I wished I'd waited until Chad was away for good. While my return home was nice, the jungle's safety was better. Warm nights filled with chirping crickets and singing cicadas, falling stars, and cold showers underneath the waterfall…and Hunter… He made the special place so much more than a vacation. He'd given me a home, safety, and the best moments of my life. We made a baby there, and he didn't know it.

My heart ached. What if he didn't find me? What if Chad got what he wanted?

"I'm not gonna let him hurt you," I whispered to my poppy seed baby, and shifted in discomfort. Although I'd lost count of how long it had been, my bladder had filled a few hours ago. I sat up in the bed, gently hopped to the furthest corner of the room, and tried to lift my dress.

"Fuck."

Crouching with hands and feet tied was impossible.

"I'm gonna piss myself."

Footsteps drummed overhead, and I hopped back to the bed, waiting. He opened the door with caution, saw me on the bed, and stepped further inside. A smug smile tugged the corner of his face.

"It's time to go."

"I need to use the washroom."

He reached into his back pocket and removed a switchblade, flicking it open with one twist of his hand.

I recoiled.

A puff of satisfaction streamed out his nose as he approached. He crouched in front of me and lifted the blade to my throat, pressing the edge against my skin. I tilted away, but he kept his hand steady.

"You try anything funny and I won't hesitate, you hear me?"

My nod was almost imperceptible, but he lowered his hand between my ankles, slicing through the ties at my feet. Cold air kissed the burns on my skin. I held in the relief because the moment I let go, I'd pee.

"Let's go."

"Washroom?" I whispered.

"Upstairs."

Chad grabbed my arm and yanked me to the first door, then through the next. He didn't bother locking the one behind us or slowing as we scaled a staircase. We emerged from the basement into an old bar. Stale cigarette smell hung in the air. Yellowed newspapers covered the front windows, letting through late afternoon air, and I recognized the place beside my salon. It would have been a perfect addition to my business.

"The washroom is that way." He pointed to a door.

"It'd be quicker if I got these off. You said you'd get them off when we leave."

"Manage with them or piss yourself."

Shit.

"They're cutting through my skin."

"Shut the fuck up."

"Chad, you also said—"

I stopped when I saw him march over to the bar, grab a roll of duct tape off the counter, and pull a piece off.

"No, no..."

I took the last breath in as he stuck the tape over my lips.

Fucking asshole.

"You have two minutes, and then we leave." He pointed to the bathroom again. I walked with caution, eyeing the side door I knew led to my salon on the other side. The chance it was unlocked was slim, but it was still a chance. I switched my route from the bathroom at the last minute, and launched for the connecting door. I turned around, back to the door, and gripped the handle, watching Chad's face turn bright red.

"Don't you fucking dare!"

I twisted the doorknob and pushed the door open. The beautiful sound of an alarm blared through the building. Chad grabbed me, twisted my arm, and pinned me to the wall. He pushed his full body against mine, his brute strength forcing my limbs to comply as he secured my wrists tighter.

I cried out through the duct tape. At this rate, he'd cut off my hands.

"That's a good girl. You're not so different from me after all, are you, Gracie?"

His cheek pressed to mine, holding my head firm against the wall. I recoiled at the smell of his disgusting breath.

"You're as feisty as all the Hartleys. That's good. Means our sons will flourish. Have I ever told you how much I love feisty women?"

God, he stank worse than a dog.

"But do you know what I love more? Breaking them."

Chills ran down my spine. He grabbed me by my arm and pushed open the back alley door.

"Don't make this more difficult than it has to be, Grace."

He yanked me so hard, my bladder let go. I made a noise in the back of my throat, thrashing in his grip as piss ran down my inner thigh. He clicked on a car key and the trunk lifted open. Police sirens sounded too far away in the distance.

Fuck, fuck, fuck!

"Get in, Gracie."

I stopped the pee and tried to buy time, kicking him in the crotch. His elbow responded by slamming into my gut, and I bent in half. Wheezing air fizzed out my nose as he lifted me off the ground. My bladder let go again, flowing down my ass and onto his arm, but I had no strength to stop it. He threw me inside the trunk with a grunt. My lungs crushed inward. I fell onto my face before twisting to my side.

"I should have done this before."

The asshole ripped the duct tape off without warning, covered my face with a cloth, and finally faded from my view.

I woke up, feeling like I'd rolled down a hill over a thousand rocks and landed in a pit of spikes. My skin hurt everywhere, and my limbs felt like they'd gone through a chopper. I lifted my hand to my head and immediately sat up on a king-sized bed.

"I'm free."

Visible cuts marked my wrists and feet. Wooden beams stretched horizontally, forming the scaffolding of a cottage that barely held on its foundation. Dated furniture hung crookedly, and dust covered everything.

I coughed. The faint sound of running water sounded from the outside. I hopped off the bed and hurried to the window. I pulled the drapes apart, flicked the latch, and lifted the window's lower part. The crisp forest air carried the smell of pine and wilderness past the steel bars. Beyond, darkness swallowed the outside world.

"Fuck."

The door opened, and I whipped around to face my twin, Chad Hartley.

"Glad to see you up. We have a lot to do."

Chad closed the door behind him and removed a banana from his back pocket. He was wearing the same pair of stained jeans and the same checkered shirt as last night. Or was it still the same night? It was dark outside, but I wasn't sure how much time I'd lost.

"Are you hungry?"

"No," I lied.

He waved the banana in his right hand, while I eyed the glass of water on his left.

"Want this? You get it after you clean up." He pointed to a door I assumed led to a bathroom. "And you will eat dinner with me in thirty minutes. I'll push it down your throat if I have to."

"Why bother to feed me?"

"You're gonna be the mother of my child, and he'll need nutrition. You're too thin as it is. Go."

He pointed with his chin, and I hurried for the bathroom. The door had no lock, and he'd nailed plywood over the only window.

"I can't hear the shower running." He banged on the door and I jumped, hurrying to turn on the water.

"And wear the clothes I brought. They're on the back of the door."

My gaze was drawn to a white nightgown on a hanger, a set of panties and a bra strung over the hook.

"Fuck you, Chad," I whispered, and quickly stripped.

The shower was one of the fastest I'd taken in my life. I didn't bother for the water to warm or steam to rise, left my hair out of the shower's way, and washed myself with soap. The wounds on my wrists and ankles sizzled with pain. I lifted my foot. A cut near my ankle was getting infected. I rinsed, turned off the shower, and hopped back into my dirty dress from the party just as Chad pushed on the handle.

I threw my back against the door.

"I swear to God, if you don't start treating me with respect, I'll kill myself before you see you me again. I'm not done. Where's the toothbrush?"

"You'll earn one with time. Now step away from the fucking door."

He burst through the door, and my body bounced off. I flew across the bathroom and smashed my hip against the sink. I slipped and fell to the floor.

"I told you to put on the clothes I brought."

He stepped toward me, and I pushed my feet into the floor, sliding backward on my ass until my back hit the wall. He grabbed a fist full of hair near my scalp and pulled me to my feet.

"Ouch," I cried, grabbing his hand with both of mine, but he didn't budge. I followed him to the bedroom. He held firm until I ended up back on the bed, still in my stained dress.

The smell of grilling steak and something else brought nausea to my gut. I hurled over the bed and onto the floor, spilling my insides. He strode to the dresser, brought the glass of water, and passed it my way.

"Rinse. I don't want your vomit all over my cock."

I took the glass from his hand, filled my mouth and spat everything in his face. His hand flew to my cheek, stinging.

"You cunt."

I pushed my feet into the mattress until my back pressed against the wall, watching him remove the switchblade from his pocket. He hopped on the bed and pressed it against my throat.

"We were going to eat, but it looks like you're not starved enough." A cocky grin painted his face. "I am, though."

He opened a dresser drawer, grabbed two new zip ties and a rope.

"No, no… Please, they hurt."

"Hands over your head."

Snot ran freely down my nose. I wiped it with the back of my arm before lifting both arms to the railing above my head. He fastened my wrists to the frame and moved on to my legs.

"You kick me, and I'll kill you."

Light reflected on the switchblade as he spun it between his fingers. He tied rope around each ankle and stretched my legs apart, tying each end to a bedpost.

"Chad, I'm… I'm not going to run, I promise." My gasped plea stuck in my chest. I couldn't let him go through with it. I couldn't let him hurt my baby.

He flicked open the top button of his jeans and lowered the zipper.

"My father wanted a pure heir. Denying him a dying wish would be wrong."

"Wrong? What about what you're doing? Isn't that wrong? He's already dead, and he doesn't care about a stupid wish. I'm your sister, for God's sake!"

He held my stare for what felt like forever, but once that smirk lifted the corner of his face; I knew I had lost.

"He may not care, but I do."

I writhed on the bed, desperate for a miracle, or a heart attack for Chad.

"Please, Chad, you can't do this to me."

"Don't worry, Gracie. I'll give you everything you want and need. I'll make you my queen."

"You don't get to call me your queen." I pulled in a sniffle.

My dress rose between my legs. He grabbed the switchblade and swung his arm forward, piercing the fabric between my thighs.

I screamed.

"Fine. *Whore* will do as well."

The dress ripped as he pulled the blade down to its hem. I was desperate, and my fight wasn't only for me. I screamed.

"Shut up!"

He ripped a piece of duct tape off a roll.

"No, Chad. You can't because I can't give you a baby. I'm... I'm pregnant."

Chapter 19

Hunter

Adrenaline shot through my veins, flowing with purpose and fury, maintaining my alert level at high. We took the house from the front, which made sense since there was no back door. Rachel picked the lock like a pro while I kept guard. My heart raced and my senses focused. An owl hooted in the distance. Grace had less than a minute, if she stalled. Rachel tapped at my leg. She was done, and I turned off the night vision while going over the plan in my head. She'd distract Chad, and I'd sneak up from a blind spot.

I twisted the doorknob, and gently pushed away from the frame. The hinge threatened to squeak, and I slowed the door's momentum. Low light glowed from a corner lamp. I scanned the room. Cigarette smoke rose from an ashtray on the table. Five feet in, cans and bottles lined the hallway leading to the back bedroom, like soldiers.

Fuck.

I moved further in. Rachel stepped past me and stood at the first row of bottles.

"We can't remove them all. There's no time," she whispered into my earpiece.

"Plan B?"

She nodded, and I launched across the room. Bottles shattered and cans clattered as we kicked our way through the space. I crossed the hall and made it to the wall by the kitchen. Rachel slid to the floor on the left. I pressed my back against the wall and counted.

Five, four, three… I didn't finish. The ricochet of a gunshot echoed through the house. Bullets flew through the wall above Rachel's head. I dropped to the floor, but not before a one grazed my arm.

"You hit?" Rachel asked.

"No, all good." Something clicked on the other side. "He's changing the load."

I rolled over the debris with a grunt, positioned myself in a shadowed spot, and aimed my gun. Rachel kicked in the door. The smell of sweat and fear seeped out, but Chad and Grace were gone. He hadn't been changing the load; he'd been escaping. A dresser stood slanted near the wall. Behind it stood a kid-sized hidden door.

"It's an escape hatch. They're in the forest."

We ran through the front and around the back. A gunshot echoed through the night.

No!

I turned on my night vision. Two bodies were moving toward the river. Grace still had her arms behind her back. He pulled on her arm, and she tripped. "Northwest heading. Keep on this track, and I'll cut him off."

I swerved left into the forest and trailed around a house-sized stack of boulders. I lost sight of Grace and Chad for a minute, but when I reached the other side, I was ahead, and Chad was heading my way. Rachel wasn't far behind them. I set myself on the ground and waited for the perfect shot.

"Okay, Rachel. I'm ready for that distraction."

My partner removed a flare gun and shot it up into the air. Chad's and Grace's heads flew up, and I pulled the trigger. The bullet pierced Chad in the chest, and he fell to the ground. I shot to my feet and darted through the forest like a boar, encasing Grace in my arms.

"It's okay. It's over. It's all over."

She mumbled through the duct tape.

"It's all right. We'll get that off. Hold on."

I opened my clippers and cut through the zip ties around her wrists. Her injured arms flew around my neck. I held her shaking body against mine and kissed her head. She clung to me like a monkey, her face pressed against my chest. Rachel reached us and checked on Chad.

"Unconscious but alive. Not sure how long he has, though. There's a lot of blood."

She took the gun from his hand and emptied the load.

"Call for a medic," I said. "Death is not enough for that bastard."

"Already done."

"And let the team know—"

"Done as well."

I forgot how great it was working side by side.

"I need a heat pack. Grace has duct tape over her mouth."

She threw the bag off her shoulder to the ground beside us, removing a rectangular packet. She snapped the sachet in half and passed it my way. Warmth spread through the contents.

"Keep this over your mouth. It'll help loosen the tape. Here… Sit in my lap, and I'll hold it."

I bent to lift her. A shot echoed through the forest, and I closed my arms around Grace, taking her to the ground. Another shot echoed seconds later..

"It's okay. He's dead now," Rachel said. "He had another gun."

"You killed him."

"Would you rather he killed you? I thought you wanted him dead."

I did, and I didn't. A dead Chad would never hurt Grace again, and I couldn't deny the instant relief in my chest. Then the piercing pain through my thigh replaced my second of solace. The spot burned, searing into the muscle and spasming down to my toes. My leg buckled underneath me and I fell to the ground, nearly taking Grace down with me.

I'm shot.

Grace dropped to her knees at my side. The sky had cleared, and I finally saw her beautiful face. Her swollen eyes filled with tears, and I smoothed my dirty hand over her cheek. Dirt from my fingers stained her flesh, but she still looked like the most beautiful woman in the world. I lifted the warm packet back to her mouth and held it against the duct tape.

"I can't feel the pain when I look at you, beautiful," I said. "But I should probably fix my leg. Can you hold this?"

She grasped the packet and her eyes fell to my leg, where Rachel injected a pain reliever into the muscle before looping a belt around my thigh. The bleeding stopped, but I felt woozy. Grace lay down and settled at my side. We watched the stars twinkle above the canopy.

"I'm so sorry about everything, Grace."

She unzipped my vest and slipped her injured hand underneath my shirt. It was almost like in Costa Rica—just me and her and a million stars.

"Let's try removing the tape." Rachel helped Grace sit up. She lowered the heating pad from her mouth and held the tape's end, gently peeling away.

Grace's first breath was deep and long. She closed her eyes and took a moment before she looked at me from above.

"Are you all right?" she asked.

"Me? I'm fine. I've got drugs, so it's all good. I see rainbows and unicorns. Maybe some toads." I pointed to the sky. "Hey, Rachel, what did you give me?"

"Unfortunately, I had no horse tranquilizer."

Grace snickered. It was so good to hear her voice.

"Did he hurt you? I mean, I know he hurt you, but—

"Just some scrapes and bruises. Nothing time won't heal."

"Good." I took in a deeper breath. The stars were moving across the night sky, and I knew whatever Rachel had given me was fully kicking in.

"Hunter?"

Her beautiful face came into view again.

"I'm pregnant. And it's your baby." She lowered her gaze to her belly, where I was already holding my hand.

"I know, my love, and I'm so sorry I assumed otherwise."

"Stop apologizing and kiss me."

She lowered her mouth to mine, and the pain was finally gone.

"Was I right, or was I right? You're gonna have some beautiful babies," Rachel said. "Come on. Let's get you guys moved closer to the house."

"What about him?" Grace asked.

"I never want to see his face again," I said.

"You can't see his face because it's not there." Rachel stepped sideways to block the view, though we couldn't see much in the darkness.

"You shot him in the face?" I grunted, lifting to my feet. Grace draped my arm over her shoulder on one side while Rachel helped me on the other.

"I aimed for the head, but it was dark," she said.

"Are you saying your aim is off at night?"

"Shut the fuck up or I'll find the horse tranquilizer, because it certainly sounds like you don't have enough morphine."

The beautiful sound of helicopter blades whipped in the distance. The medics air-lifted us to the hospital. A unit was dispatched to collect Chad's body, and altogether, the night was the worst and best one of my life.

I SAT BY HER BEDSIDE, watching her sleep. A gentle smile curved her face. Her eyes moved underneath the eyelids and her fingers fluttered over her belly where she rested her hand. Grace's wrists and ankles were healing, but the wounds and the sizeable bruises over her skin, shaded in green, purple and yellow, were a gruesome reminder of the kidnapping. Grace had begged Chad not to hurt her and at the last minute, told him she was pregnant. He'd said he'd make sure she'd miscarry, but the front lock clicked just then, and he'd changed his plan. He'd dragged Grace out the back moments later. I jerked at the memory.

Grace shifted in her bed, bringing my attention back to her beautiful face. Our joint hospital room was filled with bouquets, teddy bears, and a couple of stuffed toad plushies. I'd strung get-well cards across the ceiling, and made sure Grace had all the makeup and hair accessories she needed. It turned out all she needed was rest, and me.

She remained under observation while I healed from my surgery. The doctors removed the bullet lodged in my thigh, sewed me up, and ran the new tests I requested. We were both scheduled to be discharged this afternoon, and I couldn't wait to take Grace home. She stirred, and I sat higher in my chair. Her eyes opened, closed, and opened again, like she couldn't believe she was here. Her mouth stretched wide when she saw my face. I leaned in as she reached out to touch my longer facial hair, her delicate fingers stroking affectionately over my jawline.

"Your beard is re-growing."

"I wouldn't call this a beard, but I'll keep it if you'd like."

"It reminds me of Costa Rica. It's where I fell in love with you all over again."

I rose and shifted my weight to my right, uninjured leg, and bent down to kiss her. Her warm lips welcomed mine, and I whispered against her mouth, "It's where we made our baby."

Her smile pressed to my lips. "Sit back down and don't strain."

"And how long do I have to wait until you let me strain?" I kissed her again and lowered myself to the chair.

"Knowing you, Tarzan, not long."

"Good. Because there's something I must tell you."

She reached for the control at her bedside and pressed a button. The bed buzzed and lifted her into a sitting position.

"What is it?"

"I had something done while you were asleep."

"Let me guess… A tattoo? No, it can't be a tattoo because you don't have any bandages…unless it's underneath—"

"It's not a tattoo." I moved closer. "It's way better. The doctor ran some tests, and I can confirm I'm not sterile."

She bubbled with laughter. "I thought we already established that."

"But you know what this means, don't you? We can definitely make more babies."

"The first one isn't even born yet, and you're thinking of more?"

"Why waste time? Life is too short, and I want a family. With you."

She reached out and tapped my nose with her finger. "We're already a family. Speaking of which, have you called ours? Did you tell them we're okay?"

"You're kidding, right? I threatened them with restraining orders so they'd leave us alone for a few days."

"They're just worried."

"I'm sorry I kept them out. I didn't realize you wanted visitors."

"Actually, I do appreciate the quiet. Reminds me of Costa Rica."

"Sounds like a lot reminds you of Costa Rica."

"Especially the wild man who took me there."

I rose and crawled into her bed, squeezing in beside her. She cuddled into my side and placed her palm over my chest.

"Any way we could fly to Costa Rica before the baby arrives?"

"What about the salon?"

"I made Frankie a managing partner. I'm sure he can handle it. He runs the place anyway, and I'm just a name—which I will change, by the way."

"Why change it?"

"Chad called me Gracie. It doesn't feel right anymore."

"Chad was deranged."

"Do you think I should change it?"

"Whatever you choose will represent a strong business-woman who perseveres. What Chad thought or what anyone else thinks doesn't matter, because you're more than a name, Grace. You're my Queen, and I'm never letting you out of my sight again."

"But Chad is dead."

"Exactly what I'm trying to say. Fuck Chad. But I'm still not letting you out of my sight."

She settled in my arms and let out a breathy exhalation.

"Hunter?"

"Yes?"

"I do need a vacation."

"Me too."

WE MET Scar in the hospital parking lot. I held the door open for Grace, but Scar stopped me.

"She's riding shotgun."

"Something happened?"

"Nothing to worry about."

I crawled into the back seat and positioned myself in the middle to hear the conversation. Grace buckled her seatbelt, and Scar handed her an envelope, then turned on the ignition.

"What's this?"

"Legal documents, deeds mostly, and new bank accounts now belonging to you."

"What?"

"Chad was the last Hartley to die, and everyone else from the family is dead. The entire estate and all finances now belong to you, which puts you in a legal predicament with Infinity."

"That's the business you took over after Brad Hartley—"

"Yup. Now, obviously, it's up to you whether you want to continue the lawsuit."

"Against my brothers? No way. But I'm not the only Hart... Oh, God, I can't even say it. I'm not the only one left. What about Simone Hartley and Candice Watson?"

"Simone's serving a criminal charge in a care facility. She hasn't spoken in years. The estate cannot pass to a mentally incapacitated person. As for Candice, she divorced Jeff years ago and has no claim."

Grace sat quietly, thinking as Scar drove. He waited with more patience than I would have given him credit for.

"What's the likelihood I'd be alive if Candice hadn't remove me from that family?"

Scar didn't reply, but we all knew the answer to that. I touched Grace's shoulder, and she startled.

"I'm sorry. Didn't mean to scare you. You can think about this. You have time to decide."

She turned in her seat to face me. "But I already know. The house where Chad held me is the only thing I want—because I'll tear it down and I'll plant trees in the spot. I don't want anyone on that property ever again. It will stay wild."

"Okay, but are you sure—"

"There's more. Chad purchased a unit beside the salon. I want that too. And Simone and Tristan have a son, so he should get something, but that will be up to Candice. Everything, other than the cottage and the unit, will go to Candice. She can decide what to do with the properties and the money. That's what I want. "

"We'll get it done," Scar said, and Grace settled in her seat with satisfaction.

Fifteen minutes later, Scar pulled into Cougar Court, and then Grace's driveway. He parked the car at the curved entryway by the fountain. He opened Grace's door and passed me the crutches. Grace stepped out, wearing my sweatshirt and leggings. Her face glowed, and her eyes shone bright. In less than a minute, we'd be alone in our house, and I couldn't wait for proper alone time. I set my crutches beneath my arms and swung my body forward.

Scar followed behind us to the front door. Grace pushed on the handle and stepped into a hallway.

A chorus of voices cheered, "Surprise!"

Our family and friends had gathered in the foyer and stacked the Scarlett O'Hara staircase. I lifted my gaze to the *Welcome Home* sign hung across the hall, and my shoulders dropped.

Fucking Emma.

"Did you know about this?" Grace turned around.

"Trust me, I didn't," I said, dejected. "But I know who did."

Emma ran over with her arms wide open and slammed into Grace.

"Hey, hey. Be careful. She's still healing."

And she's pregnant.

"Sorry."

We welcomed the unexpected party and joined them in the backyard, where Emma had set up what looked like a wedding venue. A white tent stood propped near the pond, with potted hydrangeas lining the perimeter. Tables filled with food were stationed on one side, and Olivier's grill was smoking in the corner. I tried to count the number of Silver kids and grand-kids this family had spawned, but Allie and Tristan's twins started a game of tag, making the task impossible. I left Grace on the loungers with Beth and Candice, and joined the Wagner brothers for a toast of tonic water.

"Congratulations on the case."

"We always knew it would close the moment you killed that bastard." Axel lifted his glass.

"Technically, Rachel killed him. Where is she?"

"She flew back home. Told me to give you her best, but her spouse found out they're expecting."

Axel's son, Trevor, ran up to his father. "Can I get some money for ice cream?"

"There are three tubs full in that freezer by the window." Axel pointed.

"But they're not from an ice cream truck."

Jolly carnival music tinkled in the distance.

Axel removed two fifties from his wallet and handed the cash to his son. "Get one for every kid."

Trevor ran off screaming to his cousins, and nearly half the yard emptied as they followed him down the driveway and out onto the court.

"Is that what I have to look forward to?" I asked.

"That, less sleep, loss of privacy, and a never-closing fridge. Wait—is Grace pregnant?"

"She'll kill me if she finds out I said anything, so keep your mouths shut. She has this thing about waiting until the second trimester." Grace waved me over. "Excuse me one sec."

I grabbed my crutches and a cold can of tonic water, tucked it in my pocket, and joined Grace by the fire-pit. While Candice hugged Grace, Beth unexpectedly leaned into my ear. "Thank you for saving my daughter."

"You're welcome."

Candice stood up. Emma plopped down in the spot beside Grace I'd been ready to take, crossed her legs and, exhausted, took a sip of her wine.

"Love what you've done with the place, Ems," Grace said. "You should add venue decorator to your resume."

"What I need on my resume is experience, and my brothers are making my life hell to get to the good cases."

"So you fill your time decorating?"

"No, I gain new skills because one day, when they fire my ass, I'll need a backup plan, and Eric Waters deserves a woman with a job."

I spat out my tonic water, wiped my mouth, and grabbed an apple fritter off a platter. Aunt Wilma made the best fritters.

"What's so funny?" Emma asked.

"You've played it too safe with Eric," I said, chewing my fritter.

"What are you talking about?"

"He still sees you as a girl and his best friend's little sister. He needs to see you as a woman."

"But I am a woman. What's it gonna take for him to see that?"

I munched my fritter again, chewing between my words. "You're a private investigator. You'll figure it out. Isn't that Eric over there?" I pointed to the guy in the cowboy hat.

"Holy shit. I gotta go." She jumped out of her seat and ran off.

I swallowed the last bite and took her spot beside Grace,

wrapping my arm around her. "Finally alone. I'm sorry, I was expecting a quiet evening. I didn't know about the surprise. How are you feeling? Any nausea?"

"No. I'm great. Actually…do you know when the party's over?"

I lifted a brow. "No, but if you're tired, I can ask the guests to leave."

She fidgeted.

"How's your leg?"

"Good.."

She bit her lower lip and held the teeth there, scanning the crowd.

"Are you trying to ask me what I think you're trying to ask me?"

"I have a new set from Aunt Mary to try—"

I stood up, disregarded my crutches, and lifted Grace into my arms. Searing pain shot down my leg and up my spine, but nothing would stop me from seeing her new outfit.

"What are you doing?" she screamed.

"Taking you upstairs."

"You're injured, and we have guests."

I shut her up with a lingering kiss. She peeled her mouth away from mine, relaxing.

"And you're my Queen."

Her Epilogue

grace

I swung back and forth in the egg chair, watching a pair of teal and yellow macaws clean their wings. They were perched on a tree branch that extending over our eco-lodge. A light breeze blew through our home, carrying the smell of passing rain. Droplets trickled down the leaves, making a sound like it was still raining. I loved the sound of rain. It had taken six months to organize the paperwork, set up the additional salon space, and hire new staff, but it was worth it. Frankie would manage the business while I took time off for maternity leave. We'd flown to Costa Rica two months ago, and my due date was now only one week away.

My nose wiggled, and my stomach rumbled. Hunter rushed around the kitchen making breakfast. He was still wearing the shorts from his swim out in the rain…and nothing else. My gaze drifted from the macaws to his beautiful, strong body, remembering how skinny he had been at eighteen when he came to fix my bike. The kid who saved toads from my pool had grown into a beautiful Tarzan.

He looked up and his mouth curved, sinking his dimple. Arousal stirred through my body.

"I made omelets, Belgian waffles, vegan sausages, and

there's a bowl of fresh fruit on the table. Green tea with your breakfast?"

"Tea would be lovely, but I'm not that hungry."

"Five minutes ago you were asking for burgers and steaks."

"I'm pregnant, and I'm eating for two."

"You're a vegetarian. It's why we settled on vegan sausages with other options for breakfast." He motioned with his hand.

The hormones hit me like a train, made a U-turn, and the floodworks started.

"It's not my fault my taste buds flipped upside down. I'm craving turkey breast slices and salami sticks. I remember my father eating them when I was a kid, and they smelled so good."

"So you *are* hungry?"

"No, I said I... I... I don't know what I want. I barely slept because the baby kept kicking and pushing on my ribs. And my bladder feels like it has space for three teaspoons at a time."

The baby kicked, and I winced in pain. "Ouch, not so hard. I swear, if I push out a little caveman or a bear, I want a re-do."

He dropped the spatula and hurried my way, crouching in front of me. He cupped my hands in his. "I don't think that's how it works, and I'm so sorry you're uncomfortable. What can I do to make you feel better?"

"Uncomfortable? Hunter, I look like I'm having triplets, and I know we're only having one."

"Why don't we do something relaxing?"

"We just had sex..."

The baby kicked again, and I jumped from my seat right into Hunter's arms, knocking him over.

"I'm so sorry," I cried again.

"I was thinking about taking a walk by the river. I'll set up a blanket and maybe catch some fish for dinner. It's not too hot outside."

"Okay..."

"Eat first."

"I'm really not hungry."

Truthfully, I had no space in my stomach and had no appetite since last night. The delusional plea for steaks and burgers was just that: delusional. But the doctor had said to walk and move as much as possible. I rubbed the side of my belly where the baby's foot pressed against my skin, the imprint of its tiny toes visible. Hunter's smile showed a full grid of teeth.

"That's so cute."

"My shifting liver is not cute." I massaged the baby's foot into a new position. "Move, move, move, please, move."

The baby turned, and I breathed out in relief, "All right. Let's go to the river."

I pulled up my pregnancy joggers and adjusted the sports bra. Since we'd moved back to Costa Rica, Hunter had built stairs so I could easily walk up to the house. Or wobble. He still preferred the rope, as it was quicker.

He cleaned up the food, gathered his fishing gear and a blanket, and minutes later, I was sitting near the riverbank, watching his muscled back twist every time he cast a fishing line. This was so much better. Beautiful arms, a tight behind, strong trapezoid muscles stretching from shoulder to neck... He was a caveman... No, a bear, because the hair on his back and chest regrew. I'd wax him when bending over was no longer an Olympic challenge, but I didn't really mind the cuddly growth.

I cracked my head to the side. The sound of rushing water eased the tension in my shoulders, and the soft breeze cooled my skin, but it didn't take long for a cramp to tighten around my belly as the baby pushed its foot into my ribs. I lay down on the blanket, stretching and seeking comfort. Just one more week! Tomorrow, we had a visit booked with the doctor in the city, and I was not looking forward to the five-hour trip.

The leaves rustled in the bushes on my left, and I rose to my elbows, scanning the area. I sat up higher as Hunter cast his line. He was standing knee-deep in the water, concentrating on the flow. The leaves rustled again, and I startled. A cougar's head popped out from within.

"Oh, my God. Hunter," I whispered. My heart lodged itself somewhere in my throat, halting my voice.

"Hunter?" I said louder, but he couldn't hear me over the flowing water. Kali stepped out from within the bushes and slowly approached. I sat frozen, unable to speak or breathe. Her stomach stuck out on each side, swollen and large.

She's pregnant.

We held eye-to-eye, the distance shortening until the cougar stopped a stone's throw away and sat. She was panting, and I still couldn't breathe. I slowly inhaled as she extended her front paws forward and stretched out onto her side, her round midsection lifting like a balloon.

"Oh, you poor girl. Hunter, get some water." But I could barely voice the words.

Hunter was still focused on the line, unaware of Kali's presence. I slowly stood and wobbled as eloquently and non threateningly as I could to the shore, squatted like a duck, and filled the bowl Hunter had brought for the fish with water. I went back to the cougar and set the bowl a safe few feet away from her head. She sat up and I stepped back, hurrying to the river and into the water. The cougar bent down to the bowl and drank the water. I smiled while walking backward until I reached Hunter and tapped his shoulder.

He tugged on his line and turned around with a huge grin on his face. "Perfect timing. I just got one."

He reeled in the line, and I folded my arms over my large breasts, waiting until he finished. The fish flapped, and he hooked it by the gills, dragging the trout out of the water.

"I could have been eaten alive, and you wouldn't have known it."

"What are you talking about? Are you feeling better?"

"I'm talking about the cougar." I pointed to the shore.

"It's just Kali."

"She's still a cougar."

"Kali protects us. You think I would have left you in danger? I saw her pacing along the river, but she took off when I set up the blanket."

I slapped him lightly on his arm. "You could have told me."

"But you had nothing to worry about. See?" He pointed to the cat.

"You still could have warned me. I've never been near the cat. She loves you because you feed her."

He burst out a laugh. "You're so wrong about that. She's been wanting to meet you since we came back."

What?

"What about the father? She's obviously pregnant. Is he around?"

"I've seen him, but Kali keeps him away from the house as well."

"Any other cougars around here I should know about?"

"Only the beautiful one I'm looking at."

He lowered his head to mine, and what began as an innocent kiss turned fervent within seconds. The fish flopped in his grip and jumped back in the water. He pulled away from my mouth.

"Great. Now we lost dinner."

"You'll catch another one. I think Kali's in labor. I gave her some water."

"You gave her water?"

I nodded. "She was panting. I think she may like me."

His smile swung free. "What's not to like?"

"You should check on her. Is this her first cub?"

"Yes, but she'll be fine. She's wild."

I shook my head, and Hunter hooked my arm into his,

helping me to the shore. We stopped by Kali, who was on her side again. She sniffed my foot and nudged her nose against my sandal, then turned sideways, glancing back at Hunter.

A sharp pain zapped from the bottom of my spine and to my belly. I gripped Hunter for support as it twisted around my stomach.

"Ahh,"

"You all right?"

Wet fluid leaked down my inner thighs, and I looked up with wide eyes.

"My water just broke."

He looked down, as if to double check, and looked back up again. "Wait here, I'm gonna get the scooter."

I gripped his arm before he could run off. "Hunter, I can't ride the scooter now. And you're not leaving me alone with a cougar in the jungle."

Kali growled out in pain, her stomach visibly contracting.

"Rainforest."

"Whatever. Ahhh," A stronger squeeze tightened around my abdomen, strangling my breath. I bent in half, bracing myself on my knees.

"All right. Let me help you to the house, and we'll figure out how to get you to the village. There's a nurse there, and Abuela has delivered dozens of babies."

I stopped, feeling another contraction coming on. They were too close. They weren't supposed to be this close so soon, for a first baby.

"This is not part of my birth plan," I screamed.

"That's okay, Grace. I won't leave your side, I promise."

He held me as the contraction zapped through my body. I squeezed his hand, breathing through the pain. This one lasted longer, and I was afraid we didn't have much time. I was told we'd have plenty of time as first time births took longer.

I hurried my pace to the house, and had another one on my

way up the stairs. Hunter helped me to the bed, removed my underwear, propped up a pillow, and got in touch with the village on a shortwave radio.

"Abuela's on her way. We need water. I'll go down to the river."

I felt pressure between my legs and the urge to push grew.

"The river?"

"No, you're right. We need hot water. The river's a bad idea."

Oh, God. He was running around the room like a confused chicken. A chicken with a bear's body, and I'd never seen him this scattered. I started laughing so hard at the image that I was crying, and Hunter finally stopped.

"Are you okay?"

A fresh contraction tore through my abdomen. I rose to my knees, bent over like a dog, and took a position on all fours. The urgency to push forced me into a squat.

"What are you doing?" he asked.

"I don't know, but it feels right. The baby's coming."

"What?"

"It's coommiiing right nooow," I cried, feeling the stress around my belly compress my organs.

Hunter positioned himself underneath my legs. Thankfully, he'd had the mind to find fresh swaddling cloths and held them ready. I pushed, my face tense and hot. Sweat streamed down my face and body. I panted at the moment of relief, but then the pressure surged again and I pushed harder.

"Catch it," I said to Hunter.

"It's not a football."

"Are you a doctor?"

"No, but I'm not a football player either. I watched YouTube and read some books."

"When?"

"Push, Grace. Push."

I gripped his shoulders for support, released my breath, and tightened my jaw, giving into the pain and ache.

"It's gonna pop!" I screamed.

"Genies do it all the time."

"What?" My head flew up.

"The head's almost out. Give me a strong push on the next contraction."

The last push flushed the pain away. Relief and a need to hear a cry surged through me. Hunter removed the baby and wrapped a cloth around her—or him.

"What is it? Is it okay?" I lowered to the bed with my legs spread wide, watching him maneuver not like Tarzan or a caveman. He looked like a doctor.

"Give me a sec."

He clamped the umbilical chord, cleared the baby's nose with an aspirator we had ready, and passed me the swaddled bundle. The baby finally cried.

"Congratulations, Mamma. We have a daughter."

The waterworks came down my cheeks, and I couldn't stop them.

"It's a girl?" I held her against my chest, cooing until she settled. She had Hunter's nose and dark head of curly hair. "Hi, baby girl."

She opened her tiny eyes and pressed her cheek to my skin, settling in my hold. She definitely had his eyes. The tiny blue gems sparkled. A soft smile spread over her face. Hunter wrapped his arm around me as she pressed her cheek to my skin and closed her eyes.

"Oh, my God. I love her so much." I looked up at Hunter. "And I love you both." He kissed me. "You were amazing. What are we gonna name her?"

"I don't know. She doesn't look like a Lorelei."

"We can think about it. Abuela should be here soon."

Abuela, along with two of her daughters and a guide who

stayed on the ground floor, showed up fifteen minutes later. Hunter cut the cord. Abuela cleared the placenta and didn't leave until our daughter latched onto my breast. She suckled, making cooing noises. Hunter sneakily recorded the beautiful moment, and my heart was full for the first time.

My clock didn't run out, and my Hunter made all my dreams come true.

Grace held Geneviève in her arms. The moment we called her our little Genie, "Lorelei" was out the window. But we saved the name for our second one, growing in Grace's belly. Our daughter was suckling on Grace's breast, making the cutest swallowing sounds, and I couldn't pull my eyes away. She was beautiful, with a head full of curly hair and bright blue eyes. Grace had told me they were beautiful, but not this beautiful. Genie's eyes sparkled each time she laughed or giggled. She started walking on her first birthday. Strike that: she started *running* on her first birthday, and keeping up with her around the eco-house was a challenge.

Grace had the maternal instinct of ten. We hadn't planned to stay in Costa Rica for so long, but there was something special about raising our kids out here. We flew to Montana for our annual family Christmas, and joined the Silver barbecue in July at my aunt and uncle's, Wilma and Fred's. Emma's parents were the best hosts. But returning to our home out here always felt special, and there was nothing better than watching Grace thrive.

The sound of paws on leaves drew my attention to the river's edge, where Kali showed herself down the path.

"Hey, girl," I called out. "Where's Koko?"

The cub pounced from behind her mother at the mention and galloped toward me. Young sprinting cubs were as cute as suckling babies, except Koko had nearly caught up to her mother's size. She nudged her head into my arm, grazing her face.

"You're growing up fast. You want a treat?"

Koko sat like a dog, patiently waiting. My training had been going well. I removed the chicken from the cooler, and she gently grasped the bird and pulled it from my hand, walking away to eat.

"Koko," Genie squealed.

We had originally named the cub Kona, but the day Genie started babbling "Koko," it stuck.

"Koko's eating breakfast." Grace lowered our daughter to the blanket's edge. Genie sat in position, grinning from ear to ear, waiting for Koko to finish and play. Babies, cougar cubs, and gorgeous Queens were my life now, and I couldn't have been happier.

"Hunter," Grace whispered.

"Yeah?"

"Kali's staring at me."

I turned back to Grace. "The same way she did yesterday?"

"No, differently."

Kali had been trying to win over Grace for years.

"It's not different."

"Then why is she doing that?"

The cat rolled onto her back, paws up, stretching over the grass.

"She wants you to trust her."

"She's a cougar."

Kali stretched out her long body over a sunny patch.

"She protects our family. And should I mention your daughter plays with her cougar cub?"

"That's different. They have a bond. They were born on the same day. Kali can take down an animal seven times her size."

So could Koko. Maybe not seven just yet, but close enough.

I sighed. We could argue all day about why it was time for Grace to trust Kali, or I could make her trust Kali.

"Hey, Kali. Bring me the box."

The cat rose and ran off toward the tree base of our house where I'd left a package. We practiced the move for two days. Fucking smartest animal I ever met.

Grace's head whipped my way. "What box?"

"It's a gift. From a friend to a friend." I winked.

Grace's eyes grew wide, and her head jerked back to the path. Moments later, Kali reappeared and trotted up to Grace, who sat stiffly on the blanket. My accomplice took her spot, holding the box in her jaw.

"Stick out your hand, Grace."

"No." She pulled her hands behind her back.

"Stick out your palm or she won't leave."

Grace didn't budge. I glanced back to Genie and Koko, who were sitting two feet away from me at the river's shore, splashing.

"Did you know cougars can smell fear? You want to show her you're weak? Do you know what they do to weak prey?"

Grace's mouth fell open. "I'm *prey* now? Hunter, this isn't helping."

"I'm kidding. Will you just please stick out your hand? If you don't trust her, trust me."

Grace swallowed visibly and turned to Kali. She extended her shaky hand, eyes widening. Kali gently placed the slobbery box in Grace's palm, then backed away.

"Open it," I whispered from behind and knelt on one knee. The box clicked open.

"It's empty," she said.

"Oops, I think she got the wrong one."

Grace turned around with a gasp. I held the open box with the ring out in front of me.

"Grace, my Cougar and my Queen, will you be the Queen of my jungle for the rest of our lives and marry me?"

She held still for what seemed like forever before the tears broke out. I couldn't tell if she was laughing through the tears, or crying.

"I thought you said this was a rainforest."

"Not the answer I was looking for." My eyebrows stayed high on my forehead.

I stood up, and she threw her arms around my neck. "Yes, of course I'll marry you."

My mouth met hers in a lingering kiss. Her body melted against mine, soft curves, round belly, and full breasts, and my blood flew south. I pulled away. If we consummated our engagement, we'd be late and I couldn't wait to make her my wife.

"Good, because we have five hours to get ready."

"Get ready for what?"

"For our wedding."

"Again—what?"

I lifted our daughter from the shore, and she squealed.

"Come on, Genie. Daddy and Mommy are getting married today."

Our family was gathered in the front row, our friends behind them, and everyone from the village stood in the back. We'd designated an area for the kids beside the beautifully decorated gazebo with a side view of the ceremony. I thought I had this in the bag. Flowers, check. Guests and accommodations, check. Decorations, check. Food, check. Music, check. My heart hammering in my chest like a jackhammer and knees shaking: not on the list!

Genevieve shifted in my arms and pointed across the river. "Koko."

I shaded my eyes and glanced at the riverbank. Kali and Koko were stretched out flat on a thick tree branch hanging over the shore, watching the commotion on our side.

"Are those the cougars Grace mentioned?" My best man and brother James was standing beside me.

"Kali and Koko."

"Are they friendly? Is it true you let the cub sleep with Genie?"

I laughed. "No, we don't. They know us, but they're still wild. It's why they're over there, not here."

When he didn't answer, I explained. "The locals wouldn't hesitate to kill a cougar in the village. But Kali's smart. She knows to stay away."

"But you pet her?"

"Pet her?" I laughed again. "We spend time together. They protect us."

He shook his head. "I don't get it. I see the beauty of the place, but I don't know how you can live here."

I kissed Genie's cheek. "It has its rewards. I'll give you the tour of the lodge tomorrow."

Emma brushed her hand over my shirt on my other side. "I don't see it either. The bugs out here are the size of rodents. No, thank you." She shuddered.

"There are a lot of bugs out in Lord's Valley where Eric's at."

"Yes, but they come with horse-riding cowboys. Have you thought about what I said?" she asked in a lowered voice.

"I have. If you want the case, Eric needs to ask for you. Your brothers can't say no to a client. And try to act professional around him."

"You try acting professional around a broad-shouldered,

sexy cowboy in well-worn jeans, with swagger. He rides horses shirtless, and—"

"Ems?" I cleared my throat. "Maybe save it for later?"

The music chimed, and Emma composed herself, standing proudly in her position as the maid of honor.

I took my spot with Genie in front of our Abuela, who would officiate the ceremony, and I focused on the end of the path. Grace stood behind a row of her brothers, the four of them shielding her from my view. I hadn't seen Grace since the moment Paula swept her away for hair and makeup. Aunt Mary had flown down with the wedding dress, promising a perfect fit. Truthfully, I didn't care what Grace wore, as long as she'd be my wife by the end of the day and naked tonight.

The Wagner brothers parted, and Grace came into view. Axel and Scar each took her by an arm, and I was hypnotized. A breeze fluttered the silky dress flowing down her body, whisking her hair over her face. She connected her gaze with mine, and I couldn't remember much after that moment. I couldn't stop counting the seconds until she vowed to be mine and made me the happiest man alive. She walked down the aisle in slow motion and I went down a path of memories. Somehow, we managed to build a life. She was my best friend, my lover, and was about to become my wife.

I barely heard a word until Abuela said, "You may kiss your bride, *cariño*."

"I love you," I said into her mouth, sealing our commitment.

"And I love you."

The crowd cheered, and the party fell into full swing. I held Grace's face between my palms, kissing her in the middle of the dance floor. Genie had fallen asleep in her grandmother's arms hours ago, giving us time to ourselves.

"Are you ready to call it a night?" I spun her on the floor and brought her back to my body.

"We have guests. It's not even midnight."

"So 12:01?"

She giggled. A small boy ran up to me and tugged on my pant leg, looking up. We both looked down.

"*Papi*," he said.

"What?"

"*Papi.*"

My head flew up to Grace. "It's impossible."

Her brows narrowed. "Just like me getting pregnant was impossible?"

"Hunter!"

Our heads shipped to Paula, who waved us over from underneath the fairy-lit tree.

Shit.

"Maybe you should sit this one out?" I stepped in front of Grace.

"And miss the part where she reveals he's your son? No way. I'm your wife, Hunter. We've been through enough shit, and I'm ready to take on more, as long as you're by my side."

I took her hand. "All right. Let's go."

The music faded into the background. It felt like forever as we crossed the dance floor. Paula hugged Grace, congratulating her, then kissed me once on each cheek. "*Felicitations, cariño.*"

The boy tugged on my pants again. "*Papi.*"

"*Qué pasa*, Paula?" I asked.

She shrugged a shoulder, then burst out in laughter. "*Estoy bromeando contigo.* Kidding. I am joking with you. *Es el hijo de mi primo.*"

"Your cousin's son? This is your cousin's son? Paula, you almost gave me a heart attack."

Grace laughed. She was laughing so hard, I couldn't hold on to my anger.

"You know I'll get you back for this." I pointed, and she swatted my hand.

"*Gracias*, Hunter. Thank you for your help." She turned us both away, pushing us back to the dance floor. "Go, dance."

"What did you do?" Grace asked.

"Her cousin's husband was killed before their son was born. I helped a little, that's all. I've never seen the boy before, though."

Grace smiled, and I cupped her face with one hand, brushing my thumb over her cheek. The gentleness in her eyes flooded with love.

"I thought you changed, Hunter, but you didn't."

"No?"

She shook her head. "You are the man who fixed my bike. The man who saved frogs from my pool and turned my weeds into a beautiful garden. Your loyalty and devotion were always there. You were a man before I saw you, and thank you for not giving up on me. Thank you for not giving up on us."

I kissed her again, grateful I'd be able to do so for the rest of my life. Someone on the dance floor whistled. More whistles followed, but I could no longer hold back. My tongue swept over hers as I brought her body to mine. We pulled apart, her eyes begging and breath shortening. I bent down, tucked my arm underneath her knees, and swept her off her feet, carrying her away to our home to consummate our marriage.

If we made it that far.

ABOUT THE AUTHOR

USA Today Bestselling Author Lacey Silks crafts riveting romantic suspense filled with heat, spice, and pulse-pounding tension. Many of her endearing characters are inspired by her own life, and her loved ones often find themselves playfully woven into her tales. Her two children and her dog, Kygo, keep her days lively with homework queries and affectionate slobbery kisses (courtesy of Kygo, of course).

Outside of penning intense love stories, Lacey is an avid camper and skier. Naturally an early riser, she often finds herself reaching for coffee over water, crediting her billionaire heroes for her packed schedule.

Lacey's characters, replete with flaws and quirks, evoke laughter, sass, and emotion on every page. She cheekily measures men by their foot size, has a penchant for sultry lingerie, and harbors dreams of exploring the nation in a motorhome.

ACKNOWLEDGMENTS

Silver Hunter wasn't a planned novel in this series but I'm so happy with Grace and Hunter's story. Navigating through love and life is never easy. Societal expectations cast doubt in our hearts and shift our desires, but if we're lucky, love can conquer all. Grace and Hunter had such luck <3

I couldn't have done the work without my reader support or the ever-inspiring indie author community filled with a wealth of knowledge. The continued encouragement and faith in my work, along with the outpouring of love, replenished my muse.

To my amazing editor who always finds the time for me, thank you for making my life easy and my writing understandable.

To my beta readers, thank you for your keen eyes! Once I read a story twenty times (or more), the details aren't easy to spot. Your feedback is invaluable and makes the novel what it should be.

To my family, the past few years have tested us in more ways than we would have liked, and I could not do what I love without you. Thank you for your support, faith and encouragement.

Maya, thank you for your artistic eye and cover design. I'm honoured to watch you grow and develop as an artist. Alex, your loving heart and sense of humour are a constant inspiration.

To my parents, this book would not have happened without you. Thank you for believing in my dreams.

9 781999 306220